BFC

ANGUS DISTRICT LIBRARIES
WITHDRAWN
FROM STOCK

Tell Me My Name

ANGUS DISTRICT LIBRARIES
WITHDRAWN
FROM STOCK

Tell Me My Name

ANGUS DISTRICT LIBRARIES
WITHDRAWN
FROM STOCK

Mary Carter

GEORGE PRIOR PUBLISHERS

London, England

G.K.HALL&CO.

Boston, Massachusetts

1976

Library of Congress Cataloging in Publication Data

Carter, Mary.
  Tell me my name.

  Large print ed.
  1. Sight-saving books. I. Title.
[PZ4.C32396Te3] [PS3553.A7824] 813'.5'4 75-43671
~~ISBN 0-8161-6345-6~~

Copyright © 1975 by Mary Carter

Grateful acknowledgment is made to Random House,
Inc., for permission to quote four lines from "Leap
Before You Look" by W. H. Auden from *Collected
Shorter Poems 1927 - 1957,* copyright 1945 and
renewed 1973 by W. H. Auden.

All Rights Reserved. No part of this book may be
reproduced or utilized in any form or by any means,
electronic or mechanical, including photocopying,
recording or by any information storage and retrieval
system, without permission in writing from the
Publisher.

Published in Large Print by arrangement with William
Morrow and Company, Inc.

Available for sale in the British Commonwealth from
George Prior Publishers, 2 Rugby St., London,
England

British Commonwealth rights granted courtesy of Paul
R. Reynolds, Inc.

ISBN (U. K.)   240844203   0-904000-88-5 ✓

Set in Photon 18 pt Crown

For Helen Arkley Janeck

The characters in this book are fictional. Any resemblance to a specific person, living or dead, is coincidental.

PART I

One

Sunday afternoon, Nov. 3. Dear Porter: I'm sitting out here in the little cabin — I remember when your mother first showed me around she said it had been a slave cabin, but added that the McPhails bought the land after the War, which bewildered me until I realized she meant the Civil War — anyway I'm sitting out here (I was going to do some weeding but it's too muddy and that damn goat is in the veg-garden again, somebody left the gate open as usual, and that goat knows I'm scared of her which is why I'm the only one she tries to butt) thinking, as I say, about all sorts of things, amongst which our 16th wedding anniversary two weeks from today. So I thought I'd write you a *billet-doux* to say how much I

Dear Mama: Two weeks from today I'll have been married 16 years. And you dead 18 years. It doesn't seem much like yesterday. More like History. You always talked about Historical Perspective. I could use some. Lately I've thought a lot about what you used to say. Like a true Maine native you didn't say much but it was always to the point. You said to count my blessings, to remember that Charity is the noblest virtue, to never apologize never explain, and when receiving a compliment to just smile and say Thank you. I know these are all to the point, but I'm beginning to wonder *what* point. I'm beginning to wonder if all that I should be is bounded by these four precepts. Like the four walls of this old house — it has more than four walls of course, being so big and rambling, I've never counted the number of actual walls

Stop whining, Emily. Count your blessings:

4

— a roof over my head, food, security, etc.

— 3 fine sons

— a loving husband

We interrupt this list to bring you a news bulletin. Emily McPhail has just flung her bonnet into the race for state delegate. Mrs. McPhail, wife of Prof. Porter T. McPhail of the University of Virginia at Charlottesville, has for the past several years been active in Albemarle County civic groups (having served, upon the decease of Maj. Owen L. Platt, as acting Chairman of the Taxpayers' Association, as well as a member of the Grand Jury and of the School Board). Mrs. McPhail lives with her husband, their 3 sons (Porter, Jr., 13; Stuart, 11; and Timothy, 6), and Prof. McPhail's Uncle, Tyler T. Talbott, on the McPhail Family acres, now operating marginally with a small herd of black angus cattle which with the Christmas privet crop is just enough to pay the taxes and to keep on the 2 old farm retainers, Mr. Garrett and Will

Jackson, both slowing down some, plus the putative assistance of Jeannie and Mike Katz who are former poetry students of Prof. McPhail's and who wish to return to the soil and dig the meaningful eco-agricultural life-style and its reactivation of self-identity

Dear Jeannie & Mike — Just a swift note to remind you, Mike, that Mr. Garrett had to chase 3 of the heifers back from down the road this morning. This is the 3rd time since Thurs. so *please* can you fix that fence the minute you get back from revival meeting. Mr. G. threatened to fix it himself, he was that upset, but you know his bad back, so I told him you were planning to do it *today*. Also Jeannie, hate to nag, but yr goat got into the veg-garden again. She's going to *have* to be tied, or everybody will be fit to. — E.M.

Sun. Nov. 3. Dear Porter: You're over in the house watching the football on TV, and the boys are heaven knows where (I'm beginning to wonder about this lack of interruption), and I guess Uncle Tyler's up in his study translating something Greek, or working on that Family History he's so secretive about (makes one wonder if there are skeletons in your family closet), and I'm sitting here in the cabin making a list of my blessings. Of which your name, like Abou Ben Adams' (sp?), leads all the rest. What you think of as my New England reserve makes it hard for me to say some things to you, but as our 16th anniversary approaches and I look back over our years together

The dream: it came again last night. *Tomorrow's Sunday the third of November,* I thought as I was wrenched awake. How many years I've had it, this same dream. It always comes this time of year. I start awake in the middle of the night and it's as if I were strangling. The sadness stays with me for days, and an aftertaste of panic. I can never remember the details of the dream, but I awake with the terrible sense of having left something outside, something very delicate and valuable that I've been playing with and carelessly forgotten to bring back in the house when nighttime came. And it is lying out there in the dark, all unprotected; and I will awake in the morning and go outside to search for it, and it will be lying ruined in the garden under a hedge all covered with dead leaves and trampled under the hoofs of those terrible black cows that are always getting out because somebody — could it be me? — has left the gate open

it seems like only yesterday that we were married. I was very young then, and scared of everything. And you were so steady and gentle, and becoming your wife was like coming into a warm house from a cold night and finding a family of my own. After my mother died I felt so abandoned. Anyway, I want you to know what a good husband you've been to me all these years, patient of my faults (I know I'm a lousy housekeeper, despite your mother's efforts to train me in the high Southern tradition), and kindly toward my needs (I know all my civic activities these last couple of years, my trotting off to so many meetings, particularly in the evenings when you're home

Greenwood Va. Nov. 3 Dear Governor: As a concerned citizen it is my duty to call to your attention that the head of the County Board of Zoning Appeals is about to award a multizillion-$ contract to his brother-in-law to rip up a beautiful & historic stretch of county, reroute into miles of concrete culvert a creek which irrigates 22% of township, imperil agricultural land with zooming subdivision taxes, all in order to build an entirely unnecessary freeway, bridge, and shopping plaza. Although several groups of concerned people have begun to fight the proposal, they are disorganized and no match for these developers with their powerful contacts and backing of certain lobbies at state capital. Good government begins at

home. A word from you could give it a
nudge. Respectfully,

Emily H. McPhail

Dear Mama: Another thing you always
said was to come to the point. Muddy
talk shows a muddy mind, you said.
Know what you know, you said; and
know what you don't know.
Here is what I know:

— if I went out after it, devoted most
of my time to it for the next year, I
stand a fair (good, no; but *fair*)
chance of being elected State
Delegate from this district.

— circumstances: old Harry Griffin,
who's owned the seat since Nought
One, is retiring after this last term.
Opposing party has no real candidate
or organization: nobody's ever been
crazy enough to run against Griffin.
Our party has no real candidate
because the man everybody, including
Griffin, assumed would be his
successor has just been named
"corespondent" in a scandalous
divorce case, and we don't 'low no

sexual scandals 'round here. Several growing, active women's groups, plus the usual Liberal groups based in the University (slowly gaining ground in the old Town/Gown battle), are determined to push a woman candidate. My last few years' involvement with local concerns has made me "visible," they say — particularly says Catherine Tupper, who's been dropping strong hints to me for several months, last week all but came out and asked me if I'd consider being a candidate. She packs a lot of social (and therefore, political) clout around here, is known as the velvet glove inside Harry Griffin's iron fist (one would suspect an old, er, relationship if Mme. Tupper were not so imposingly the Grande Dame in high old South'n Style). She says Harry would be "persuaded" to back any candidate she might seriously propose to him. And unless some unknown factor (like the divorce scandal) appears to blow the candidate's image, nothing known to history can dislodge the Party's seat: whomever Harry backs is a shoo-in. I'd have to work with Tupper to "persuade" Harry — but that would be easy if Tupper were persuaded I could work with her.

And here's what I don't know:

— if I could persuade Porter to let me take a leave of absence from my commitments to him and the family, in order to commit myself to this.

And here's how I feel about it:

— guilty.

Guilty. Face it, Emily: that's how you feel about yourself. For sixteen years — no, almost eighteen, is it possible it's been all this time — guilt's been in you like some chronic disease. Malaria maybe, it's caused by a parasite in the bloodstream, it lies dormant for a while and then it flares up into another attack, fever, with night sweats and terrible dreams and shaking all over inside. That's what it is now, another attack and trying to shake it sitting here on an apple crate scribbling crazy notes as if they were prescriptions for medicine but they're just placebos, sugarcoated pills that can't cure anything except make the patient feel something's being done about it. CURE THYSELF the Bible says somewhere, if only I were a Catholic I could go to Confession and come out all absolved and clean. How can killing be so clean and love so dirty

Dear Porter: If I confess to you would you absolve me? God knows I'm penitent, Porter, and I love you. Does love pile up points for absolution? It's you I love but it's you I sinned against — twice, if you count the Original Sin plus all the years of hypocrisy. Strange but nowadays Original Sin doesn't seem to be considered as unforgivable as hypocrisy, except among throwbacks like me. There's a kind of Fundamentalist streak in me maybe inherited from my New England ancestors, it makes me susceptible to this particular disease of guilt. All the modern doctors say guilt is very bad for you, it's a disease they feel they've

13

licked, so it's become unmentionable in polite society, the way cancer and VD used to be. Well, I've got this unmentionable disease and I can't face the cure which is confession. What you don't know may not be hurting you Porter but it sure as hell is hurting me. Guilt invades every area of my life, it drags me down just where I want to rise and expand and find out who I am as a person and what I'm capable of on my own. Every chance I've had has been burned out in another attack of this fever, look at me right now wanting so much to see if I can really do something, really *be* something besides a wife and mother, and all I can think of is would it be another betrayal of my duties, my commitments to love and care for

you. Oh my darling who has loved and cared for you all these years? Not me, not me all these years

There was a staid matron from Maine
Who was seized with a very weird pain.

"But what is it?" she cried.

The stern doctor replied,

"First apologize, then I'll explain."

It is hard for me to express my feelings of gratitude to all you people who had confidence in me, and voted for me, men as well as women (*pause here for polite laughter*), and I promise you that insofar as I am capable, I will fulfill that confidence. It has been said, in the course of this campaign, that politics is no place for a lady (*pause for polite protestations*), which is to imply that there is no place in politics for a lady (*pause for confusion occasioned by Porter's thundering from the back of the hall "THAT WAS NO LADY, THAT WAS MY WIFE"*)

● ● ● ●

"There you are."

A shadow falls over the open doorway, blocking the last of the pale late-afternoon sunlight. Hunched on the apple crate with the binder on my lap, I startle. The paper crumples into a ball. I am surrounded by a litter of crumpled-paper balls.

"What on earth are you doing in here?" says Porter. Even with his head thrust forward and his shoulders hunched he fills the tiny cabin doorway. Guiltily I blink up at him, a presence whose features I cannot make out in the blocked light, whose face I suddenly cannot quite remember. Guiltily, I try to reconstruct the features of my husband's face one by one: the blue eyes, the blond brows, the shapely nose — the McPhail nose, his mother used to emphasize, looking proudly down her own — the wide mouth and even teeth. A handsome face, a pleasant face, at forty growing a touch plump about the jowls, but an amiable face, a decent face, the face of a reasonable man, a responsible man, a man who is a good sound Professor of English at a good sound University, who prefers to teach rather than to perform the additional duties of Chairman of the Department, a man with good sound tenure, which means hold, in his profession, in his community (the McPhails are an old, sound name here), in his family seat, in the bosom of his family . . . Why then — I think guiltily, blinking up at it — can I not at this moment quite recall this man's face in its entirety, in its effect? Because, for the moment, it seems to have no effect on me?

"I've been looking all over for you," it says. "The Peterses are here."

"The Peterses?" One last blink and the face comes into focus. It is patient, slightly frowning: the patient aspect of a husband of almost sixteen years, who has learned to live with a somewhat disorganized and occasionally abstracted wife.

"The Peterses. Good heavens." I stand, knocking over the crate; stoop, scrabbling for papers on the dirt floor. "What time is it? Lord, I didn't invite them for supper, did I, and forgot —"

"Five-thirty. Honey, they just dropped in." The slight emphasis on the last word is Porter's way of chiding me for my inability to remember (after all these years) that people in these parts just drop *in* without a formal invitation. And he is not so much chiding me as resignedly noting (again) how flustered I get at the prospect of guests, invited or not. In a place where hospitality is transmitted in the genes, like eye color, my inability to take it — or maybe dish it out — in stride is puzzling to Porter. It is as if in this respect I had not quite evolved into womanhood. But Porter is a patient man. His patience fits him like an old shoe. It sometimes pinches me.

"Oh. Well, but at this hour," I say in pinched tones, "I suppose we should ask them to stay for supper?" His raised eyebrows signify, Yes, of course we should, and will. I kick the papers into a little pile, lift the apple crate, and bang it down over them. "The boys get ravenous at six," I mutter.

"They can hold on while we have a leisurely drink. They can entertain the Peters girls."

"All four?" I groan. "They brought all four?"

"Emily, it's just a family group, for heaven's sake, not some kind of dress-up ball. No call to fuss. Just give 'em soup or something," he says vaguely, ducking

18

back outside, "and some hot bread, or whatever." He is already ambling back across the drive, in no rush, hands in his old tweed pockets, sneakers scuffing up dead leaves.

Soup and hot bread. Like hospitality, the ability to provide these things instamatically (I think as I trot after him) seems somehow to reside in the genes. Perhaps the same Southern gene. Cooking doesn't come all that naturally to me. When I was first married I got the impression from Porter's mother that the lack was indicative of some early distortion of my natural instincts. Oh, I am competent enough, after all these years, and diligent in my fashion. But I have to concentrate. I have to be able to think ahead. I cannot get a meal together swinging by my knees from the chandelier. My grocery lists tend lately to get shuffled in with other lists, like Roberts' *Rules of Order*, or summaries of county tax rates. Porter once inquired why mealtime always arrived as such a big surprise to me.

The raw wind scours my cheek, rustles

the dry gold of the great maples. The cones of the old magnolia by the back porch are beginning to drop on the uneven brick of the drive. I perch a moment on the lower step to pry off my muddy boots. The cones are studded with lacquered red seeds that look exactly like sleeping pills. The last of the cold sun glints on the dense green of the privet; the hedge is tall as two tall men. Everything here is so old, so tangled, with an order long ago abandoned; once tended, now not. The trunk of that elm over there is cracked halfway up; whole limbs have died and should be cut away; high beneath the graceful gables of the roof the gutters have rotted and are hanging precariously against the red brick. There's not enough money, not enough hands, not enough will, not enough time — with all the other things there are to do just to keep ahead of the seasons and in touch with our own vigorous life demands — to care for the old, the beautiful, the irreplaceable, the outmoded. Life here, in a place like this, is outmoded.

So think ahead: soup and hot bread. I

stand, briskly knock my boots against the iron scraper, shoulder open the kitchen door (which after almost two centuries still swells stuck with the first fall rains), drop the boots on the spread-out newspaper on which the dogs' water bowl has been overturned. After the cold outside it feels stifling in here; the ancient furnace, groaning away in its cell somewhere in the labyrinth of cellar, is either Off and polar or On and tropical. The kitchen is huge, bare — Lord, Sunday night and I am Mother Hubbard again. I hurry across the peeling linoleum in my stocking feet, clutching my binder against my chest with one arm while I try to get the other out of the sleeve of Porter's old plaid jacket I wear to garden in. I scrabble about in my mind wondering if I could get away with giving visitors canned tomato soup (now hear this: this is not a dress-up ball), and if there's enough cornmeal for a double batch of bread, and —

"Emily?" It is Porter, his easy, drawling company voice, approaching the pantry door. In a moment he'll push it open and there I'll be, caught flatfooted, stocking-footed, unprepared, one arm in and one arm out of my husband's old jacket.

"Coming, I'm coming, Porter!" I barrel through hastily, one arm trapped, and Lord, Lord, the goat ate the last of the greens I could have made a salad with.

• • • •

"Don't be ridiculous, you don't have to change just for us, Em," booms Lucy Peters, who is standing with her back to the library fire, legs akimbo in whipcord trousers. "No call to gussy up just for family." Lucy is a big horsey woman with bluff red cheeks and short graying hair and very blue eyes, who scared the liver out of me when I met her, at the first of the series of parties my mother-in-law gave to introduce Porter's new bride, namely me.

Lucy was standing exactly the same way before the same fireplace when Porter introduced us. "I s'pose you know that all the females in the county are prepared to hate you on sight," she said. Porter put his arm around my shoulders.

"Come on now, Lucy, you exaggerate. Only half the females in the county." She nickered horsily, in a way that would take some getting used to. "You're too modest, Porter, for all you're considered such a plum. You plucked him right off the tree," she said to me, "and around here we're sufferin a shortage of eligible plums. Most of this year's crop has gone soft. Haw. Haw." She elbowed Porter chummily. She may have glimpsed something in my face — Porter had turned away to receive the felicitations of an olderly couple — because she said to me in gentler tones, "Don't let these county gals bother you overmuch. Their mothers'll forgive you eventually, after they get 'em all married off. I went through the same thing with Weston. These women" — she glanced around the room — "they're my friends now, most of 'em. Friendship's important in this part of the country. So you're a New England gal. I understand you and Porter met in Boston. That's what comes of sendin our men up to Harvard." Porter told me afterward that Lucy herself had come from Illinois just five years before, when she married Weston. I began to understand Lucy's exaggerated Southern accent: a good disguise for a Northern woman whose drier tones might grate on Southern ears. I began to perceive something about survival amid the alien corn.

"Frankly, that skirt never did much for you." Lucy is eyeing me with the privileged stare of Oldest Friend. "Makes you look too up-and-down. If you turned sidewise you'd disappear." Lucy could never disappear, neither in sight nor sound. She is, well, commanding. She is always commanding me to put on weight ("I swear, Em, you look like a waif on *purpose*"), to get some new clothes ("How you can manage to wear bucket-sprung skirts when you haven't even got a bucket to spring 'em"), to do something about my hair ("Honestly, goin around in a ponytail held back with a rubber band, when you've got hair that nice dark red, and curly too, you could have it cut some, and shaped, and what with your bangs you could look sort of like Margaret Sullavan.

Now don't tell me you don't remember who Margaret Sullavan is''), and giving me a subscription to *Town & Country* each Christmas so I can get a clearer picture of the gracious living it is the duty of us Southern women to uphold. I have given up trying to explain to Lucy the ways in which it is impossible for me to live graciously, much less find time to study *Town & Country* or go to movie matinees (which Lucy is addicted to) to check on Margaret Sullavan's hairdo. Lucy asserts it is simply a matter of organization. After years of trying to organize me (a task she felt she inherited from my late mother-in-law) Lucy had all but thrown in the towel — until two years ago, when she (and I) discovered I could organize a committee meeting with the same ease and dispatch with which Southern womanhood organizes its gracious living. Since then she has resumed her mission, under the impression that I am willfully hiding my domestic lights under the public cracker barrel. "If you can manage all that committee stuff so efficiently," she says,

"I can't for the life of me see how you can have so much trouble organizin one household and one little ol' farm." Lucy has no farm, only big ol' well-tended acres, on which she raises not scraggly cattle but sleek Irish setters. And Lucy has four daughters; and daughters are more amenable to domestic order than riotous sons. Having a daughter would be like having a comrade-in-arms; not just a helpmeet but a womanly blood-spirit, I often think . . .

"Get a drink," Lucy commands. "Porter fixed us up a batch of his daiquiris. Whereall are the boys? The girls've gone up to the attic to play ping-pong. Where's Uncle Tyler? Haven't seen the old rascal for ages. Weston says he sees him at the University Library, just porin away over his Greek. Rachel, don't you want to go play ping-pong too?"

The oldest Peters girl is sitting in a corner, leafing through one of Porter's poetry magazines. Rachel has just turned sixteen. It is just being discovered that she will be beautiful. She is beginning to be uncertain that she can afford to live on trustfulness. Watching this girl coming into her womanhood moves me with a sharpness like pain. Although my sons move me, too, as they grow and change, I cannot feel in me this same sharpness, this pain of recognition. I remember coming into my own wariness. They call it awareness now.

The girl smiles and retreats back to her magazine. I would like to offer her something — what? — but she seems so remote. "Cheerio had her litter," Lucy announces. "Six of 'em, my gawd, practically killed the poor bitch. She's got a narrow pelvis, y'know," she says to Porter, who looks politely concerned; "I was up all night with the vet, didn't get a lick of sleep." I suspect the Peterses fuss more about their dogs than Weston does about his teaching — Accounting Principles — or Lucy her daughters, who seem quite cheerfully to be raising themselves.

Raising themselves —

"You look as if you could use some sleep yourself," Lucy is saying. "You're doin too much runnin around to all these meetins of yours." She hauls me over to the sofa and sits me down for a lecture. She says I should be more tactful about Seward Creek or I'll "make it hard" for myself. "Y'know what they say about catchin more flies with honey than you can with vinegar," she says.

"Seems to me they could use a little vinegar around here to cut all that honey." I feel my face heat. "That's part of the trouble. People'd rather go on being polite and letting a few greedy old entrepreneurs run things, just because they're everybody's cousin twice removed."

"Once in a while you do act pretty redheaded, you know that?" Lucy says tartly. "All I'm sayin is you don't want to set up resistance by bein so blunt. At the meetin the other night for instance —"

"When Chauncy was honeying everybody along about how we need the taxes from new development? All I did was outline a proposal for raising them equitably by reassessing —"

"Oh, nobody'd argue it didn't make sense. It's just the way you cut across old

J.J., made him look, well, insincere."

"He *is* insincere. He's a cynical old walrus, and he doesn't care if —"

"Well, *you* care too much, and it makes people nervous. You —"

"They damn well *should* be nervous, they're going to wake up some day and find Seward Creek and their good land and the whole county paved over with useless concrete —"

"— told him I could put that new dog run in myself, with what he's chargin me just for the concrete," Weston is saying to Porter. "The way prices have gone up around here is a scandal. Why, I remember —"

I have to get away. I have to find a quiet place where I can get some perspective, think things through. I can't do it here, where sixteen years have laid down in my mind an accumulated clutter, the way two hundred years of occupancy have laid down the clutter and dust and treasures and disorder of this huge old house; not here, where a thousand tiny duties snag at my distractible mind, interrupt my thought every time I'm about to break through to a glimmer of insight; not here, where well-meaning friends harangue me, tell me what I can or can't do, define what I *am*. I have to get away from other people's vision of me, if I'm to find my own.

"— vet says we may lose one, a male," Lucy calls across to Porter. "The runt of the litter, of course. Weston, don't take another drink, we have to go shortly."

"Lucy," I say, leaning close to her, "where would you go if you wanted to get away for a couple of weeks?"

"Don't want to leave Cheerio for long. Where? Would I go? Why, the Bahamas I s'pose, if we could afford it. Someplace sunny. Why? You and Porter thinkin about takin off over Christmas? You takin the kids too? Take my advice, don't. A vacation with kids is like bein home with four times the laundry and ten times the cost. And in the *Bahamas* —"

"Sh. We're not — we're not going to the Bahamas, or anything like that. Never mind, nothing's settled anyway. I ought to get supper started. You are staying for supper? I hope you don't mind something very simple —"

"Nope," she says, "can't stay. Got to get back and check on Cheerio. Rachel, go find the girls and tell 'em to come put their boots on. Emily, take my advice, don't take the kids with you. Put 'em up somewhere. Listen, I'll take 'em. Christmas, it's confusin enough, three boys'd just add to the riot. Besides, they're mannerly and helpful. Why don't you do that — you and Porter go on, be by yourselves for a change, have a second honeymoon." She winks. "I s'pect you could use one, what with you workin so hard on all those Concerned Citizens committees. Seems to me you've got enough concerns here at home, as I b'lieve I frankly told you often enough. You know me, frank's my middle name. Could be Porter's beginnin to feel neglected, and you know what they say when a husband starts feelin neglected." She winks again. "Anyway, think it over about us takin the boys. WesTON! We got to be off, honey. Girls, say thank you to Mrs. McPhail for her hospitality."

She marches her daughters out the

31

door. Weston pecks my cheek, follows them. Porter and I stand hand in hand, as hospitality prescribes, watching them drive out from the portico, around the circle, down the hill, and beyond the curve onto the county road.

"There." Porter releases my hand. "They didn't stay for supper after all." He sounds a trifle disappointed. Porter enjoys company; he is a hospitable man. "Speaking of which, I'm starved. What're we having?"

"What you suggested, Porter. Soup." Perhaps he has forgotten that he also suggested hot bread.

"I wish," says Porter, "we could have something else sometimes. Like curry. We always used to have curry on Sunday nights. It was a family tradition. Funny, I just remembered it. Didn't Mother teach you how to make curry?"

"She gave me the recipe," I say after a moment, "on her deathbed. Don't you remember that, Porter?"

"I don't think," says Porter after another moment, "that that was a terribly kind thing to say, Emily."

It wasn't. Oh, it wasn't. Where is my charity? I flee to the kitchen. Never apologize; and how could I ever explain?

• • • •

"Carpemus diem," Uncle Tyler proposes, "and pass the ammunition."

"What's a carp-moose," Timmie wants to know. Timmie is, after Uncle Tyler, the family scholar. He pursues bits of data as they flutter by, like a lepidopterist would impale them for later inspection. Uncle Tyler informs him that it means Grab what one can oneself, instead of carping at God all day.

"Carpemus diem," Porter supplies professorially, "means Let us seize the day. Uncle Tyler is making a pun."

"Stretching for it, as the ammunition in question is beyond my arm's reach," says Uncle Tyler.

"I guess that's what you mean when you're always saying that what the body can't do, words must," Stuart puts in brightly. Stuart is the bright one, blond and sunny, tactful. He has doubtless noted that the mood of the adults around the table is tonight a bit glum. Porter is brooding on curry (while Porter is large in large things, he tends occasionally to be small in small things). I am fretful with relief, and accompanying guilt, that the Peterses didn't stay (I probably should have insisted). Uncle Tyler is always bored on Sunday nights (unaccountably, as Sundays and weekdays must be all the same to him).

"Hand that young man a see-gar." Uncle Tyler pours himself some Burgundy from the bottle I've passed him. Wine is Uncle Tyler's ammunition against Sunday nights.

When I arrived as a bride I got the impression that Uncle Tyler "drank" — it was a Sunday — until as the weeks went by it was borne in on me that his peculiarities were not fueled by alcohol or by any external event. His metronomic swings between exuberance and melancholy were directed by some internal pulse. You could say he dances to a different piper — if anybody so stout as Uncle Tyler could be imagined dancing. It is odd, because snapshots of him in old family albums show a slender and elegant young man, usually lounging against some veranda pillar or seated gracefully on the grass at the feet of some lady in a lawn chair. In every picture it is summer, and Uncle Tyler is wearing white tennis flannels; and in every picture he has just noticed the camera, and his smooth handsome expression is beginning to knot into an angry glare. This is odder: Uncle Tyler has never, since I've known him, exhibited either anger or aversion to notice. His corporate — or corpulent — image is one of amiable vanity. Uncle Tyler is my (deceased) mother-in-law's brother and has been a member of the McPhail household since she married into it. He claims to have been part of her "dowry" and — when I became a McPhail — part of Porter's. "I go with the house," he told me. "Fortunately for us all, it is a big house." He has always occupied two rooms upstairs in the west wing. Uncle Tyler was originally expected to take over the cattle part of the farm — it was much larger then, and devoted mainly to the raising of horses — but he claims to loathe animals. "Particularly," he says with a fastidious shudder, "black Angus." This doesn't strike me as odd. I am terrified of cattle. I never know what animals are pondering, or what they're going to do. You don't admit things like that in this part of the country. Not even to Uncle Tyler, who is fond of remarking that next to innocence, timidity is the least attractive of the so-called feminine virtues. But Uncle Tyler makes remarks like that only when he is in the grip of melancholy, and at those times he mostly keeps out of the way, holing up in the west wing. When he is in the grip of exuberance he spends much time in the kitchen, whistling and humming and occasionally breaking into operatic arias you can hear even upstairs in the east wing. Those are trying times for us all. Uncle Tyler fancies himself a Creative Cook, and his creations strike dismay into even our cast-iron stomachs. The boys begin to whine about why can't we just have plain canned soup the way Mother makes it.

"What this needs," grumps Uncle Tyler, "is a dash of character. No offense, Emily, but tomato soup tends to be somewhat pious.''

''It is Sunday.''

''Oh *good* one, Mother.'' PJ (that's for Porter, Jr.) rolls his eyeballs upward to indicate vast ennui. ''Oh good *one*.''

Porter is aroused from his curry-brooding. ''Watch that smart-aleck tone of voice to your mother,'' he says sharply.

PJ and his father knot up their foreheads and glare at one another. Lately there is considerable of this knotting-up, butting stance. I guess this is what happens when the oldest son gets to the stage where his horn-buds start to grow, and itch. There is the sense of snorting and pawing and nostril-flaring going on over at the edge of the meadow, which the grown bull finds irksome. Porter has always been indulgent, even tender, with the boys; still is with Timmie and Stuart, but with PJ I suppose he is beginning to feel challenged in his manhood. They say this is a normal thing, and that women and their adolescent daughters feel the same sort of challenge. Well, that I will never know about.

''Please,'' I burst out, quite surprising

myself with how angry it sounds, "I can't stand you two picking at each other. Not tonight."

Porter eyes me with elaborate astonishment. "I was not 'picking,' Emily. I was merely protecting you against impudence."

"I hardly need protection against my own son."

"Bit of chopped persimmon, maybe. Or some yogurt," muses Uncle Tyler tactfully.

"Yogurt, ugh. Mother, do we have any Rice Krispies or something?"

"I don't think so, Timmie. Have some more soup."

"Not with *yogurt* in it." Timmie's left eye has begun to wander, as it does when he gets tired. The doctor says it's a weak muscle and he's supposed to wear a patch over the other eye for a few hours daily. The patch is held by an elastic ribbon that goes behind one ear and makes it stick out, and goes over the top of his head and makes his hair stick up in a tuft that looks like a red feather.

"There's no yogurt in the soup,

dear. Just milk."

"*Quod vide.*" Uncle Tyler sighs.

"Wuzzat mean?" Timmie blinks his one sleepy, wandering eye.

"Which see. PJ," Porter says, "where are you going?"

PJ stares at his father as if the man has lost his wits. He props his gangly frame against the doorway. "Up," he mutters wearily, "to watch TV. OK?"

"I didn't hear you ask to be excused, and don't you have homework to finish?"

"Dad. It's. Sunday. Night." PJ's tones are massively fatigued. "You always let us watch TV on Sunday night. Mother, may I please be excused?"

"Yes. Take your dishes out to the kitchen. Timmie, you too. You're all but asleep in your plate. Up to bed."

"Just a minute there, young man. You haven't answered my question." Porter's face seems to be swelling. It is a handsome face, but engorged with righteousness it somehow becomes a tedious face. I would prefer — it flashes to me — if the face were stripped-down, instead, by the purity of anger. I don't believe I've ever seen Porter's face naked: i.e., purely angry. Sixteen years, and never seen my husband naked. The insight is dazzling.

"*What* question?"

"And you will not take that tone of voice to *me.*"

"Mother-may-I-be-excused?" says Stuart swiftly. As I say, he's the bright one, he slips his bright voice like a blade into the argument, slicing it in two. Oh, they're all bright, of course, the boys. They are good boys, *dear* boys. Dear Stuart, so friendly and tactful and loving and chubby, like a pup; dear Timmie, so scholarly and intense and interested and scrawny, practically asleep with his tufted head (the eye-patch has slipped up) in his soup dish; dear PJ, so rawboned and big-footed, so assailable in the burden of his new malehood with his voice cracking open around its tough protective edge.

And Porter. Yes, dear Porter: see him there at the head of the table, *his* table. Is it his fault that a man must have his own territorial table to preside over? Shored up behind it, is it his fault that he feels besieged and set upon, all his offerings to his family — his protection, his love, his house, his name, his awesome responsibility to provide — all he owns and cherishes and *is*, held in contempt by this raw kid, by this rude challenge to his authority? Is it his fault — whose fault is it, anyway? — that his wife of sixteen years can look at his face so objectively as to wish (for just a moment, an appalling and irrational moment) it were blazing with anger instead of decency?

"You come back here, young man," he thunders, "and you sit down, and you look me straight in the eye, and you answer my questions in a tone of *respect* —"

● ● ● ●

"Em. You awake?"

No. I'm trying to think. Where can my body take my brain where it can be alone and think

"Honey? Em?"

No. Please Porter no. Not tonight

"Yes, Porter."

"What was that I overheard Lucy saying? Something about our going to

41

the Bahamas.''

Would it ever be possible to *under*hear Lucy. I open my eyes. ''I was just asking her about something and she misunderstood.''

''But why the Bahamas? What made Lucy think we'd be going there? Or anywhere, for that matter?''

''I don't know what makes Lucy think things. She just jumps in.''

''Well, what was she jumping into? What were you asking her about?''

Now. Tell him now. Lay it all out to him, lovingly. Isn't bed supposed to be the best place for wives to

''Lucy wouldn't just pull the idea of the Bahamas, or whatever, out of the air.'' His voice is edged with patience. He is prepared to be offended. He is trying to reverse the regret he feels for the shouting match with PJ. In family politics, as well as the other kinds, the best defense is still

the offensive position: could I take that? Could I put it straight out to him that I, like PJ, am at a stage in life where there is a need for private space to rediscover our separate selves, rethink our priorities? Could I

"Emily. I asked you a question."

"I'm sorry, Porter. I was trying to remember."

He turns to me, raises himself on one elbow as if to study my face in the dark. (Does he, too, long to see my face stripped naked? What does he yearn to see on it?) "Were you thinking of taking a vacation?"

He found my note. Or notes — dear Lord, those crazy notes, but I crumpled them, surely he wouldn't have found them, but Oh what if he did —

"Because if a vacation's what you want, you could have mentioned it to *me*," he is saying in tones of swelling offense he has plainly worked hard to achieve, "instead of airily discussing the Bahamas with Lucy. You're so damned secretive sometimes, Emily —"

I cut him off. I roll on my side, fling an arm around his neck, pull his head close, and kiss his ear. It is the old, old trigger, and it triggers the old, old response.

"Em," he says somewhat later, "you asleep?"

"No."

"I was thinking," his voice says out of the dark, "that it would be nice to take off over Christmas vacation. Someplace like the Bahamas — Lord, it'd be so nice. It'd be damn expensive. I don't know if we could manage it. But Lord, wouldn't it be nice," he says softly, "just the two of us maybe, having a couple weeks to ourselves with nothing to do but swim and loaf and lie in the sun. You'd look so pretty with a tan . . ."

The moment is past when I could bring myself to negotiate with him.

Presently he says, "Emily? Did you hear what I said? Maybe we could arrange a vacation, if that's what's been on your mind. I mean" — he clears his throat sternly — "I realize how tied down you probably get to feeling, what with all you have to do to keep up this big house, and the boys, and me. I want you to know I realize that, honey, and I appreciate all you — Where're you going?"

I don't know. If only I did. I don't know,

I say; go to sleep, Porter. I go in my nightgown out of our dark bedchamber, through the dark halls and down the dark stairs and more halls and the dining room and the pantry into the big dark kitchen where the two dogs scrabble to their feet, spooked. Spooked, I fumble for the light switch, growl, "Hush. It's me." Their ruffs up, they duck their heads sheepishly, thump their tails once, sink back down, watch me with their heads between their paws. The linoleum is icy under my bare feet. Shivering, I sit down at the table in the middle of the huge empty-feeling kitchen and put my head between my hands. I sit there a long time. The old house groans in its sprawled, far joints. The dogs watch me, waiting. Presently the clock above the stove crawls past midnight. Another November third is over. This was always a bad date for me, anyway. Who besides me, remembering it, might possibly remember me? Nobody. For surely over all these years it must have been their task — as well as my own — to forget.

Two

"Labor omnia vincit." Uncle Tyler negotiates the piles of books, the rolled-up old library rug. "But precisely what you are trying to conquer with this — uff" — he tries to squeeze his stomach between the sofa arm and the hall doorway — "spasm of domesticity remains elusive. Two centuries' accumulation of dust, perhaps?"

"Hardly two centuries. I cleaned last spring. Would you mind going around? I just waxed the hall."

"Last spring? How merciful is memory's ability to deselect. I would be enchanted to go around, Emily, if the terrace doors were not also blocked." He wheezes with the irascibility of a man who, like all men, loathes having furniture shifted.

"OK, play through. But watch your step."

"Would that I still could. May I observe, Emily, that in my experience only three things tend to plunge a woman into such abandoned paroxysms of housecleaning. One: the last stages of pregnancy. Two: —"

"Wait, I'll move the sofa."

"I am waiting. Two: guilt. And three: —"

"Guilt? I don't know what you —"

"Guilt, my dear. You know, *mea culpa*. Of the order *materfamilias*." He waves a hand grandly. "Woman decides she's been neglecting her, ah, natural duties of late, hasn't been throwing her full weight into it. Symbolically and literally punishes and purifies self by drastic purging of dust, et cetera."

"Uncle Tyler, are you implying that I've been neglecting my, whatsit, natural duties?"

"My dear Emily, how would *I* know?" He hoists his eyebrows. "I was merely making a philosophical observation. Why must people insist upon inferring the

47

specific from the general?'' he inquires, in the measured diction that presages a discourse on the classical disciplines. "Syllogistically —''

"There,'' I grunt, heaving at the sofa. "You can pass.''

"Thank you. And three — Where was I? Oh yes. And three: imminent departure.''

"Imminent —''

"Departure. You know, absence. Yes, that's the third.''

"Third what?''

"Reason for all this'' — he flaps both hands — "activity. I don't believe you knew Mollie Ackeroyd? Before your time. Mollie came back from *uff*'' — he squeezes himself between sofa and doorway — "from Mayo's with the diagnosis of an inoperable tumor. That very day she started cleaning house. Turned it out from attic to cellar. Didn't quit until she finally had to take to her bed. The story was that her last words to Randolph — Randolph Ackeroyd was Molly's husband, dreadful bore, looked like a walrus, can't think what Mollie saw in him — her last words were a plea for him to bring her one of the old cartons remaining in the attic, so she could sort through it. Well. *Varium et mutabile semper femina.''* He chugs off down the hall, stately as the *Queen Mary,* unvarying and immutable in *his* ways, he would have me know. Not for *him* pregnancy, guilt, or imminent departure.

Through the open windows and from far down the hill the tootle of the school bus, discharging with a relieved gasp my three boys, who will in a moment be skidding over my fresh-waxed hall, busting out of their skins with energetic devices, and starved. And I have forgotten to go to the market. Dear Lord, do we have bread? Do we have milk? Do we have peanut butter

● ● ● ●

''What'd you do,'' Porter grunts, struggling to close the lid on the old freezer chest that sits like a coffin on the utility porch, ''buy out the General Store? Is Mr. Page retiring, or what?''

''The A & P in town was having a meat sale. And some other stuff. I thought I'd stock up.''

''You drove seventeen miles into town

49

and seventeen miles back just to save a few pennies on — What's this?"

"Potatoes. And some onions. We never have quite enough from the garden, and I told Jeannie and Mike they could share, in exchange for doing some weeding."

"Stoop labor? Them? It's hard enough to get that kid to mend a fence," grouses Porter, "unless you want to spend an hour discussing the transcendental implications of man-made barriers."

"Oh, they helped weed," I lie (the goat might have devoured some weeds along with the greens). I am forever trying to defend the indefensible, i.e., the young Katzes' philosophical stance, which could be described as supine — or perhaps I should say prone more to contemplation than to gross action. "Could you take the sacks down to the root cellar for me, Porter?"

"Emily, you've been laying in stuff as if you were expecting a siege."

"Well, but it'll all be used, dear. And you know how you hate to market."

"I don't hate to market, I just don't like having to stop on my way home to pick up stuff you've forgotten." This grousing of Porter's is mostly formality. He does it quite amiably. He grunts, heaving at a sack.

"Porter?" I come to stand before him, my hands awkwardly at my sides. "Porter? You know I love you, don't you?"

"Lord, this thing weighs a . . ." He straightens, turns to stare at me. "Why, sure I do. What brought that on?"

"I . . . just wanted you to know."

His face looks suddenly youthful, abashed. *How little it takes; how little I do.*

He puts his hands on my shoulders, slides them down my arms, gives them a quick squeeze. "I love you too," he mutters. He ducks and starts wrestling with the potato sack.

● ● ● ●

— dining room drapes to cleaners
— dentist: cleaning & checkup
— meeting Thurs. 8 pm
— Tim: eye app't Thurs 4:30
— attic

● ● ● ●

"Miz McPhail?" Voice on the phone, summoning me up from the recesses of a basement cubicle where I am sorting through maybe fifty years' accumulation of Mason jars, trying to find enough with lids so I can put up two crates of applesauce — still in the form of apples — which for the first time in my life it seems imperative to do. "Thishere's Ida? Over to Dobbs Flat? You got some of your cows wandered loose over here, looks to me like maybe seven . . . ?"

I thank her and hang up. Rush out into the cold gray wane of the afternoon, up the lane back of the house skirting the edge of the woods and all the way up the slope past the pasture (broken fence) to the barn, where I find Mr. Garrett forking hay off the tractor wagon. His red old winter-apple face turns even redder and sourer. We scramble into the old truck and bounce back down the lane, peeling off behind the veg-garden to the shack, where I leap out and pound on the door, which Jeannie eventually opens. "Gee," she says, "I don't know where Mike is. I mean maybe he's over at the barn or something?" I say No he's not and Will's way over by the creek bed cutting up a dead tree and there's some cows loose and we need another hand. "Oh, wow," she says in her wondering voice, "I've got this yogurt I'm making. . . ." "Come on. I'll *buy* you some yogurt." I scramble back into the truck and haul her up by the hand; she has trouble with her fringed shawl and her long flowered skirt but she is wearing, I note thankfully, her mocassin boots. Mr. Garrett shoots her a look of baleful Blue Ridge contempt — hippies! Bums! Don't know the meanin of an honest day's work! — as he guns the rattling truck down the hill.

The cows are straggled out in the road and along the ditch. This is the season when the calves start coming, and they are mean and skittery. One of them looks about ready to deliver; her tail's high and stiff and a thin, opalescent balloon has begun to appear; she backs away, lowering her head and shaking her horns. The three of us spread out, arms wide. My cowardly heart is banging around fit to choke me. Protected only by my T-shirt, arms spread and sacrificial, I have to dig for every ounce of will I possess to take one slow, cautious step forward, and another, and another . . .

Until finally the wretched beast lets out a bellow, breaks, turns tail, and bolts through the nearby gate that Ida Whosit has ambled down obligingly to open. The rest of the strays, bawling, follow. They'll be OK in here until Mr. Garrett can round up a couple of the neighbors to help herd them back the four miles to our place. "Mike was gonna fix the fence yesterday," Jeannie says amiably as we rattle back home, "only he couldn't find those big thingies, you know, those wire cutters." Mr. Garrett's wizened old face is flaming with rage. Someday he's going to have a stroke. Then where will we be?

● ● ● ●

"Emily?" Voice on the phone again, 8:30 P.M., summoning me down from Stuart's room, where I am being counseled in the correct way to sew the First Aid Merit Badge on the uniform. "I hope I'm not interruptin your supper," it says softly, charmingly, not needing to identify itself; who but Catherine Tupper would assume a family doesn't get hungry before time to put its youngest to bed? "I'm goin over my appointments and I see we've got the taxpapers' meetin on Thursday, and if it's not too inconvenient I'm wonderin if you could postpone it until after Thanksgivin. What with the holiday season comin on, we're all gettin terribly busy. Also I'm wonderin if you could drop by for tea Friday afternoon around four? There's some people comin from Richmond I think you'd be interested in talkin with." She pauses, then adds in a portentous murmur, "And Harry's comin for a few days. It'll be an awfully good time for us to have a little council of war, don't you think? There'll just be the three of us."

"I —"

"I've been discussin things with him, of course, and he's *most* interested in meetin you again and havin a *real* talk." There is another loaded pause.

"That's nice of you, Mrs. Tupper. But I'm not sure yet that I —"

"My dear, I understand. Perfectly. Why

don't you bring that nice husband of yours along next week, by the way?''

''I'm afraid he has classes in the afternoon. And I —''

''We'll make it in the evening, then. Yes, let's do that. The Richmond people aren't all that necessary yet. It's always a delight conversin with your Porter — so intellectual — and I know he'll be interested in, ah, what we have to propose. . . .'' She trails off into a sociable little laugh. Out here we're always aware that we're speaking on a party line.

''It's not just him, Mrs. Tupper, although that's a, uh, consideration. Frankly in my own mind, the question of whether or not I'm qualified to —''

''Why not just let *us* make that judgment?'' The laugh takes on an edge. ''Bein not entirely inexperienced in these matters.'' The edge smooths again. ''Your modesty's most refreshin, though. It's goin to be a real asset. So you just stop frettin, and we'll be lookin forward to seein you *and* your charmin husband on, let's see, Wednesday evenin? Shall we say around nine?"

"Mrs. Tupper." I fortify myself with a deep breath. "As you say, Thanksgiving is coming up, and what with the family and everything, and vacation, and . . . everything, I'd rather wait until afterward." To ward off further negotiations, I promise her I will, I really *will,* call her then.

•   •   •   •

"Ah-prease, honable ah-Mista Blur Fox, not to fringing humble labbit into bliah-potch." The Golden Oldie, delivered in my interpretive Japanese hiss, fails for the first time to break Timmie up. He continues to recline cold-sober against my arm, sniffling occasionally when he remembers to. He has — for some reason I haven't diagnosed — decided he has a severe cold and cannot attend school today. I have — for some reason I haven't diagnosed — decided not to call his bluff, and to grant him credibility. "Humble labbit request ah-prease to fringing onnyprace else but bliah-potch," I hiss.

His hair smells like dry oak leaves, his breath like apples, his room like sneakers.

57

It used to smell like talcum in here, and the faint ammoniac tang of diaper pails. *Sic transit,* I think with a pang curiously composed of regret and anticipation. But why curious? That a mother may both regret the departure of the baby and anticipate the approach of the man? Surely it is Nature's wisdom that we must eventually, lovingly, free each other?

● ● ● ●

"*La donna è MO-bi-le*" rolls, like far thunder, from the kitchen. "*La la la LAH-la-la . . .*" Uncle Tyler can never remember the words after the opener.

"Crissake. Mother , do we *haf*ta eat supper with you tonight?" PJ, kneeling in front of the fireplace it is his duty to haul logs to from the terrace, scowls up at me. His inadvertently pleading posture grabs me. My stance on the partaking of Uncle Tyler's Gourmet Specials is We're all in it together, sink or swim and no survivors left to mourn. But my maternal instincts, which tend to snooze if not to slumber, have of late been uncommonly wakeful.

"Tell you what. As long as Timmie's feeling poorly, maybe you and Stuart could have a quiet supper with him in the TV room — just soup, or something." I will have to negotiate this somehow with Porter, who has always upheld the tenet that eating is not a spectator sport. Maybe — ah, my female cunning is aroused along with my maternal instinct — I will put on some eye shadow and get into that velvet housecoat Porter gave me (rather wistfully) two Christmases ago, which has always made me feel uncomfortably like a female impersonator, and propose that we have a candle-lit *adult* supper, just the three of us.

"We get to eat in front of the TV, oh *boy!*" Stuart gives me a hug; even PJ forgets himself enough to bring in an extra load of logs without even being nagged.

● ● ● ●

Somebody — it couldn't have been Mama; but I get the impression it was some matronly authority on Respectability — used to say, "Think of how embarrassing it would be if you were in an automobile accident and your undergarments were unclean, or repaired with a safety pin?" I know she wasn't directing the question specifically at me (Mama's training on *personal* cleanliness, at least, took hold) but I pondered it; and now I find myself suddenly aware that if I were ever to depart this house (for where? For what?) I would want to leave it in order. I would want to leave it well stocked: in provisions, in affection.

● ● ● ●

"Emily. You might as well confess." Porter, who's been sitting at the card table in front of the library fire, correcting midterm exam papers for his Introduction to English Poetry, throws down his pen.

I jam the needle into my finger.

He stands, shuffles papers. "Don't you think it'd be easier if I knew?"

The drop of blood spreads slowly over the white silk of my slip, whose ripped lace I am mending.

"You don't really want to handle this alone. It's not the kind of thing you do easily," Porter continues, tidily arranging sheafs in his briefcase.

The slip is silk because it was part of my trousseau. Sixteen years ago you could still find a silk slip. I found this one in a dresser drawer I was cleaning out. I found I couldn't bring myself to throw it away.

Porter snaps the briefcase closed. "All this work you've been doing, it's unnecessary. Nobody's going to care whether or not the curtains are washed."

Although why I'd keep something like a silk slip, which nobody in this house of men could ever want . . . The pretty little stitches (who would ever see them? Who would ever care, or know?) swim under my stare.

He comes to stand before me. "Let yourself off the hook, Em. I could be of some help, you know."

". . . help . . .?"

"Em, come on. Now that I've figured it out, you may as well admit it. You're fixing to throw a big surprise anniversary party." He chuckles. "It's pretty obvious. All these elaborate preparations, this cleaning up and marketing — You never could get ready for a big party the easy way, honey. Which is why I figure I'd better step in and give you a hand. Otherwise you'll be so exhausted you'll spend the party in bed. Now, then. How many have we got coming?"

•　•　•　•

"That's the night of the Dog Breeders' Association meetin. I don't see how we could —"

"Lucy, please. It's our anniversary. How could we have an anniversary party without you and Weston?"

"Seems to me you could've planned it a mite sooner. Or did you just happen to notice the great event was comin up?"

"It was, uh, going to be a surprise for Porter, but he —"

"You were fixin to surprise the guests too?" But Lucy relents. "Well, shoot, if it's your anniversary and all. Nowadays I guess we have to celebrate if people manage to stick together sixteen years," she says tartly.

•　•　•　•

"If you weren't going to make it a supper party," Porter protests, "how come you put in all that food?"

"I got so busy cleaning the house, I

don't have the energy left to plan a banquet," I say pleadingly.

"That's what happens when you don't consult me." But Porter pats my shoulder. "Never mind, honey, it was the thought that counts. I'll get some champagne, make it festive." Porter loves festivities.

• • • •

"Forgot to tell you." Porter sticks his lathered face around the bathroom door. "I asked some of my students."

"Oh Porter, that's fine, but they *eat* so much —" Guilty about not serving a real dinner, I've made a last-minute run to the market for hors d'oeuvres, canned ham and rye bread and cheese and nuts and hideously expensive stuff like artichoke hearts and smoked oysters.

"Never mind," he says expansively. "Oh — and I asked Vernon Crouse."

"Vernon . . ." I grope in my closet, snag my best dress, wonder — too late! — if I should've pressed it, know I should've sewn on the button which I secured, how long ago, with a safety pin. Mama said I should never use safety pins but sometimes I do. Oh guilt.

"Crouse. I *told* you, the visiting poet."

"Oh." Visiting poets drink a lot. "Porter, are you sure we've got enough champagne? And how about the kids —"

"Emily." Splash. "Honey." Splash. "Relax. It's a party. People come to parties to have a good time, remember?" Porter goes to parties, Porter gives parties, to have a good time. I'm not all that good at parties. I can never think of amusing things to say. Only controversial things, like "What is *your* stance on the destruction of Seward Creek?"

Porter comes out, swabbing at his face with a towel. The face is smooth, anticipatory, handsome. "Honey, it's your anniversary party. Hell, sixteen years together is an occasion for celebration nowadays." He grins, eyes me in my slip, comes over to kiss me. It is a long kiss, and we have only a short time. Why is it husbands become amorous when one is struggling to get a dress — or supper — on? "You're so damn pretty," he murmurs, "with your hair like that around your shoulders. Don't pull it back,

OK? And wear the earrings."

"But —" The earrings are an heirloom. Although they're not worth what used to be called a "fortune," they are handsome ruby teardrops in a dangly Tiffany silver setting. When Mother McPhail presented them to me — a solemn ceremony indeed — she quoted that passage from the Bible about Who shall find a virtuous woman, her price is above rubies. I have always felt uneasy wearing the McPhail ruby earrings. I am not the svelte, dangly type. "— but Porter, if I don't hold my hair back with a barrette the earrings wouldn't show. And besides, with this green dress I'd look like Christmas."

"Christmas." He laughs. Porter can get high on parties even before he has a drink. "Now there's a thought. We can make it a combination anniversary and Christmas party." He is high on excitement as a schoolboy, standing there in his boxer shorts. I will say this for Porter: he has handsome legs, even if he's added an inch or two to his waistline. "What the hell," he says, "I was going to wait until afterward, when we were alone, but why not do it now."

"Porter! We haven't time —"

He bends upon me a boyish leer. "No, and isn't it too bad. I meant, give you your anniversary present. It's partly for Christmas, anyway."

"Oh Porter dear, not now! Afterward —" Afterward, when we are alone, I am going to give Porter his anniversary present. I am going to open my bureau drawer, where under my fresh-mended silk slip I have slipped an envelope, and in it I have laid out my plea, as honestly and lovingly as I know how. It is (I have at last perceived) a matter of trust. What could honor a husband more than his wife's trust that he will understand? "— afterward, Porter, when there's time for us to be alone together, and talk —"

But he is already opening his bureau drawer, and has brought out . . .

". . . an envelope?"

"Open it." He holds it out to me, shy and impatient and delighted with himself. "Open it, Em."

Inside are two round-trip airline Christmas Excursion Package tickets to the Bahamas.

• • • •

"Carpemus diem, my dear." Whom has Uncle Tyler got trapped in the pantry, and what is he proposing they seize? Not — I smile in a vague hostessy way as I sidle past a clot of students surrounding the punch bowl and hors d'oeuvres — Margaret Chauncy again? *"Nunc aut nunquam,"* continues the voice in an intimate roar, "now or —"

"Never." I push open the pantry door. Uncle Tyler is sauvely peering down Margaret Chauncy's cleavage.

"What, never? Hello, Emily." Uncle Tyler smiles sauvely at me. "No, never, or hardly ever," he finishes with a philosophic shrug, winks at me, clicks his heels to Margaret, and moves off in a stately way to the kitchen.

"Amazin," breathes Margaret. "All that energy at his age."

Amazing, all that coquetry at Margaret's age, fifty if it's a day, and wouldn't you think that she'd have learned not to get trapped in pantries? If Margaret Chauncy wishes to be trapped it will not be in my pantry or with my uncle-in-law, who is still gallant enough to make a fifty-year-old woman feel dangerous. Jeffrey J. Chauncy's jealousy is dangerous. And Jeffrey J. Chauncy, as head of the County Board of Zoning Appeals, is dangerously powerful.

I draw Margaret back out into the dining room, seeking somebody safe to unload her on — clot of students, mostly bearded, thus male, thus unsafe — and steer her through to the library where another clot, female, has coagulated around the sofa in various seraglio poses, which means that Vernon Whatsisname, Louse, the poet, is holding court; and what with all that youthful competition Margaret, and/or the poet, should be quite safe. So I drag her over, which given Margaret's dimensions versus mine indicates how strong two strong drinks can make me, and dump her squalling with joy ("Oh Mr. Louse I am such an admiruh of youah work!") into the poet's magnetic field.

Donning the hostess expression which signals crab puffs burning in the kitchen, I tack past a ladies' group discussing the upcoming Art Tour of Historic Houses (ours is historic but in too far gone a decline to have been included), a cluster of Porter's colleagues gossiping about the Department Chairman's finagling of funds to lure the poet, an *ad hoc* meeting of student wives deploring the boost in soybean prices, and a mixed brace of County discussing new techniques of flash-freezing sperm for artificial insemination.

I am ambushed by Nancy Benjamin. She gets a lock on my arm and my eyeballs and says in conspiratorial tones, "Emily. I see *every*body's here tonight. Practically the entire county. And on such short notice. What's the *real* occasion?" Nancy's manner gives the impression of a female spy. The impression is correct. "You can tell *me,*" she murmurs.

"I did tell you, Nancy. It's our anniversary."

"Oh, I know what you're *telling* people," she says with a narrowed gaze, "but I get the impression that Harry Griffin's going to be here tonight. You wouldn't be thinking of making an announcement, would you?''

I know where Nancy may have picked up this impression: she shares our party line. "If Harry Griffin were going to be here tonight I s'pect I'd know about it," I say with a little laugh, "and I don't. I'm afraid the only formal announcement I have is, uh, I think something's burning in the kitchen."

What is burning in the kitchen is me. I hang around in there simmering for a while, which boils off some of my liquid courage. But I am the hostess; I have responsibilities. I square my shoulders and march back out, elbow my way through the beards, and am splashing myself a bit of whiskey when I lose half of it to a jar on the elbow.

"Sorry," mumbles the jarrer, a quite young boy — no, girl — student whose mouth is very full. She is holding a loaded plate just under her chin, which cuts down on the distance needed for the transfer of fork to mouth. She is wearing an overlarge army battle jacket and patched blue jeans and she looks starved. She keeps her gaze starvedly on her plate, keeps shoveling.

"Have some more," I say as I edge off. "Have some crab puffs, or something."

"There aren't any crab puffs."

"Well . . ." I wave my glass vaguely. I am feeling disoriented; I rarely have more than two drinks; tonight my courage keeps draining away along with the whiskey; I need to think myself back to courage, slip away and reexamine the reasons that sounded so logical in that letter lying in my bureau drawer. ". . . they must've burned. Try the clam dip."

"Are you the hostess?" She has stopped chewing. She lowers her plate. She raises her gaze to mine. There is a click as she gets an eyeball lock on me. "Are you Emily McPhail?"

"Yes," I say, wrenching my eyes free, skittishly edging off, "but if you'll excuse me, I must, uh . . ."

"Wait. Can I talk to you —"

I manage to slither away. Porter's little girl-students, the few who bother to talk to me, want either to impress me (and

71

thus Porter) with their mature insights into Eng. Lit. 311 or else they want me to "free" Porter, with whom they have decided they are in love, for "alternative confrontations." If you've seen one undergraduate insight you've seen 'em all. If there is anything I do not wish, in this crisis of nerve that seems to be bringing my house down around my ears tonight, it is to tackle the problem of alternative confrontations.

. . . There is Porter: standing over by the fireplace, one elbow on the mantel, listening to Harvey Plante. Harvey would be propounding on flood control. Harvey is County Engineer and is beginning to talk about the necessity of rerouting Seward Creek. Harvey will recommend that over my dead body. (Or the body of my marriage? Porter? Would it have to be that?)

Why should it have to be that? What law of nature says it would have to be that?

Dear Porter. If only gratitude were all I needed to feel, were all you needed to receive. Standing here looking at him across the crowded room, I feel my eyes flood with maudlin tears. That is what two and a half drinks do: liquefy what is left of the brain and swirl it out through the eyes.

"Emily McPhail? Are you really Emily McPhail?"

It is the little girl who looks like a boy and eats. I stare at her and her image refracts, swirling. "No. I mean not *now, please.*" I push past her and flee for the stairs.

•   •   •   •

Dearest Porter: For weeks I have been wondering what to say to you, how to approach you so that you will understand. Now, on the occasion of our sixteenth anniversary together, it has come to me. I must *trust* you to understand. For that is what a great part of love must surely be: trust.

Dear Porter, I have a decision to make, and I can't make it without your help, and your blessing. What I have to decide, and very soon, is whether or not to consent to run for political office in this district. It would involve most —

maybe all — of my time and attention. It would demand the total cooperation of you, the boys, the family

The bedroom door is opening. I slap my hands down, guiltily, over the paper. Huddled beneath the bedside lamp, I stare out into the dimness beyond it. "Who is it?"

"Me." A girl's voice.

"You could've knocked."

She approaches. It is the little short-haired girl. "I wanted to talk to you," she says flatly. She stops. She stands just beyond the rim of light. I can feel, rather than see, her eyes pinning me inside it. "I have to talk to you," she says again.

"I'm sorry. I'm busy right now."

"You are Emily McPhail. Right?" she says without moving.

"Right. And you're a student of Porter's, right?" The slight threat is intended.

"Wrong."

"Well, a student, then. Anyway. I'm glad you could come to the party, but the party *is* downstairs."

"Your daughter," she says flatly. "If you're Emily McPhail, then I'm your daughter."

Three

— Where? I asked her.

— Boston. Mass. General Hospital, she said.

— When?

— November third, 1957. A Sunday morning, she said, turning her face into the light of the lamp, at 3:37 A.M. Baby girl, she recited, weight six pounds five ounces. Born to Emily Elizabeth Hughes, age eighteen, unmarried.

— How did you find me? How could you ever have found me? The records are supposed to be sealed. They sealed everything away, nobody ever can find anybody again, they seal us away. And my name, my married name, how did you find me here, way out in the country, with a married name?

— My name, she said, is Alexandra. She

would not tell me her last name. That has nothing to do with you, she said. To do with me: her red hair. Brighter and more golden than mine, but red. Unmistakably: mine.

• • • •

"We'll say you're my niece." I sit on the bed shivering and rocking with my arms wrapped around my breasts as if to protect myself from a bitter wind. Cold, cold; I will never again be warm. "Yes, that's it," I chatter, "we'll say you're my niece, my brother Robert's daughter, come unexpectedly to visit, on your way through from — where is Robert now?" I ask her and she doesn't answer. "Still in Maine, I suppose, he planted himself so firmly in that town, he must own it by now, if his father-in-law corked off and left him to manage the mills, which is why he married that girl, he told me as much. I can't stand the thought of my brother," I chatter with a stinging in my eyes like lye, "he turned out to be such a terrible man, there was nothing of charity in him in spite of all Mama's teachings — I went to him when I found I was pregnant

77

with you and I asked him what I should do and his face turned hard and cold and I saw that I disgusted him. He was afraid of scandal. 'How could you have been so stupid and cheap?' he said. He was the only family I had left then, eighteen years old and Mama dead just after I went off to Radcliffe, and never really knowing Daddy except a photo of an officer with wings on his chest. He would've been your grandfather," I babble, "only his plane was shot down over the Pacific when I was four. Military officers have always been mythic figures to me —" I stop.

I tighten my voice like a tourniquet around my words. "We'll have to say you're my niece. If I don't know anything about Robert now, neither does anybody else here. So nobody will question it. We'll have to tell them you're my niece."

Her silence is massive. The space between us fills with a slow, glacial pressure. How can such a slight figure, standing there at the rim of light, impose such a sense of mass and volume and weight, so that it seems to occupy the entire room? Perhaps it is the pressure of seventeen years' absence, become all in one moment a presence. She stands motionless just outside the light. If she took a step nearer I would have to stare seventeen years in the face.

I close my eyes. "Please," I say, rocking with my arms wrapped about myself, "tell them you're my niece."

Somewhere below my feet it seems there are boulders being slowly ground together, pulverizing what was once acres of serene meadow. "Why did you have to come? What do you want of me?"

"You're my mother."

"But you have a — an adopted mother. You were adopted. I signed the papers. Isn't she — she nice? My God" — and my cry sounds thin and far — "hasn't she been good to you? Hasn't she loved you all these years?"

"You're my blood."

"But hasn't she — been good? Oh, if she hasn't —"

"You wouldn't have known." The voice is flat, uninflected.

"Please, I can't stand it. How can I

stand thinking they haven't been good to you?"

"You could stand not knowing."

"You don't know. You have no idea. All these years. I wake up in the middle of the night and it's as if I've been drowning, trying to know and trying not to remember —"

"Why don't we just cool this for now. I'm sorta . . . tired."

"Tired . . . Yes. Oh, you must be tired." I pass the heels of my hands over my eyes. "Coming all this way from Boston —"

"I didn't say I came from Boston."

"Where, then? Did you take a bus, or a plane, or . . . How did you get here? How did you find me?" My voice is tightening again. "They sealed the records. There was no way even for me to find out who took you, where you went —"

"Did you try? To find out?"

Another massive silence descends. Her voice cracks through it wearily. "You got an extra bedroom in this place?"

"Yes. Yes, I'll make it up for you." I haul myself up from the edge of the bed.

Bones heavy as boulders, they feel. I haul them up to look seventeen years in the face at last.

. . . Seventeen? Almost a woman? How then so slight, so very childlike: not over fourteen she seems to be, in the boy's jeans and oversize jacket and her cap of ruddy ringlets and her stripling length. She has to raise her chin to meet my gaze: she too is staring at seventeen years. The chin is pointed; the mouth wide and firm-set; the nose straight, short, a bit sharp; the eyes

Dark. Dark, like his. Surely it's only a trick of the shadows, the lamp striking the edge of her cheekbone, the tangle of hair over her brow that way, like a faun's, like some sort of half-dreamed creature you can never see clearly

"Emily? There you are." Porter? Oh God, Porter. "What're you doing up here so long? Everybody's asking —"

"I'll be down in a minute. I was just coming, Porter, I really was." Something cracks against my teeth: my mouth, stretching to a grin. "I was just — just having a little talk with — with Alexandra here. You know, Alexandra? My niece? My" — I haul a steadying breath in around the grin to keep it in place — "brother Robert's girl?"

"Oh?" says Porter blankly.

"Yes" — I grin — "Robert's daughter. Isn't that a surprise? I didn't even know I had a niece."

"I'm not sure I knew you had a brother."

"Certainly you did, Porter." I turn my grin on him like a spotlight, so that he blinks. "Remember, I told you about Robert once. It was right after we met and you asked me if I had any —"

"Oh. Yeah. I guess I remember something about that." Porter blinks again. "You said you never wanted to hear his, uh . . ." Good manners reassert themselves. He turns to the girl, smiles. "So you're Emily's niece? Well. You have your aunt's pretty red hair. It must run in the Hughes family."

Please, I plead wordlessly. *Only this one thing. Do this one thing for me and I'll never ask another.*

She wraps her arms around her frail

chest. I sense that she too is very cold, trying not to shiver. Unmoving, she seems to shrink under Porter's friendly regard.

"I guess I'm your uncle Porter, then."

She continues to shrink, staring down at her sneakers.

Please. Please. Just this one thing.

"Well," says Porter, a bit overheartily, "welcome to the McPhail house. It's nice to have you."

She doesn't move. She doesn't look up. Finally, "Thanks," she mutters.

I close my eyes. *Thanks.*

● ● ● ●

"Please, Porter, couldn't we just leave everything? I'll clean it all up in the morning."

"I don't feel like going to bed." Porter winds high on parties, likes to unwind slowly. "You go if you're tired." He piles glasses onto a tray, empties ashtrays into the embers of the fire.

Tired: Lord, Lord, I've never before known what it is to be tired. I haul my granite bones through the rooms, swiping at table tops with crumpled napkins. Find myself at the kitchen table, sitting and staring.

"Funny thing, her just appearing like that." Porter appears in the kitchen with a loaded tray. "Emily, there's no use your just sitting there. If you're all that dead on your feet you might as well turn in." He piles plates onto the sink, rolls up his shirt sleeves. "Funny she didn't write, or at least phone, first. Or did she?"

"Did she what?"

"Write or phone to let you know she was coming." He squirts in detergent and turns on the tap. "I'm talking about your niece, Emily. You really are out of it."

"She . . . said it was just an impulse. Porter, you're not going to wash all these now? It's after one-thirty."

"I'm not sleepy. She came on 'impulse'? Why would she get an impulse to see *you,* if you and her father have been estranged all these years?" He scrapes scraps into the dogs' bowls. They creep up, sniff, begin to wolf the mess down. "You don't suppose the girl's run away, or something?"

The sound of the dogs' eating is making me queasy. "I don't know. I . . . didn't quiz her, Porter, we didn't have time really to . . . She was so tired, you saw how tired she was. Porter, I'm sorry, I'm tired too. Can't we leave everything until tomorrow . . ."

Go to bed, he commands; so I drag myself up the stairs. I have this drugged sense that if only I can go to sleep, I will wake up tomorrow with this confused nightmare over, and my world all orderly around me again. Maybe — I think as I fumble with the earrings, get out of my clothes — that is what this is: only a new version of the dream, so urgent and powerful that it seems a waking one, a kind of breakthrough of the imagination.

Imagination: It was like telling myself a story seventeen years long. What is she doing now, at this moment? What has she, at this moment, become? Imagining, I tried to fix her image in an orderly succession of stills. In a series of time-lapse snaps, she unfolded like a flower: starting with the tight little bud which was the only image I possessed, she expanded from that one intense glimpse into a seventeen years' album of images, each evolved from its predecessor. (She is two months old today. Her eyes are darkening now, like his; the straight, delicate shadows of her brows are being brushed in; the new, drowned aspect is clearing, firming. What does she see? What face, bending over hers, absorbs her wondering stare? Does my own image, first-planted on her retinas, fade, supplanted by these others'. . . ?)

November 3, 1958: a late Monday afternoon, cold and sleeting; dodging the traffic across Harvard Square, hurrying to meet the man who'd just become my fiancé, I bumped into a young woman with a baby in her arms. The baby's head bobbed at her shoulder; its face inside its little furred hood was close to mine and just beginning to startle; its wide-eyed glance locked with mine for a moment. *Birthday;* I thought; *one year old today.* The baby's gaze unlocked and blurred as it bobbed away. I scurried on with my chin down in my upturned collar and presently Porter's face appeared — eager; his face was young then, it lit with recognition — and it seemed stranger than any stranger's face to me. I understood then that no matter how long I lived with it or how familiar every aspect of its features became to me, this man's face would remain — in a way having to do with a trick of light — strange to me. Strangers are those who are not entirely known. Strangers are also those who do not entirely know. Maybe it was out of this understanding that I blurted to him, "Porter? Let's get married now? Not wait until Christmas?" He was taking me to supper at Cronin's and there was a bottle of red wine, I remember, and there was a candle in another bottle. Two points of flame caught in his pupils as he stared across at me. *Maybe those will be enough to warm me,* I thought; *maybe they won't go out when he knows.* When he knows: I could not bear to wait to have happen what might happen when he knew about me. It would be better, whatever it was, than having a stranger's face the only face that looked at me with love. (*Stupid,* my brother said when he knew, *and cheap . . .*) We were married two weeks later, after Porter had passed his orals for his Master's degree. There was no man to give me away. I remember waking up in my college dormitory room the morning I was to be married, thinking *He will ask me afterward, and I'll tell him then. Then, no matter what, his face won't be a stranger's.* Porter did not ask me. Perhaps it was because I wept, unexpectedly and stormily, just as the moment broke. "What is it? Tell me — Ah there, honey, there, don't," he gasped. "Did I scare you? Was I too — Ah, Emily, my own Emily . . ." Or perhaps it was because he was borne up into a kind of rapturous innocence, claiming what he loved; and sensing this, I wept the more bitterly, that this good man should, all ardent and unknowing, be thus duped.

That first moment lost, it became the only moment. What moment, in all of sixteen years, could have arrived when it was possible to say to a good man's face, "You have been duped"? Each moment of ardor strengthened the innocence, compounded the injury, made strange (for the moment) the familiar face of love.

• • • •

"Cousin *who?*" PJ blinks over his orange juice.

"Alexandra. Your mother's niece. Timmie, wipe the jam off your hands before you get it on your shirt." Porter winces slightly in the morning sun. His face looks heavy, a bit swollen.

"Where is she?" Like his father, Stuart loves company.

"Still asleep. You'll meet her when you get back from school. Speaking of which, it's time you boys get ready."

"Ale*xan*dra." PJ rolls his eyeballs ceilingward. "What is she, some kinda princess, with a name like —"

"She is a very nice girl," snaps Porter, "and you will not make fun of her name. You will be courteous to your cousin, young man, and remember she is also our guest."

"How long's she gonna stay?" Stuart says.

"How come she doesn't hafta go to school?" Timmie says.

"Who wasn't being nice? Jeez, I was only re*mark*ing," PJ says.

"Emily," groans Porter, "will you kindly see that these boys get ready for the bus? I'm already late." He lurches off. "Boy," mutters PJ, "he must've really got drunk last night." "Did he?" Timmie says in tones of scientific inquiry. "Mother, did Daddy really get drunk last —"

"No. Boys, please," I plead weakly. "Daddy and I were up very late, so we're a bit tired. Be big boys and get yourselves ready for the bus . . ."

I am left, at last, in the wan sunlight of the breakfast table, shakily pouring myself the dregs of acrid coffee, trying not to wake up. I lean my elbows on the table, raise my cup with both hands, close my eyes. It was only a dream, Emily, Mama used to say; go back to sleep.

"And who," Uncle Tyler's voice booms from the hall, "are you, my dear? A charming item left over from the party?"

You could put it that way.

•　　•　　•　　•

— Please, I said, consider what you're doing. Two families are involved in this

— How do you know the other is a

family? she said.

— How can I know anything, when you won't tell me?

— You don't need to know these things. You don't need to know anything except that I'm here, she said. The afternoon sun spilling palely in the library windows splashed on her face but did not warm it.

— But *why* are you here?

— I don't know how many times we have to go over this. I'm here because I'm your . . . niece. She smiled, coldly.

— I don't know what you want. If only you'd tell me what you *want* from me.

She didn't answer. She stood looking out the tall windows, her hands shoved into her jeans back pockets. *How small she looks,* I thought with a flick of terror.

— Are you hungry? Wouldn't you like something else to eat?

— I just had lunch. Don't you remember, you just gave me lunch. Is this whole place yours? All these pastures and gardens and barns and things? You must be rich.

— It's a lot of land, a big house, but it's old, it's all gone to seed. Places like this, there's a lot of them around here; very few people can afford to keep them up or run them anymore. We're anything but rich . . . Did you think I might be?

— Did you think that's what I wanted? She looked over at me then, slantwise across her shoulder. Under the boy's cap of short curls her face was faunlike, inscrutable, hungry.

— I don't think . . . anything. I don't know anything. I don't know what you want from me, I repeated, helplessly.

— How about your instincts?

— Instincts?

— You know, motherly instincts. She smiled. Only the mouth curled, long and pretty like a ribbon, matching the slant of her stare.

— If I've got motherly instincts, you've got . . . daughterly ones. Is that what you're trying to tell me?

— I'm not trying to tell you anything.

She turned back to the window. The smile was gone. Her face, the inscrutable childlike profile, was pale and cold in the pale cold sun.

Four

"Ju-UH suis Ti-TA-nia, la la-la la-la — Emily my dear, if you'd fetch a larger bowl, it seems the dressing has begun to expand before it's in the turkey — *Ju-UH suis . . ."*

The kitchen door bursts open with a rush of chill air. Stuart, trailed by Timmie, all apple-cheeked and muddy-footed. "Take off your boots on the paper, boys," I command. "Where's PJ? You were supposed to've cleaned the fireplace and got that wood in."

"We were, Mother, only we were showing Alexandra around and she and PJ went off somewhere," puffs Stuart, "and we couldn't carry it by ourselves."

"What's that smell? Ugh, what's that —"

"Oysters, Timothy my lad, the delicate

93

scent of the iodine deeps, the very *esse* of the sea. Close that door before that wintry blast reactivates your poor old uncle's arthritis."

"Where did PJ and Alexandra go?"

"We dunno. Mother, what's a voodoo?"

"You weren't supposed to *say,* Stuart," Timmie hisses. "She said not to *tell.*"

Stuart reddens. "I didn't tell. I just asked."

"Emily, if you'll hold the bird now, I'll stuff in the stuffing."

"Tell what, Stuart?"

"About the voodoo. What is it?"

"Voodoo's a form of superstition. What weren't you supposed to tell?"

"Nothing," Stuart mutters. "She just said there was a —"

"STUart!" wails Timmie.

" — voodoo ghost in the cabin."

"Now it'll *getcha,* you dumb Stuart!"

"Timmie, don't be silly. There's no such thing as —"

"*I* just said what *she* said, Mother," says Stuart.

"Well, then, she was silly to say it. She was just teasing, I'm sure," I say lightly.

"How about some lunch?"

"Not overmuch," Uncle Tyler warns. "Part of the Thanksgiving ritual is to starve all day and then feast. Recapitulates the occasion. Pilgrims and Indians et cetera."

"It's gonna getcha, Stuart. *I*'m not ever going *in* that cabin ever anymore!"

"Ew, Timid Timmie, scared of what a girl says —"

"What's all the fuss in here." Porter wanders in from the half-time break on TV. "The bird looks great, Uncle Tyler. Say, what's that smell?"

"Oysters. And a dash of saffron. Et cetera. Porter dear boy, you're just in time to lift this noble bird into the oven. My arthritis . . ."

"She said if you told, it's gonna getcha —"

"Lissen, baby Timmie, Mother said there's no such —"

"Boys! Stop that howling this minute. Is that any way to act on Thanksgiving?" Porter, wrestling to get the huge turkey into the oven, turns to holler over his shoulder. The pan tilts. The turkey falls to the floor with a great squishy thump. Dressing oozes out of its split seams.

An appalled silence. Uncle Tyler clutches his chest, staring at the spreading gobs of slippery oysters. "The voodoo ghost," quavers Timmie. "It got out of the cabin." The quaver rises to a wail. "It's all Stuart's fault! She *said* if we told you, the ghost'd get out and —"

●   ●   ●   ●

"For that which we are about to receive, may the good Lord make us truly thankful." Will Jackson's soft voice stills the babble at the table. It is Will's turn, this year, to deliver the Thanksgiving grace. It has a special grace, this year, emanating from the gentle folds of Will's dark old face, the dark old suit (once belonging to Porter's father, a considerably bigger but no better man). I am not sure what Will Jackson has, this year, to be specially thankful for; his beloved wife Carrie died in the spring; but Will Jackson's grace asks to be truly grateful, and that grace and gratitude shine out over the table.

"A-*men.*" Jeannie and Mike Katz, only

recently Into Jesus, sing out rather self-consciously. "A-men, brother!"

"Brothuh." Mr. Garrett sitting on my right, emits a muffled snort. He is wearing stiff new overalls, a red cotton shirt, a black patent-leather snap-on bow tie, and a scandalized expression. Mr. Garrett does not hold with calling a colored person brother (although he and Will have worked amicably side by side — Will a little to one side, as is proper — for over thirty-five years); nor does he hold with eating with the family (although he has done so every Thanksgiving for the fifteen years since he was widowered and I, bride-new, invited him); and, further, he does not hold with the Katzes ("don't know the meanin of a honest day's work") in general, or particularly The Religion expressed outside the confines of the Baptist Church, Batesville.

"Well." Porter, moved, clears his throat. He rises from his chair, picks up the carvers. "They say," he says, as he always says, and his father before him said, "that a carver is either a fool or a knave. I, for one, have never been accused of being a fool." He smiles, gently mocking himself.

Everybody smiles, with the exception of PJ, who rolls his eyeballs, and Alexandra, who is sitting at Porter's right ("The place of honor, honey," Porter said gallantly as he seated her) doing what I've come to think of as her Shrinking Act. She has a curious way of seeming to get smaller by withdrawing into herself, so that she begins to look ephemeral, transparent, drifting away feature by feature until there is only the sense of her presence — hardly visible but permeative somehow, the way a thin draft of chill air eddying through a room permeates the bones.

"Which is your choice, Alexandra? Light meat or dark?" Porter's wrists flick powerfully, sharpening the carving knife with a *shhhk shhhk shhhk* against the long, elegant steel. The blade has been honed over a century to a bare half-inch width. Porter loves this ceremony, inherited from his father and his father's father. "Breast or thigh?"

"Neither."

"Neither?" The blade pauses in midair. "Don't you like turkey?"

She doesn't answer.

"Maybe she doesn't like oysters," Stuart says helpfully.

"Pro tanto," says Uncle Tyler in hollow tones.

"Maybe she's, like, a vegetarian," chirps Jeannie. "That's really cool. I mean we'd be vegetarian, actually, except Mike has this low blood sugar condition."

"Hypoglycemia. It's a medical condition," Mike says. He says to Alexandra, "You a vegetarian out of humanistic principles, or only dietary? I mean, what's your position on eggs?"

"Let's get her position on turkey," Porter suggests. "Surely you'd like a bite, Alexandra? A nice thin slice of —"

"No. Nothing. Thank you."

"She could eat the sweet potatoes," Jeannie says. "I brought them. There's acorns in them. So they're, you know, ecological."

"I don't want anything. Thank you."

Mike squints across at her. "You're fasting, right?"

"Fasting," breathes Jeannie. "Oh, that's cool. That really is. Mike, isn't that cool? She fasting."

"Cool indeed, if you are referring to the dinner," Uncle Tyler says irritably. "Come come come come. Fasting? On a feast day? Contradiction in terms. Day to give *thanks,* y'know, for the harvest, et cetera." He says to Alexandra, "Surely you understand that, my dear, coming fron New England and all. Pilgrims. Indians, and so forth."

"And the Vietnamese?" Alexandra's smile is thin, chill, disembodied as the Cheshire Cat's. "And the people of Bangladesh? And the Ethiopians?"

"Oh, of course, the Vietnamese, and the other poor unfortunates. One must remember them, of course. One must do what one can, send checks, et cetera. Remind me to send a check, dear girl. But *after* Thanksgiving, when it is appropriate. Today it is appropriate to celebrate our blessings, and give thanks for them in an appropriate manner. In this case, feasting."

"What she's saying," says Mike, "is

where is the Vietnamese Thanksgiving? Where is the Thanksgiving for all the other victims of starvation and war? What've *they* got to be thankful for?''

''Isn't the Vietnam War all finished? Maybe they're grateful for that?'' Stuart hazards, bravely.

''A lot *you* know, Stuart,'' PJ snarls. ''Their whole place is a mess and *we* did it.'' He shoots an agonized glance at Alexandra and subsides, sliding deeper down in his chair.

Mr. Garrett snorts. ''They ain't hardly Americans, them Vietnese.''

''Hold it,'' Mike says tensely. ''They may have yellow skins but they're human beings.''

''Ain't Americans,'' Mr. Garrett snaps.

Porter clears his throat. ''I think we're really all in accord here. What we're saying is that Thanksgiving is a purely American tradition. So right now I don't think we need to —''

''Worry about stuffing ourselves,'' murmurs Alexandra, ''while the rest of the world is starving.''

Uncle Tyler groans. ''My dear, you have

resurrected the classical specter of prosperous societies. One recalls the Starving Armenians —"

"Starving?" Timmie's eye has begun to roll anxiously.

"Didn't they tell you?" Alexandra lifts her wondering smile. "Didn't they tell you, Timmie, about the Vietnamese, all the men and women and little children we dropped bombs on, and burned up their houses, and all their crops, so nobody has anything to eat? Didn't you know that all over the world people are starving? Didn't you know about that?"

"Mother? Do we know about that?" whispers Stuart.

"Everybody knows about that, stupid." PJ's face is raw and bleak. "It's a fact of *life*."

"Yeah." Mike folds his arms across his chest, looks around the table. "And what're we doing about it? Sitting around a loaded table. What're we doing about *any*thing?"

"Well, we could march on Washington," Jeannie says, "only we're not into violence."

"The rest of us are not into starvation," snarls Uncle Tyler, shifting his bulk in his chair. "And the turkey is congealing."

Porter picks up the carvers again. "OK. Let's shelve the question until later. Who wants light meat? Jeannie?"

"I dunno . . ." The Katzes exchange a deep, troubled look. "I guess maybe we'll pass it up this year," Mike mutters. "Yeah," says Jeannie. "I guess we sorta need to meditate . . ." They excuse themselves, drift out in a levitating, meditating sort of way.

"Boys?" Porter says tensely after a moment. "I've got this nice big drumstick —"

"I'm not very hungry, Dad." Stuart's anticipatory flush has paled. "I guess I don't want . . ." he gulps, ". . . anything."

"Me either," whimpers Timmie.

"Crissake." PJ shoves his hands in his pockets. "Who wantsta *eat*."

Porter carefully lays down the carvers. "Am I to understand that you boys are asking to be excused from Thanksgiving dinner? Because if you are, you may leave the table. Now."

They do so. One by one, without looking at us, they slink out of their chairs and shuffle out.

We finish the meal in silence: Porter and Uncle Tyler and Will and Mr. Garrett and I, presided over by Alexandra's thin, disembodied smile.

• • • •

My size-8 skirt hangs from her boy's hips like a sack. It has been a hassle to get her out of her jeans, which she has been wearing these five days since she arrived, and into something, anything, else so I can wash them. And her shirt, and her underwear.

"Her suitcase was lost on the bus," I have told Porter.

"You've got to get her something else to wear," he has told me.

She has told us nothing. When Porter asked her, politely, how long she was planning to stay, she muttered that she didn't know. Porter is renewing his suspicion that she's a runaway. "It may be a good idea to contact your brother," he says to me. A lurch of terror makes me blurt, "How can I contact him when I'm not even sure where he lives?" "Emily," Porter says, "All we have to do is *ask* the girl that." "Oh Porter no! I mean if we — if she *has* gone off for some reason, she'll think we're trying to turn her in, if we . . . I think we ought to just wait, and let her — I mean can't we just leave things *be* for a while?" He stares at me. "Your brother must be some kind of monster, if the idea of contacting him puts you in this state. OK, we'll let it ride for a while. But you've got to get her something else to wear besides those ragged blue jeans."

As I say, my skirt hangs on her. My shirt bags on her. She looks even younger, more like a waif, hunched down beside me in the car. She resists me in silence. She is the personification of passive resistance. What is she resisting? She tells me nothing, not even the most innocent fact about herself. What is she protecting of herself?

She does not even allow me a glimpse inside the huge fringed shoulder purse she carries. She thrusts her hand under the flap, withdraws a pack of cigarettes. She lights up, settles into a deeper slouch, turns her head to look out her side window.

I would like to comment that seventeen is too young to be smoking. I say nothing. *No rights,* her manner says. Rights imply responsibilities; therefore I could claim *No responsibilities.* Yet her very presence, here beside me in the car, is an intense, willed imposition of responsibility. *You are responsible for my presence in the world,* it signals; and at the same time, *You have no rights over me. You abandoned me. You signed over your rights.*

Ergo: I have no rights, only responsibilities. What are they? What has she come to me for?

I sneak a glimpse of her profile next to me: delicate and vitreous as a chip of flint, turned stubbornly to the window, watching the landscape — surely unfamiliar to her, with its gentle hills, lush meadows, an occasional manor glimpsed behind genteel groves, always commanding a rise, long white fences coursing gracefully for miles. What does she feel, down here amid the alien corn? Memory of my own first views makes me break the silence. "You've never seen Monticello, have you? Thomas Jefferson's house. It's very beautiful, very historic. Would you like to go there sometime? They have tours."

"Tours," she says flatly, "are for tourists."

• • • •

"Well, Emily. What on earth are you doin in the Teen Miss department?" Lucy Peters' voice booms over the howl of rock stereo. Lucy has her arms full of packages, ethereal Rachel in tow. "Try and find a decent-lookin dress in all these racks of decorated pants. Rachel's going to be a junior hostess at the Hunt Club Christmas Tea and all she's got that's halfway presentable is her wool suit. What could *you* be looking for in here?"

It had to come sometime. I introduce my "niece."

"You never mentioned you had a niece," Lucy booms reproachfully. "Where you from, Alexandra?"

"She's from New England," I put in.

Alexandra stands staring impassively at Rachel, whose pretty, polite smile fades. I add, "She's just down for the, uh, holidays."

"They must start early up there. Where in New England, honey?"

Alexandra is busy staring at Rachel, who drifts behind her mother. I mutter something which Lucy cannot hear over the stereo. She waves her head irritably. "Damn racket, they do it so a person can't think, buy anythin just to get away from it. Rachel," she bellows to her daughter, who has drifted away, "see if you can find a salesgirl. Well, Emily, we must get Alexandra together with the girls while she's visitin. Rachel's group's a little older of co'se, but maybe we can fix up somethin with Joannie's crowd . . . By the way, I haven't found out when you're leavin for the Bahamas. Weston says Porter mentioned it to him. Wish *we* could afford to go with you. I s'pose that means we won't be havin Christmas Eve together this year? Well, anyway, let me know about taking the boys — phone me, y'hear?" She steams off.

"You could've told her," Alexandra says with a curl of the lip, "I'm older than that Retchel of hers."

• • • •

She leans back into the corner of the booth, lights a cigarette, and slowly blows out a plume of smoke.

No rights, I remind myself shakily. It has been a shaky morning. "Don't you want the rest of your hamburger?"

"If I did, I'd eat it." She regards the smoke.

"Some ice cream, then? A milk shake?"

She blows another plume. "You're not going to fatten me up much. Or make me grow big and tall with strong teeth and bones and all that. You're not going to make me look more mature, no matter how you feed me."

"I'm not trying to make you look more mature." I hoist my coffee cup. I am weary, bone-weary, battered-weary from battering against this massive, passive resistance. She must have tried on everything in three stores. In everything she looked — I swear it was deliberate —

more waiflike, tinier, engulfed. She is forcing me into forcing her into my choices; she will make none of her own.

"Oh?" she murmurs. "Wouldn't you be more comfortable if I looked twenty-one instead of twelve?"

"Wouldn't *you?*" Her shrewd, cruel insight snaps some of my patience.

She lowers her cigarette, taps the ash onto the remaining half of her hamburger bun. "I don't know how old I look. I haven't checked that out lately."

"You mean you never look in a mirror, or what?"

"Why should I look in a mirror when I don't know who it is looking back?"

She lifts her head, meets my gaze. Over her chill, still smile the eyes are dark and unblinking. Something drawn over them like a black sheet of glass seems to bounce my own image off it resistively, like — Mirrors? What does that mean? Is she trying to tell me she can't see herself, doesn't know who she is?

(Maybe she's sick? Mentally ill? A breakdown — a lot of young people nowadays — Drugs? Oh God, LSD, or)

She raises her cigarette, draws on it, lounges back again.

Unlocked from her gaze, I fumble for my purse, busy my shaking hands. "Well," I hazard, and back down. "Maybe we should, uh, try the Shopping Plaza now. Unless you're too tired? Or — anything?"

"Why should I be tired? I'm never tired."

(Look, she said, *can we just cool this for now. I'm sorta tired.)*

"Are you sure?"

She doesn't answer. She crushes out her cigarette in the exact center of the bun half. She slides the strap of her bag across her shoulder, slides out of the booth, and ambles away without waiting for me.

●　　●　　●　　●

coat
nightgown/robe/underthings
shoes
slacks
dress

She has been in that dressing room a very long time. She does not want me to come in with her, but I go to check. I push the curtain aside and she is standing naked except for ragged bikini underpants, stepping out of some slacks. "Hey!" she cries, flicks a terrified glance, crouches protectively with her hands across her breasts. "It's just me," I say.

She turns her back to me, begins dressing. I edge out through the curtain, mumbling something about trying the store across the street.

(The nape of her neck, bending as she turned from me, was downy, humble; the curve of spine, of slim thighs, of tiny round breasts — so unexpectedly female, assailable, maidenly, that some hard dry pellet in my chest liquefies. *Daughter. Almost-woman. Flesh of my flesh.* That flick of terror: what terrifies her about that flesh?)

• • • •

"May I say," rumbles Uncle Tyler, "that if the clothes do not make the young lady, the young lady looks quite fetching in the clothes? I see, Alexandra, that you have legs. One can never be sure nowadays, what with all these trousers women wear.''

She rewards his gallantry with the flick of a cool smile, continues to eat in silence.

''When're we gonna put up the Christmas tree?'' Timmie wants — again — to know.

''It's not even the middle of December yet,'' Porter says.

''Jeannie and Mike already have theirs,'' Timmie says.

''Yeah, we helped cut it and carry it,'' Stuart says.

Porter says, ''Where did they cut it?''

''In the woods behind the south pasture. When're *we* —''

Porter puts down his fork, looks across at me. ''I told them to check with you first. Did you tell them they could cut over there?''

''I thought it'd be OK,'' I lie. The Katzes have neglected to check with me. I seem forever to be protecting them. I seem forever (a flare of anger lights my weariness for a moment) to have to lie.

Porter nods, takes up his fork again. ''OK,'' he says, ''just as long as they checked.''

"That's strange," Alexandra murmurs. "I mean, the boys and I were walking with Jeannie and Mike, just sort of rambling, you know, through the woods behind the south pasture. And Jeannie stopped and said, Hey, look at that tree, it'd be perfect for a Christmas tree. So Stuart went back and got the saw . . ."

• • • •

"Emily? I hope I'm not interruptin your supper. This is Catherine."

"Who?"

There is a pause. "Catherine Tupper. You do remember me?" There is a little laugh like the tinkle of ice. "I've been expectin you to call. I hope you've not been taken ill?"

"I . . ." Forgot. Good Lord, forgot. ". . . *have* been sick. It was terribly sudden. I woke up this morning with, with chills and fever, and a bad pain in my —"

I apologize. I explain. I lie. Out of all this I manage to squeeze my assurance that I will be recovered shortly, in time for an appointment with Harry Griffin. Between Christmas and New Year's, perhaps?

114

Five

"... as one by one the Little Match Girl lit her matches, each tiny flame warmed her numb, stiffening fingers for a moment, and into her widened eyes brought dazzling visions of angels, and tables laid with all manner of goodies, and she seemed to feel the warmth of hearth-fires, with loving voices laughing merrily ..."

Passing Timmie's door I pause: the voice is low, throbbing, hypnotic. Despite myself I am once again caught up in the sentimental, voluptuous cruelty of the Little Match Girl's story, in which even as a child, even as I wept buckets, I recognized something morbid.

"... and on Christmas morning a passerby found her there, a poor pathetic bundle of rags, huddled beneath the store window; and on her pinched little face, frozen to death, a beatific smile —"

"She *died?*" Timmie's voice rises, cracks.

"Frozen to death," come the low, insistent tones. "See, she was an orphan, and poor and alone and hungry, because there was nobody to take care of her. And she was out in the cold, and everybody else was inside eating their Christmas feast and opening their presents —"

"I don't wanna *hear* any more." Timmie begins to sob.

"— and all she had was these matches, see, she had to sell them if she wanted pennies to buy food with, but she was so cold she had to light them to keep warm, and when they were all gone she froze."

"But what about her mother and father? Why didn't they —"

"I told you, she was an orphan. That means she didn't have any mother and father. Or else they just left her."

"Left her?" Timmie wails.

"Just went away and left her. Abandoned is what they call it. Sometimes mothers and fathers don't want their kids —"

"But mothers and fathers *love* their kids! They don't —"

I push open the door. "There you are, you two," I say brightly. "I've been looking for you, to help go cut the Christmas tree —"

"Noooo! I don't wanna go! And I don't want *you* to go, Mother! I want you and Daddy to stay here in the house —"

It takes some time to straighten that one out and to convince Timmie that (1) it was only a fairy tale, not a true story, that Alexandra was telling him, and (2) there aren't any Match Girls anymore, and (3) people no longer allow children to freeze to death, and (4) we will never ever abandon him, not for anything in the world.

While I am doing this I can sense the silent mass of her presence, sitting on the edge of Timmie's bed, smiling her inscrutable smile.

●   ●   ●   ●

See the blazing log before us
Fa la la la la

"Where's the star? Mother, we can't find the star."

"Hold the ladder, PJ. Damn, how did these strings get so tangled just lying in the box?"

"Hey, here's the camel I made in second grade." Stuart draws it triumphantly out of the box.

"Camel?" She is lounging on the couch, smoking one. It looks more like an ostrich."

Stuart reddens. "Yeah, it's pretty dumb. I was only a little kid then." He drops it back into the box.

Strike the harp and join the chorus
Fa la la la la, la la

"Mother! Stuart's stepping on the angle!"

"Angel, stupid! Don't you know what an angel is?"

" 'And it came to pass, there were shepherds abiding in the fields, watching over their flocks by night,' " Uncle Tyler recites, in his plummiest Charles Laughton delivery. He traditionally

118

presides thus over the Decoration of the Tree, standing with the old family Bible propped over his embonpoint. " 'And lo, the Angel of the Lord —' "

"Lo, here's the eggs! Who gets to hang the eggs this year, Dad?"

" '— and the glory of the Lord shone around them, and they were sore afraid —' "

"Mother?" Timmie pulls at my sweater. "What were they afraid of?"

"Who? Oh, the shepherds. Well, they were sleeping, and there was a beautiful bright light that woke them —"

"And a loud spooky voice coming out of the sky," observes Alexandra, "which would scare the liver out of anybody."

" '— and the Angel said, *Fear not,* ' " roars Uncle Tyler supportively in Timmie's direction, " 'for I bring you tidings of *great joy!* ' "

"For unto you is born this day in Bethlehem an illegitimate child," Alexandra intones in exquisite imitation of Uncle Tyler.

"Mother? What's an illegi —"

" '*For unto you a son is born, unto*

119

you a child is giv'n!' "

"Hey! It doesn't have to be so *fortissimo,* Uncle Tyler," Porter calls, *fortissimo.* "We get the message."

"You don't know what an illegitimate child is?" Alexandra flashes a dazzling grin at Timmie. "It's a child who has no earthly father."

"Like an orphan?" Timmie says fearfully.

"Certainly not. Alexandra's just teasing." I feel spots of heat on my cheeks. She turns languorously from my warning glare.

"Dad? Whose turn is it to hang the eggs?"

"Why don't we let Alexandra do it this year?" says Porter gallantly.

She says, "I thought eggs were for Easter."

"These are special eggs. Hand-painted by my mother years ago. We always put them on the tree."

"Quoad sacra," mutters Uncle Tyler, taking a moment out to mop his forehead. *"Quorum pars magna fui."*

Alexandra says, "Actually, eggs are

120

symbolic of fertility rites."

"What's fertility rites?" For Timmie, Alexandra seems to have become Miss Ripley, Believe It or Not, preferably not.

"I don't think they'd want me to tell you."

"Why not?"

"Because" — she fixes him with a hypnotic smile — "there's some things parents don't want kids to know."

"You're mixed up on that," I say to her levelly. "We tell the boys anything they want to know. We don't feed them sensationalistic half-truths. Timmie, isn't that the star over there? I think Daddy's about ready for it."

"Daddy's about ready for a beer," puffs Porter. "PJ, hold the ladder steady or there'll be a wondrous crash."

"I want to know what fertility rites is." Timmie plants himself in front of Alexandra, his eye wandering.

"Fertility rites," Uncle Tyler begins in the lecturing tones he employs to flatten boring subjects by making them more boring, "are celebrated in the spring, when the ground is prepared for seeding

121

crops. Utensils employed over the centuries are the stick, the flint, the plow, the disc, the harrow, et cetera, until we come to the modern tractor . . ."

"Oh," Timmie mutters, his attention wandering with his eye. Even Alexandra's gaze has begun to waver under the steady wash.

". . . Among primitive peoples, who have nothing more interesting to do than grub about planting cabbages, it is considered an occasion for capering about, dancing and singing, and generally comporting themselves in an idiotic manner. With the invention of the, ah, ax handle, not to mention the spur, which by the way had an important effect on history . . ."

While I tell of Yuletide treasure
Fa la la la la,
La la, la, la.

"Oooooh."
"Aaaaahh!"
"Hey, that looks really neat, Dad!"
"A rather heavy concentration of blue

lights on the right flank," advises Uncle Tyler, "but otherwise a magnificent tree. An artistic accomplishment."

"I believe it's the best tree we've had," Porter says, as he says each year.

"You did a great job on the lights, Dad," PJ says, as he does not say each year.

"Yeah, I think we did, PJ," says Porter judiciously. The two fellow laborers, colleagues, squint at their handiwork. (Let the women and children tack on the extras; we men do the structural stuff.) I feel a stir of wonder.

We sit in silence awhile, gazing at the tree. Letting the old, old magic do its work.

"Now. I have an announcement." Porter clears his throat. "Between Christmas and New Year's, your mother and I are taking off for the Bahamas. You boys will stay with the Peterses —"

"You're gonna *leave* us?" Timmie's wail is sudden and piercing. "You're gonna go away and *leave* us? That means we'll be *orphans!*"

"Orphans? Whatever gave you such an idea?" Porter's smile fades. "Our taking a week's vacation hardly —"

"You're leaving us! We'll be hungry and cold —"

Porter is gazing at me, stricken. "Emily," he says, "whatever gave the child an idea like that?"

"— and we'll freeze to death and they'll find us —"

•   •   •   •

"What do you mean, we 'shouldn't' go?" Porter, standing in his undershorts, turns from his bureau to gaze at me, stricken. How has it come to this, that I am struck with stricken gazes? "What the hell's the matter with you, Emily?"

"I . . . It just doesn't seem like the proper time to go away."

"Just because Timmie got some little kid's crazy notion — Listen, we explained it to him. He's straightened out now."

I'm not. Things will never be straight again. I will hack my way through tangle after tangle in this jungle, and find myself back in the same old thicket, lost as ever. "It just seems too complicated." Sitting on the bed, I lean over wearily to slough my slippers.

"Complicated? *You* don't have to do anything. I've made all the arrangements. Lucy's taking the kids. Uncle Tyler says he's perfectly content to have the house to himself." Porter sits down heavily on his side of the bed, begins to wind the alarm clock. "I don't see why it should be a strain on *you,* taking a vacation." There is a harsh edge to his voice. "God damn it, we have lives too. We can't let our kids dominate every corner of them, much as we love them. When have we ever taken off without them? When have we ever taken a vacation alone? How the hell long has it been since we felt like lovers, not just parents?" The clock is wound. He sets it down on the bedside table. We sit on our separate sides of the bed, our backs to each other. It is a wide bed. The distance between us seems to stretch flat and endless as a tundra.

"It's about time," Porter says over this huge distance, "we put our own needs first. We're not getting any younger."

"Porter," I hear my own voice saying, thinned and far, "right now I need not to go."

125

The silence stretches, creaks. "Porter? Maybe we could go later?" If there is a later. If something in this stretched distance does not crack and everything spill out for him to see. Why didn't I tell him at the beginning, when we first sat on this bed, our bridal couch? "Porter? Would you care all that much?"

"Yes, I would. *Why,*" he explodes, "didn't you tell me in the beginning? Why didn't you tell me on our anniversary, when I showed you those tickets? Why didn't you tell me you didn't want to go?"

"I didn't tell you I did want to go."

"You didn't tell *me* anything. You just kept talking about it to Lucy Peters."

"Oh, Porter." I stare down at my bare feet, cold as stones; I am stone-cold weary. "It was a misunderstanding."

"It was a gift. A *gift,* Emily," he says harshly. "I thought it'd please you. Christ, what woman wouldn't like a trip to the Bahamas?" I do not turn, but I know he has put his elbows on his knees, his head in his hands. "You baffle me, Emily. You honest-to-God mystify me sometimes. Sometimes it strikes me that there are big gaps in what I know of you. How could I possibly know you wouldn't *want* a gift like that."

"Oh Porter, I'm not ungrateful! It's only that I . . . I have so much to do, so many things to straighten out —"

"Do? Straighten out? What the hell's suddenly so urgent?"

"For one thing, I — I have these meetings, and for another, we can't very well ask Lucy to take Alexandra too —"

"Alexandra!" The bed lurches; he stands, comes around to confront me. "That's it, isn't it? That's why you suddenly decided you can't leave. Because she's here."

"No! No, that's not —"

"And because she's a problem." His voice is cold. I stare down at his bare knees. "It's time we admit that. The girl is a real problem. She's disruptive. Something about her — There's something wrong."

"Porter, you're imagining . . ."

"I'm not imagining. For one thing, she's incredibly defensive. She shrinks whenever I come anywhere near her, as if

127

I were going to beat her. I've tried to be good to her, make her feel at home, she won't let me anywhere near her," he says grimly. "She's been here over three weeks, and we don't know anything about her. We don't know why she's here, or what she wants. I hate to say this, but we don't even know *who* she is."

"Who? She's my —"

"Niece. So she claims. But has it occurred to you that's only her claim, Emily? We have only her word for it. Has she given you any other facts about herself? What made you simply accept her word, when she walked in here that night and said she was your niece? You're not the only family that's got red hair." He pauses. "Although I've got to admit she looks one helluva lot like you."

He ponders this, while I stab desperately around for a denial of it. "She looks more like my mother," is what I manage to bring out.

"OK. This isn't to say I don't like her." I hear the instinct for trust, for liking, for generosity and hospitality and family in his voice. "There's something appealing

128

about her, sort of like a — a lost kitten or something. But there's something sort of wrong about her too. There's all these tensions in the family since she's come. Haven't you noticed that? And now there's this business about your not wanting to go with me on a vacation." The tone turns grim again. "When it gets that messed up, that's when it's time to —"

"Please, Porter. If you'll just be a little patient, I'm sure she'll, I'm sure everything —"

"Patient. I'm sick of patience. I'm tired," he says with controlled violence, "of waiting for a few small pleasures in my life. My God, I've been teaching for fifteen years and I've never even taken a sabbatical."

"You've never asked for one." A petty quarrel: if I can find the energy to sustain it, the other may be preempted. "And you do have the three summer months off."

"Summer." He laughs bitterly. "What do I do with those so-called summer breaks? You may not have noticed, Emily, what has to be done on a farm, even a broken-down one, in the summer."

"I've noticed what has to be done on it the rest of the year, Porter, when you're teaching."

Just as the quarrel takes off and gets under way, he shoots it down. "I'm not going to argue about how much work each of us puts in," he says wearily. "The point's already there. We need a break. Lord, we're talking about one little week. And we're going to get it." He turns, goes to the closet, starts getting back into his trousers.

"Porter — what're you going to do?"

"Call that girl's parents. This has gone on too long. I don't know why in hell I didn't do this two weeks ago. Those people have a right to know where she is. And if they *do* know, they've got a responsibility for her. And we have a right to get this responsibility off our backs. What's your brother's full name?"

"Porter, please, no! You can't!"

He stops at the door. "And just why not?"

"Because —" Tell him. No other way out. "— because that's not the reason."

"What's not the reason? You're not

making sense."

"The reason, the reason —" Tell him something, anything. "— I don't want to go, it's not that. Her, I mean. The reason I, the reason is I have an appointment with Mrs. Tupper." Hauling blindly on the fishing line, I've pulled up a big flopping red herring.

He blinks at me. "You have an appointment with Mrs. Tupper."

"Yes. I promised her she could set up a meeting sometime between Christmas and New Year's. A very important meeting —"

"Very important," he repeats flatly. "A very important meeting with Mrs. Tupper is keeping us from taking a vacation. Do I understand this right?"

"Oh, its not just that," I babble while the red herring flops about and I try to get a grip on it. "I, they, Harry Griffin, that is — they want me to run for State Delegate."

"State Delegate."

"Yes, Porter, they do, they really do. They think there's a very good chance for a woman, it could be an actual *advantage* they say, and they ought to know, and now that Harry Griffin's retiring, whoever gets his nod —"

"They want you to run for State Delegate." He comes slowly back toward me sitting there on the edge of the bed.

"Yes. Of course Griffin hasn't given me the nod yet, but Mrs. Tupper says there'll be no trouble convincing him —"

He sits down heavily beside me. The mattress bounces. "You," he mutters. "My God. State Delegate." He bursts into strangled laughter.

•　　•　　•　　•

Cold sunlight fingers my face. The bed is empty. Then I remember. That fatal, give-away laughter: a hook to hang my herring on, like a prize catch. I lie a moment, remembering.

— Male chauvinism, Porter. What else can you call it?

— Emily, it's not *you* I was laughing at

— Oh? The ridiculous idea of me as an elected Delegate, then? Your little wife, Emily?

— Lord, Lord. Honey, can't you understand — those two, Catherine

Tupper and that old pol Griffin, the idea of them with their heads together deciding the time's come to exploit the Lib

— And I'm the little puppet they can exploit it with.

— Emily, believe me, I'm not putting *you* down. I have the greatest respect for your, uh, your abilities

— Just as long as they're applied to running the house and the farm.

— That's not true! The implication is I'm trying to keep my wife barefoot and pregnant, and that's not true. Have I ever complained about all those meetings you go to

— All those meetings? Since you bring them up, I assume that's what's on your mind, Porter. All those meetings I'd have to go to if I become a candidate

— Bringing them up isn't complaining about them, for crissake! What I'm trying to point out — Look, you spring this on me, something that never occurred to me, my natural reaction is to

— Laugh. Exactly. That's your natural reaction, Porter. Well, that clears up one thing, anyway. We both know how you really feel about your wife's having an outside career

— You really think that of me, Emily? You honestly believe I'm such a goddam male chauvinist pig? Or is that what you *want* to believe? You want me to feel that way so you can feel justified in striking a blow for Liberation

— What else can I believe, when your first reaction is to laugh at the very idea

And so it flopped around in circles, the classic closed circle of domestic dispute, the fish swallowing its own tail. Until the argument was swallowed up in exhaustion, with nothing decided except to abandon it until morning.

Morning: eleven o'clock? I lunge out of bed, grope for my robe, stumble downstairs. The house is empty; Porter must have left for his office, the boys gone off somewhere. Never in sixteen years have I slept so late, arisen to a house so abandoned. It is eerie, unnatural. Perhaps I too have been abandoned? In a panic I push open the kitchen door. Regarding me above the overturned garbage can, with yellow, baleful, slitted eyes: the goat.

I scream, plunge back through the pantry door, and bump into Alexandra in the hall.

She has, it seems, taken a shine to this goat. She found it in the vegetable garden. Obviously, it was hungry. So she brought it into the kitchen and gave it some celery — which was all, she points out accusingly, she could find in the refrigerator. Less coolly I inform her that I will not have goats in my house — particularly this goat, which is a mean and spiteful creature. She is to return the goat to the Katzes and to tell them that if it gets into the veg-garden one more time, there will be goat stew for supper.

"Which might be a change from canned soup," she says.

● ● ● ●

Uncle Tyler pauses, hypodermic syringe poised. "You're making a what?"

"A curry." Blinking my stinging eyes, I chop away at the onions. "Mother McPhail's recipe."

"My dear Emily. Must you?" Uncle

135

Tyler groans. The need is a long, veterinarian's model. He inserts it into the bottle of brandy, carefully draws up the plunger. "That recipe produces a ghoulish gruel that tastes like the lining of an old campaign trunk. Wherever did you find it?"

"In an old trunk. How could it be that bad? Porter's been raving about it for years."

"Memories that bless," observes Uncle Tyler, withdrawing the syringe, "tend to become confused with those that burn. Particularly as they recede into the mists of time." He plunges the needle deep into the flank of an A & P fruitcake, several of which he is in the process of "curing."

"Well," I say grimly, "whether it blesses or burns, I'm making Porter this curry."

"What you're making — if I may venture a guess — is a point." Uncle Tyler stabs the needle into the other flank of the fruitcake. "A, um, Brownie point, I believe is the expression? Trying to pile up marital merit badges?"

I throw down my knife, lurch to the

sink, splash water over my streaming eyes. "Oh, Uncle Tyler, I don't know *what* I'm trying to do. Make it up to Porter some way, I guess."

"Make what up to Porter, my dear?"

I mop my face with a paper towel. "Everything." I crumple the towel in a tight ball, stare at it there in my fist. *Everything: tell him everything.* Unload the burden of this guilty secret. Share it with him; he is old, he is wise, he is

A gentleman of the old school. Old-fashioned, correct, proper. Innocent: he is gazing at me with innocent, mild old eyes. I open my fist, drop the crumpled ball into the wastebasket. "I feel guilty," I mumble, "about not wanting to go to the Bahamas."

"Ah." He nods sagely. Turns back to his fruitcakes. "Well, my dear, I'm not sure that you can retilt the balance of power, as it were, with a curry — I have noticed that in domestic, as in foreign, relations there seem to be similar diplomatic principles at work — but you can of course *try*. The pain and suffering involved in making it, not to mention eating it" — he gives a slight shudder — "should weigh heavily in your favor. One of the great difficulties about the balance-of-power principle is that we satellite countries keep getting the squeeze. Oh well," he says resignedly, "one must make sacrifices in the cause of family peace."

I go back, sacrificially, to chopping onions.

• • • •

Porter arrives home with the air of a man who has been through the purifying fire of reason. He pecks me on the cheek, goes to the pantry to pour himself his pre-dinner bourbon, brings it back to the kitchen table, sits down to watch me make the salad, and announces that he has turned in the Bahamas tickets.

"Oh, Porter . . ."

"It wouldn't be fair," he says with the weight of Jeffersonian logic, "for one of us to insist on something the other doesn't want."

I sit down at the table, desperately unload my counterweight. I offer to renounce my political ambitions.

"Emily, good Lord —"

"It wouldn't be fair," I intone, "for one of us to insist on something the other doesn't —"

"I didn't say I didn't want you to —"

"Nevertheless, I have decided that —"

"Emily." He folds his arms on the table. "Let's table it, OK? All these offers and decisions and negotiations — why don't we just put them away for a while? It's almost Christmas. How about declaring a Christmas cease-fire?"

"I . . . About Alexandra too?"

"Alexandra too," he says after a moment. "I guess a few more days won't matter."

Across the table, we shake on it: a Christmas cease-fire. Out of my relief I say, "I love you, Porter."

"I love you too," he says, out of the relief of a peace-loving man.

"*Aaarrgh!*" PJ drops his fork, clutches his throat with both hands.

Everybody else, fork poised, pauses.

"What," says the peace-loving man,

"has got into you? Stop that ridiculous writhing, PJ, or else excuse yourself."

"*Hu-hu-hu* —" PJ claws the air, eyeballs bulging.

"He's poisoned," Timmie whispers.

Before the panic can spread, Uncle Tyler douses it: hands poor PJ his glass of water, advising that it is only the curry seasonings, which tend to be hot.

"Curry?" Porter stares at his plate. "You made curry, Emily?"

"Your mother's recipe. I must've put in too much seasoning."

"To cover the taste of the goat." Alexandra's face is whitish.

"*Goat! Yarrghh!*"

By the time this panic is doused, it is too late for anything but scrambled eggs, which I wearily serve up to the boys when they return from verifying that the goat is alive and well, too well, in the veg-garden. Alexandra, refusing anything, white-faced and silent, continues up to her room.

● ● ● ●

Christmas Eve she disappears.

We are to spend it at the Peterses'. Our families alternate each year, a tradition

140

involving a supper of oyster stew, a modest exchange of gifts, a rather self-conscious singing of carols around the piano — at our house I bumble stiff-fingered through the chords; at the Peterses' Rachel accompanies, graceful wrists arched — and, at midnight, a ceremonial bottle of champagne, of which the children are allowed a crystal thimbleful.

Six o'clock, past time to depart: she is nowhere to be found.

"You all go on," I say to Porter. "I'll wait for her. She's probably at the Katzes', or someplace. We can drive over in the truck." I force a casual air.

"Maybe she's been kidnapped," Stuart says.

Timmie blinks fearfully. "What's kidnapped?"

"Don't be silly," Porter snaps. "PJ, run down to the Katzes'. I'll go over to the barn, check around the place."

I phone Lucy to explain we'll be a little late. The scouts return to report the Katzes haven't seen Alexandra, she's nowhere on the place. "Maybe she was in

141

the cabin," whimpers Timmie, "and the voodoo got her —"

"On Christmas Eve, voodoos become inoperative," says Uncle Tyler calmly. "It is a time of holy magic, when the humble beasts are given voice. As a matter of fact, I believe I shall stay home this evening, my dears, and converse with, uh, a cow or two. In the interests of research. Run along, run along, everybody. When Alexandra wanders back, I'll phone you. It may be that she'd prefer to stay here with me, and have a chat with that goat she's taken such a fancy to."

He is so calm that I am, despite my unease, persuaded.

Round yon Virgin Mother and Child,
Holy infant, so tender and mild

Rachel's arched fingers ripple gracefully over the keys. Pretty, tapering, young girl's hands. (Hers are like mine, utilitarian and square. My unease grows. He said he would telephone when she returned.)

What child is this
Who laid to rest
On Mary's breast is sleeping?

Long, pale-blond hair falls forward like wings from Rachel's bent nape. (Hers is exposed, downy, vertebrae swelling defiantly between the two thin cables. Maidenly, vulnerable —)

Good King Wenceslas looked out
On the Feast of Stephen,
When the snow lay round about

(*Where?* Where is she? The woods, dark and deep, miles to go before she —)

No music, only a buzz. Then another, then another, a flat vacant buzz ringing in an empty house, only an old, sleeping man way up in the west wing, beyond summoning.

"Emily." Porter takes the buzzing phone out of my hand, replaces it in the cradle. "If Uncle Tyler's asleep, he couldn't hear the phone. Neither could Alexandra, so —"

"She's not asleep, Porter, I know it! Anyway, Uncle Tyler promised he'd phone and he didn't —"

"Calm down, honey. If you're that worried," he says worriedly, "I'll call the sheriff's office."

"No!" Hunting her down like a runaway slave, dogs baying through the woods. "If we could just go home, Porter. She's there, she's there somewhere, I just know she is, and she *needs* me —"

"OK. Get your coat. I'll explain to the Peterses."

The house is dark, empty-looking. Never has any house looked so dark, so empty.

Stopping the car, Porter exchanges a quick glance with me. Uncle Tyler always leaves the lights blazing.

Stuart says maybe burglars got in. Timmie starts to whimper. PJ snarls Crissake, what would burglars want with *our* stuff, but his voice quavers. Porter and I manage to shepherd the boys briskly to bed — fortunately they are half-out with sleepiness and the late hour — and go first to check on Uncle Tyler.

He does not answer our tap on his door. Alarmed, Porter opens it; the light from the hall limns a dark bulk on the bed, evokes from it a muffled groan.

It seems Uncle Tyler has suffered an acute attack of indigestion — "Quite all right now," he groans, obviously lying — and managed to haul himself upstairs rather early on, and thinks he dozed off; and so he did not hear Alexandra when she came in.

But if she came in, where is she? Not in her room; not anywhere Porter and I search. We go from room to room, turning on lights, searching closets, checking crannies I have not seen for years, perhaps didn't know existed. Porter says nothing, but he does not believe my feeling that the girl is in the house. He does not chide me; he thinks I am hysterical. He is a good man with hysteria, Porter is; his instinct for normalcy is overriding. He is at his best when I am not. He supplies me, generously, with a logical rationale for my search: "It's sensible to be sure she's not here before we call the sheriff," he

says. "Oh Porter *no,* not the sheriff —"
"I'll check the attic," he continues. "You take a look in the cellar."

The cellar: in one of the old cold storerooms I switch on the dim bulb and from a huddle in the corner a pair of baleful yellow slit eyes gleams back at me. The nanny goat clambers to its feet. The girl raises her head from her knees. Her face is gleaming with tears.

"I came back," she whispers, "and you were gone. You left me all alone. All, all, all alone."

Staring at me with her streak-gleamed face dim in the dusty light, she begins to sob dryly. The goat lowers its head and gently nudges her shoulder with its horns. Sobbing, she puts her arm around its neck and huddles there in the corner with the splay-legged goat her comfort.

I grope toward her, I kneel, I put my arms around her, and the goat jerks away and trots off shaking its horns to sulk in the doorway. My arms take her to me closely. I lay my face against her goat-smelling damp-tangled hair. I rock her in my arms, my daughter, in my arms.

Six

— Please, Porter, go on up to bed, she's OK now, she

— What about you, you're not OK — Alexandra, you owe us an explanation, disappearing like that, scaring your aunt

— Don't let him touch me

— Porter dear, please won't you just

— I'm not touching her, I'm not anywhere near her! Alexandra, I'm sorry I shouted at you, but we have to know what's going on around here, why on earth you'd disappear and then hide in the cellar

— Make him go away don't let him touch me

— For God's sake why is she so scared of me? What've *I* done

— Nothing, Porter, nothing, she's — Please, Porter, won't you go to bed now, she just needs to talk with me

147

— Fine, let her talk, that's what I'm asking, for her to explain why in heaven's name she

— Make him stop

— Porter, can't you see you're just upsetting her, if you'd only leave us alone for a bit I'm sure we can

— OK. OK, Emily, I'll go. But let me tell you, Alexandra, there's not going to be any more of this. We're not having any more of these disruptions. Whatever it is that's causing you to act this way, it's going to be cleared up. We're going to get to the bottom of all this nonsense, young lady, and you're going to cooperate. All *right,* Emily, I'm going. But you'd better be up in bed in no more than an hour — My God, Christmas Eve. And everybody in hysterics

— There. There, darling, he's gone now. You mustn't mind his sounding so cross, you must understand he was worried too, he cares about you, he's such a good man, he really is, there's no reason on earth you should be — There, darling, please don't cry like that, dearest child, my dearest daughter — Alexandra, please don't cry

— My name's not Alexandra, you don't even know my name

"Tell me then. Tell me your name."

"I can't."

She is curled in an exhausted heap at one end of the couch. I sit close, in the big chair pulled around to face her, my own knees tucked up, curled around my own exhaustion, which has become a lightness in my body.

She gathers a pillow in her arms and rests her cheek against it. In the glow of the lamp her bent neck is downy, sacrificial. "I don't think I know my name anymore." Her eyes are dazed, dark.

"But it's not Alexandra?"

She does not seem to hear. "For a long time I tried to guess . . ."

"To guess?"

"What you might have named me." She raises her head, gazes darkly at me. "When I was born, and you knew I was . . . me." Hugging the pillow, she gazes at me, waiting: a child waiting to be told a story. "Tell me my name," she says.

So I tell it to her, in the only way I remember it. Stored in my memory like old letters in an attic trunk — too secret to be sent, too durable to be destroyed by my many attempts to set fire to them in the desperate hope that a fire might cleanse and purify me — they are mostly charred fragments now. But I open them for her, one by one.

●　●　●　●

Dearest Jim: It's 4 in the morning here, I'm sitting in my dorm room trying to study but it seems unimportant now, with you gone these 2 months nothing seems important anymore. I wish I knew what time it is there — is it tomorrow or yesterday? All I know is you're halfway around the globe in some little Oriental country, Observing or Advising or whatever it is you career Military Officers do. How little I know about you, except you can speak that strange Oriental language and they sent you here to Cambridge to take some special course and you've got a wife back in California and you're the most wonderful man I know. You once said a man who is an adulterer cannot be wonderful and it scared me, because I know adultery is wrong too. Adultery is wrong but love is right — it is so confusing. If I told any of my friends here at school they would say I was neurotic and Victorian. So there is nobody I can tell. I feel so alone. But tonight I'm happy, because

Dear Jim: I'm terrified and I don't know what to do. Two weeks ago I found I was pregnant. I tried to write you but tore up the letters. I must have been crazy, all I felt was happiness. There was this child who'd be part of you and part of myself, since Mama died and then you went away I thought I couldn't stand the loneliness. But now I have to face the reality and I don't know where to turn, I went up to see my brother Robert in Maine last weekend and he says I have to have an abortion. I feel so dirty. An abortion is killing. How can love be so dirty and killing so clean? That's the way Robert sees it. Robert says I have to arrange it, I can't take care of it and think of what it would do to the family name, meaning his name I guess. I promised I'd keep it secret and I could support it with the Trust money Mama left for my education. But Robert said as Administrator of the Trust he could not in conscience distort the specific use of the small amount Mama left me, the money had to go for education. I pleaded with him and said she was my Mother and she loved me and she wouldn't want me to kill my child because I couldn't provide for it. But Robert was adamant and said Mama's trust would never go for helping me have a bastard. I think Robert hates me. He said I was a slut, he washes his hands of me, he has his position to think of. I'm glad Robert's hands are going to stay clean, anyway. Please help me. Advise me. If you say I have to have an abortion then I will, because it's your child as well as mine. Please write me immediately, your letters take such a long time to get here and you can't wait past a certain time to have this thing done

Mama you were so clear. I wasn't asleep, I know that. Lying on my bed I felt you close, my skin felt the pressure of your presence the way it can sometimes feel a wall close by in the dark. You said *Dear Emily it will be all right.* I heard your voice the way my ears can hear my own pulse. *Trust and love, and you will give your daughter life,* it said. And then I felt your hand laid against my cheek, and I fell asleep. Now it's morning and I can remember everything you said, and know it was not a dream. A daughter, Mama! Flesh of our flesh, Mama, and his. *It will be all right,* you said.

Dear Emily Hughes: This is not easy to write. I promised Jim I would, in the event something happened to him. His wife will be notified officially. He was killed two days ago. I am not at liberty to give details. He was a good man and a good officer. I am sorry. I am returning to you, unopened, a letter from you which arrived yesterday. Sincerely,

Lt. Wm. Evans, Jr.

Coll. girl seeks position live-in maid, mothers helper, au pair or what-have-you in family home. Reliable, neat, hard-working. Cambrge area pref. Box 744

Mama, what is there about pregnancy that disqualifies me from caring for children? As soon as they open the door and see me — "A baby coming? There was nothing in the ad about *that,* we've got young children here, impressionable . . ." I guess I really do understand the reasoning behind all those slammed doors. You brought me up to understand that adultery is not just improper, it's not *right.* But if Jim hadn't been married it would have been right, love that doesn't break faith is not wrong. Except, Mama, when it makes a child? A baby has a right to unbroken faith, and love? Oh Mama I do love it, and I'm trying to keep faith, but I'm desperate. I have $7.56, and no job, and the semester's about over and I'll have no place even to live, and my coat won't button across my stomach anymore. I don't know where to turn, and there's no place to hide. My Faculty Adviser called me in and was very nice, but she said I should give the baby up for adoption. She said I had no way really to care for it properly, and it wouldn't be fair to the child or to myself to try. She said I have some promise as a scholar, and it would endanger both that and my future chances (I had the impression she was talking about marriage) to drop out of school and try to bring up an illegitimate child by myself. She gave me the name of this Home where they take in girls like me and give them good care and help place the baby for adoption. But Mama, I love my baby, it's part of me and you and Jim, the only part of him that will ever be left — how can I give it up

Dear Mama, I am very tired. I got up this morning at 5 o'clock. I bathed and washed my hair and got into this dress I got at Filene's bargain basement, it's 4 sizes too large but it's like a tent, navy blue with white collar and cuffs I thought would do for a maid's uniform, but nobody wanted a maid. I put on my coat that doesn't button and went out into Harvard Square, the light was golden and warm. I thought, in a few hours the Square will be filled with girls in their summer dresses, all slim and young and walking as if they owned the world, and knew everything without being damaged or changed by it. I felt full of grief, the way I felt when you died, as if something in me were dying. I went down into the subway where it was dark, and the cars rattled around the tunnel in the underground dimness, and the doors opened with a whoosh into emptiness inside, only an old man slumped in a corner and a black woman in a maid's uniform who ran her eyes over me in a weary, knowing way. I guess she knows how it is to feel the way I do. There is a place in the tunnel just before the train plunges up and out over the Charles River where there's a pressure in my skull, like being in a vacuum tube. I held my breath and closed my eyes. When I opened them there was a dense golden mist lying close along the river. It seemed to roll in the doors as they sucked open at the Charles Street station. Then they closed and there was a rumble and a streaked glimpse of gray stone, the Charles Street jail. I wondered if the Home would look like that, and if I'm an enemy of society, too. Then we plunged down again under Beacon Hill, and the gold dome of the State House. That subway ride is the last clear thing I remember about today. I had the address of the Home on a piece of paper, and it doesn't look like the Charles Street jail, it looks sort of nice and plain but comfortable. They were expecting me and they took me to this room they say is mine, I share it with another girl and I haven't seen her yet. I guess she's quite young because there's a battered teddy bear she's got tucked between her bed sheets with only its head showing.

Dear Mama, I've been here at the Home almost 6 weeks now and I haven't done much, I can't get interested in sewing and things like that, I feel kind of dragged-out although I'm young and strong as a horse, as Mrs. Cripps the matron in charge keeps pointing out. Mrs. C. is a nice matter-of-fact gray-haired woman, kindly, but she tends to keep finding things for me to do when I'm reading, which she seems to think is a form of "brooding," but isn't. I don't have a roommate at the moment, I have to confess it's a relief, as Sharon was a compulsive talker, and I had no place where I could be by myself quietly and just think, which Mrs. C. would doubtless consider another form of "brooding." Sharon — my roommate — was 15 years old with long thin blond hair who refused to eat more than a few bites of anything, insisting that she was not pregnant but just overweight — her arms and legs were skinny as broomsticks — and she had to stay on a strict diet because she'd been offered a job as a model. She explained to me that the fat tended to accumulate over her hips and stomach because she had a "glandular condition." They finally had to take her to the hospital to force-feed her. Yesterday one of the other girls said Sharon had died giving birth to premature twins. Mrs. C. said that was nonsense, that kind of speculation was silly, we were all young and strong as horses, childbirth was the most natural thing in the world, and if we would busy ourselves with keeping our rooms tidy and doing our exercises and other useful and pleasant things instead of making idle gossip, the time would pass more quickly.

Mama Oh was that you?Just a moment ago before I woke up there was this strange stillness somewhere like the kind that settles after an explosion, I opened my eyes to a flat shadowless light and it's snowing, the first snowfall of the year. Lying here listening to the stillness and smelling the flat ozone smell of snow and waiting for the next jar of the explosion I felt in my sleep — Mama! It just came again, without any noise, and it is a Presence! Is that you, Mama? Oh now the Presence has flattened out again into stillness and I am waiting. I feel very excited, but I am very quiet, I don't want to scare it off. Mama? Are you

Mrs. Cripps just came in and put her hand on my stomach and said "Well Emily this is your day I think."

. . . Mama it's not a day it is happening outside Time alone outside Time with only me, and you, and It traveling together through the white snow and into this other whiteness with so much moving around and coming and going but they can't reach us here, we are whirling in the middle of this blizzard-white place Oh Mama was it like this when we Aah! the whiteness all explodes and ruptures Time into millions of fragments of color Can you see them Mama great swirls of color-dots, emerald and purple and gold and scarlet

"And it was me."

"Yes. You. And me. It was like washing in on a wave, whirlpools of color, like when you squeeze your eyes closed very tight —"

"I'm squeezing. Yeah . . . I think I can see! I *think* I can remember. Can you remember being born? Behind my eyelids it's like, like a movie screen, there's all this sort of flashes of green and red and gold —"

"You *can* remember! Isn't that marvelous, that you —"

"Emily. It's three-thirty in the morning."

I open my eyes. He is standing in the living-room doorway, pulling the sash of his bathrobe tight. The fringed ends swirl in a last, trailing arc of neon-blue.

"What in heaven's name," he says, voice thick with sleep, "can you still be talking about?"

She goes rigid. Her eyes are still tight-closed. "Make him go away."

I stand, put my hand on her small, tight fist. "We're coming, Porter. We're coming right now."

My arm around her waist, I support her up the stairs, down the hall, into her room. I sit down next to her on the bed. She lifts her gaze to me. Her eyes are very clear, with a dark transparency. "You didn't tell me what was your name for me."

"Sara. My mother's name was Sara."

"Sara." She is silent a moment. "You *had* to give me up for adoption, didn't you?"

"There was no other way. I couldn't take care of you properly. I wanted you to be taken care of properly . . . Were you? Taken care of properly? Did they —"

"There was no other way," she repeats, as if she had not heard me. "But you wanted me. You didn't do what he tried to make you do."

"No. I wanted you." I try to smile but I am all at once emptied, as if I had just come to after a long, fevered surgery.

"Sara," she declares firmly, "is who I am." Her gaze is still on me, clear, imperious, penetrating. It penetrates the part of me that has been opened and scraped clean by the knife of memory, already beginning to throb painfully. My throat, too, is painfully thick, with all the things given voice to tonight for the first time.

"Good night, then, Sara."

She lays her head against my shoulder. She puts her arm around my waist. "Good night," she says, "Mother." Her lips brush my cheek as she releases me. "Merry Christmas," she says.

Seven

Ding-a-ling. Alarm clock? *Ting tink tinkle.* Sleigh bells? Merry Christmas? I lift my head. DONGGG. Clapper whacks my brass skull-bell. Fall back onto pillow. Cool palm claps my clobbered forehead. I unstick my eyelids, *ponk.* Porter's face floats over like the *Graf Spee.*

"Lie back down, Em. You've got a temperature."

Too bad if not. Temp means still living. "Time'zit."

"Noon. You had one hell of a night, crying and thrashing around. I couldn't wake you this morning. Lord, you're hot as hell —"

"Noon! 'Z'Christmas! Kids wanna open presents —"

"They'll manage. You're not getting up, Emily, you're sick. I'm going to call

Jim Randall."

"No!" He'll find out. Can't fool doctors. He'll tell. " 'Mall right!" *Dingdingdingding*. Ambulance? Coming to take me to hospital? "Oh my poor babies, Christmas —"

"Lie *down.*"

Struggle frantically; useless. Surrender. Abandon ship. Ah lovely, sinking deliciously, slowly, slipping down under cool, cool waters.

"Mother?" Waiting for Mama. Hands crossed prayerfully on breast, formal position of supplication. Waiting. Her Presence there on the bed, eyes dark, tragic. "Mother? You want some tea, or something?" All these years, waiting. Mama? Please advise? She comes at last, and sits on the bed, and weeps. "Mother? Please, isn't there anything I can do for you?" Why does she weep, now that she's found me?

"Emily." Waiting. Alone, alone, all these years waiting. "Here's the doctor, honey. Here's Jim." Waiting and waiting and no answer. Jim? Oh my dearest. Oh my sweetest love, my only love and one true love, all these years, help me. "Help get her into a cool bath, Porter, we'd better break this fever." Oh my love, oh Jim. Why is love so clean and killing so dirty

"No! Don't take her away! I won't let you take her —" "Emily, it's OK, we're just taking you to the bath —" What're they doing to me, mustn't, is the baby coming now? Can't come now, everybody'll know. "No! Leave her nightgown on —" "Alexandra, I'm her husband, quit being so damn silly, either get out of here or make yourself useful. Check the bath water —" Arms. Oh Jim lovely cool strong arms, see it's snowing outside. "Jesus, she's so light. Hold up her head, sponge her neck." Small, like a faun, like some woodland creature. "Emily, honey, put your arms around my neck, can you, so you won't slip into the . . ." Water, slipping slowly into the cool delicious

"Two aspirin every four hours. Call me this evening. She should be OK now, fever's broken. See she doesn't get chilled. This kind of flu, it's sudden and pretty virulent, but we haven't seen any severe complications."

•   •   •   •

Complications:
"Anything you want before I go?" Porter stands by the bed, fresh-shaved and white-shirted this morning, vacation ended, classes beginning. His face is heavy, tired. He has aged these two weeks. "Anything I can bring you back from town?" he says, looking speculatively down at me.

"Yes. Clean hair. I feel so grungy."

He doesn't answer. Why does he look at me like that so much? Is he still worried that I'm going to have a relapse? (Blips from feverland: his face drawn tight over panic sharpened with anxiety, leaner somehow; I got a glimpse of bones.) He's not used to having me sick. Strong as a horse, I've ever been; thin but wiry. I move my unwired, rubber legs under the weight of blankets. Surely I've not been sicker than they've told me, he much more worried than he's let on? There's a secrecy in his weary face. He looks down at me as if he were trying to see through

167

me. Well, I feel thin enough to be transparent.

And brittle. "Porter," I say, "I know I must look awful, but I don't look *that* bad, do I?"

"No. You look fine. You're getting some color back. Emily," he says abruptly, "will you tell me something?"

"What?"

"Was there ever anything between you and Jim Randall?"

"What?"

He flushes. He says doggedly, "When he came and you had that high fever, you kept calling him 'my love.' "

"Jim . . . *Randall.* Oh Porter. How could you think —"

"I haven't known what to think." The flush has drained. His face is gray, bony. "What can I think when you kept calling his name, calling him 'my own true love'? How do I know what to think?"

"But surely *he* —"

"Yeah. I know, he's a doctor. Doctors can always play the brisk, impersonal —"

"But Jim Randall *is* brisk and impersonal! We've known him for years

168

and he's that way even at parties! Oh Porter, how can you possibly, how could you think I could *ever* —"

"I don't know," he says starkly. "I don't know how I can even imagine it, but there it was. I guess I can imagine his making a pass at you, but I can't imagine . . . you. Not you, Emily."

"Oh, Porter." I have begun, weakly, to sob. "How could we possibly have come to this?"

"*Madame est servie.*" Uncle Tyler puffs in, bearing my breakfast tray. "Fragrant delicacies to tempt *la belle dame aux camellias* — What's this? Good Lord, Porter, have you been bullying this poor sick girl?"

"Yes." Porter's face is a mask of misery. "Honey, forget what I said. I must've been crazy. Maybe it was because I was so terrified, seeing you so sick, not responsible for what you were saying. My imagination got out of hand. Jesus, I should've known better. I *did* know. I must've been hallucinating myself —"

"And now you're not," says Uncle

Tyler, standing impatiently with the tray, "so pull yourself together, Porter, and hand Emily that box of Kleenex —"

"Emily, forgive me, I've been so damn —"

"No," I sob. "Oh no no no, you've been so marvelous, Porter, so kind and patient and —"

"*Laus Deo,* is this a testimonial breakfast, or what? Sit up, Emily, your coffee's getting cold. Porter, the boys are waiting for you, it seems they've missed the school bus. One can only do so much by oneself —"

"Oh poor Uncle Tyler," I blubber, "doing all my work, and you so hate things to be upset and emotional —"

"Honey, it's not all that upset." Porter pats my shoulder clumsily, leans over to peck me good-bye. "You just rest, and take care of yourself, and I'll try to be home around four —"

"Da-a-a-ad! We're la-a-a-te!"

"— and forget what I said, OK?" He bends anxiously to give me another kiss, and hurries out.

"Oh, he's so good, Uncle Tyler, such a

good man —"

"Certainly he is, Emily, which is why your tears of gratitude are appropriate." Uncle Tyler sets the tray over my lap. "Try not to slosh the coffee with your sobs."

"— and poor dear Uncle Tyler, doing all my work, you're such a good man too —"

"Certainly I am good, at my age there is little opportunity to be otherwise. Stop sniveling, Emily, and eat your toast. I am *not* doing all your work, Alexandra's doing most of it. The child's a domestic gem, an atavistic throwback from the good old days when there were servant girls."

"Oh the poor child, doing all my work" — I hiccup, plucking out a fistful of Kleenexes and slopping my coffee — "and reading to me by the hour, and waiting on me hand and foot —"

"She likes to." Uncle Tyler leans over, lifts my cup, mops at the saucer with a Kleenex. "She seems to have decided she adores you. She seems," he observes casually, "to be under the impression you are not her aunt, but her mother."

My sobs dry in my throat.

"I wouldn't worry about it right now," he says gently. "When you're stronger. Something's going to have to be done about the child, Emily. Porter naturally hasn't wanted to broach the question while you've been so ill, and of course the girl *has* been like one of the family through this crisis, there's been a real change in her attitude, remarkable really. One has become" — he clears his throat — "quite fond of the child. Yes. Quite fond. However. No use pretending there's not something peculiar, is there? Been here a month, and still a mystery. Oh dear, I see I'm distressing you. Later — we'll talk about it later. Yes. When you're quite well. No hurry, actually. Such a help, the child is. Don't know what we'd have done without her. Also rather amusing. We've been playing Scrabble in the evenings, she and I. Ferocious Scrabble player, that girl, a walking dictionary. Beat me with *zyme* last night, laid over a triple. I challenged her — disgraceful, should've known it! — and there it was. *A ferment, or disease-*

172

germ. Well. Eat your breakfast, my dear. Once you're up and around, everything'll resolve itself. Always does, with the lady of the house back at the helm."

● ● ● ●

I drag myself back from my uncomplicated sickness (I can see now why some take refuge in the white, nursery shelter of a sickbed) and find myself again in the same thorny, tangled thicket. I have barely the strength to lift my arm, much less hack away with that heavy machete of lies.

She is unflaggingly solicitous, accompanies me on my first tottery walks — around the farm, down the driveway yesterday, today a braver venture down the road.

Everything looks so stunningly fresh, so exotic. It seems impossible that I once knew this country road, these hills and pastures, that fringe of sepia woods, as intimately as I know the rooms of my house. These rooms have — I suddenly see — become a prison. Released for my exercise period, I gaze around as if it were the first morning of Creation, blinking in the pale winter sunlight, feeling it finger my pale prisoner's face; under my feet the crunch of brittle leaves releases an exquisite pungency to my stale nose, floods my dulled brain like some intoxicating gas. Even the water running swift and muddy in the ditches seems dazzling, sparkling with motes of color. "Smell that," I cry "and listen — a wood dove! Oh, isn't it beautiful —"

A grab at my elbow: she jerks me out of the road as an old truck barrels by, swerving wide. "You're still sorta out of it," she says tightly. "Maybe we oughtta go back now."

"Oh no, not yet! I feel marvelous, and I'll never get my strength back unless I push myself a little. Anyway, I'm sick of the house, and it's so lovely out here."

"I'm sick of that house myself." She puts her arm through mine as we walk slowly down the road. "It'd be so great if we could just keep on going."

"Then we *would* get tired," I say lightly.

"I mean if we could just *go*. Just the

two of us. Pack up and go somewhere. Italy maybe, someplace really neat.''

''Italy? Gracious, what'd we do in Italy?''

''We could decide when we got there.'' Arm linked to mine, she matches my slow pace, looking straight ahead into some distance I cannot penetrate. ''We could go to Rome, get a room in a pensione, and a little Fiat, and just — you know, take off. Explore.''

''That's lovely,'' I say, ''only we couldn't just leave the rest of the family, could we?''

She jerks her arm from mine, thrusts her hands into her jacket pockets, walks on ahead of me.

She looks so small and so lonely, plodding along the road burdened with the secret she cannot trust herself — or me — to share. My strength suddenly drains. The landscape has turned gray, which is strange because the sun is still out. Still so much of the day to be got through; still so much jungle ahead to hack away at before there can again be any real light in our lives. *She seems to be under the impression that you're her mother —*

I force myself to plod on, to catch up with her. We walk together in silence. We round a bend and I stop.

Up there ahead — at the beginning of a rise which I realize, with a lurch, is Cooleys' Hill — a dark clot surges into the middle of the road. A frantic bawling and lowing: cattle loose. And streaking silently at their flanks, head low and ears flat, the great wolflike Cooley dog. The cows, scattered and panicked, bolt down the hill toward us.

Terror paralyzes me. Animals — the dog, the black cows bearing down with eyes rolling insanely — populate my oldest nightmares, the ancient terror of the irrational. As in those dark childish dreams I am powerless to move.

Moving me: her arms on my shoulders, her voice in my ear. "Get over the fence." A firm hand under my arm helps me leap the ditch, set my foot on a rail, boost me over. "But the dog," I gasp, "he can get through —"

"That mutt? He's not interested in you." She perches casually on the top rail.

"He's busy herding cows."

"Herding, he's trying to kill one," I chatter. "That's the Cooley dog, he's a famous dog, everybody gives it a wide berth, the Cooleys won't get rid of it, they're mean, trashy people, they claim they have to keep the dog to protect their property, it's already killed some calves, and it chases everybody —"

"Only if they run. See," she observes calmly, as the bellowing herd thunders past with the wolf snarling and fanging at their flanks, "dogs have this very simple instinct to chase things that run. So if you don't run, they don't chase. Cows are stupid," she continues in conversational tones, "which is probably why you don't like 'em. I don't mind stupidity that much, but I guess a lot of people do. You might like pigs. They're the smartest of all the farm animals, even goats. A lot of people don't realize how smart pigs are. And they're clean, y'know. They wallow in the mud to keep their skin cool and the insects off, because they haven't much hair . . ." She continues in a lecturing, casual sort of way which, despite my terror, I recognize as a technique for calming hysterics. ". . . Mike says we ought to have a few pigs around, I was talking about it with him and Jeannie last week. Jeannie showed me how to make yogurt. They're really neat, they've got this terrifically relevant outlook on living and poetry and ecology and so forth. We had a big discussion on religion. I've been talking with Will too, he's so philosophical and sort of, you know, gentle. Jeannie and Mike say he's an Uncle Tom, but they recognize he's locked into the system, he's too old to revise his consciousness. But he's got dignity, even old red-neck Garrett recognizes that. Uncle Tyler says Mr. Garrett's got dignity too, I should learn to understand him, but *I* said I'd probably like him even less when I got to understand him," she finishes, with a tartness in her voice that reminds me, for a flash of a moment, of Mama. "Are you OK now?" she asks briskly.

"I . . . think I am." I nod my head, as much in surprise as assent.

"Then c'mon." She jumps down, takes my elbow. "We'll just sort of shuffle home, OK? You really must be getting stronger," she says in congratulatory tones, "coming this far today — What's the matter?"

"The dog." My hands have stiffened around the rail. "It's coming back."

"Yeah?" She eyes it speculatively as it comes loping down the road. It sees us, stops, flattens its ears, grins, sits down to wait. "Yeah . . . Well, it's not going to give us any trouble. C'mon."

"No! It'll chase us —"

"Not if we don't run." She slips out of her jacket, offhandedly; begins to amble through the weeds along the fence in the dog's direction.

"But it can tell when we're scared —"

"And it can tell when we're *not* scared, and I'm not scared, and that gives us the upper hand, see, because dogs have this instinct to obey people. It's been bred into them, you know, over like about ten thousand years. You walk along that side of the fence if you want, he's not going to come anywhere near us. I took a special course last year, called Instinct and Adaptation, from this guy who told us all about dogs . . ." and she continues to talk, so that despite my terror I seem to be pulled behind her on the invisible leash of her voice; and the dog is right there in front of us now, and she is holding her jacket loosely like a resting bullfighter's cape, and I perceive in an abstract way that if the dog charges she will throw the jacket over its head. We walk slowly past the dog with only the ditch separating us and the fence separating me and she chattering idly as any schoolgirl, and the dog does not charge, just sits there with its flanks quivering as if it too were hypnotized by her voice.

It is not until we reach the house that I see how ashen her face is, how her hands shake as she helps me out of my coat, how her whole small body is tight as a steel coil, how — in my terror I failed to perceive it — terrified she, too, had been. "You better go lie down," she says wearily, "and I'll get you a cup of tea or something."

Wordlessly I put my arms around her.

"Hey," she mutters, "hey, it's no strain, you know. Just fixing a cup of tea.

I mean it's not *sacrificial* or anything."

● ● ● ●

"Emily? I hope I'm not interruptin your supper. I understand you've had the flu, so I haven't been pursuin you." She permits a little laugh. "I trust you're recovered now? I ran into your nice Porter downtown this afternoon and he says you're up and around. Do you think you'll be feelin strong enough to come for a little luncheon meetin next week? We *do* have trouble gettin together, don't we? Harry says he can make it Tuesday, or maybe Thursday'd be better. We've got to wiggle some, don't we, if we want to get our plans firmed up. Would Thursday noon be convenient? If you don't feel up to drivin, I can send Willis over to fetch you. Oh, and Harry thinks he can persuade Winston Langley to join us, too. It'd be a real boost if we could interest Winston — he has considerable influence, as I'm sure you know, being a lobbyist and all for the tobacco people, as well as a right smart public relations expert. We have to start thinkin about the practical aspects of campaignin, outside support and financin and so forth. Of co'se *you* won't be discussin that with Winston, best you just be your captivatin self, we'll do the groundwork without botherin you overmuch with borin details . . ."

• • • •

"Emily? There you are. I've been looking all over for you."

A shadow falls over the cabin doorway, blocking the wan Sunday-afternoon light: Porter, ducking to squint in at me sitting on the apple crate. "What on earth are you doing in here?"

"Nothing much." What I'm doing is trying to evoke the voodoo ghost. Maybe it knows something I do not know and can counsel me. I am desperate for counsel. Things are shaping up for an ambush. This unnatural suspension of reality cannot continue. "I thought I'd weed the veg-garden. I can't seem to find the trowel."

"Weeding, on a cold day like this? And you just over the flu? Furthermore it's freezing in here," he says exasperatedly, like a father to a recalcitrant child. "You'll be flat out on your back again if you don't take care."

The prospect is one I have considered, and (I think) rejected. You can't hide in bed forever. "You know, Porter, I think there *is* a ghost in here? I get these vibes."

"Vibes. You sound like one of my freshmen," he snorts. "What you're getting is chills from the cold. Emily, come on back in the house where it's warm." Concern weights his face. I am swaddled in his concern. How constricting love is sometimes, I think childishly. "Besides," he says, "I think we should talk."

A click somewhere, as of a gun being stealthily cocked: the ambush? "What about?"

"Well, there's a couple of things we've got to discuss, now that you're feeling up to it —"

"*What* things?"

"Em, you know we've got at least two questions hanging over us we've got to decide. I ran into Catherine Tupper in town the other day and she talks as if this political thing's all been decided. And then we've got to do something about

Alexandra. We can't go on ignoring — What's the matter?''

"I don't know,'' I say faintly. "All of a sudden I feel as if I'm . . .''

"Good Lord, you're shivering like a leaf — I *told* you, Emily, you'd catch a chill out here, and now look at you! I honest to God don't know why you won't take care of yourself — Here, put on my jacket and get back to the house this minute. You're going to climb right into a hot bath and then bed —''

And so back to bed, cowering fraudulently. He waives the questions for now; he says he wants me to conserve my strength.

He is right: I'm going to need it. Any time now, reality is going to have to be faced. Sometime soon, the ambush is going to be sprung.

Eight

"Four; and one is five, and six-seven-eight; and five doubled is ten, plus eight is eighteen," mutters Uncle Tyler, figuring with his pencil stub, "and double word makes thirty-six. *Thirty-six,*" he groans. "The wench is humiliating me. And with four-letter words which are *not,*" he says sternly, "in the Oxford English Dictionary."

"You agreed, common parlance is acceptable," she says.

"Common, indeed! Where does a young lady learn such language?" Uncle Tyler scowls at his tiles. They are hard at their nightly Scrabble game, played with loud cries and moans on the library table.

"From a Shakespeare course," she says dryly. "Your spin."

"What's that mean?" Stuart is hanging

over Uncle Tyler's shoulder. "F-U —"

"It means thirty-six points," Uncle Tyler snaps. "Why don't you go watch TV with your brothers, or something educational."

"You always said Scrabble's educational. So what's that word, F-U —"

"Look it up," she says. "It's more educational to look it up."

"Hah!" Uncle Tyler leans forward. "Prefix! Two and four is six and one is seven —"

"R-E — hey, wait a minute," she says, "I challenge that. I never heard that word used with a prefix."

"That is because you are young and, ah, inexperienced. Something done once can be done again," says Uncle Tyler with a feral grin. "In purely grammatical, if not, ahhh, social or kinetic terms."

"OK," she says after a long moment. She plays. "That gives me a *triple* word. Using a double prefix."

"C-O?" Uncle Tyler's eyes bulge. "*Co-re* —"

"Something done again," she says blandly, "can be redone communally. I mean in *any* terms. Speaking loosely."

"That," thunders Uncle Tyler after a shocked pause, "is where I draw the line!"

They glare at each other across the board. Their mouths begin to twitch. She snickers. Uncle Tyler snorts. They burst into volleys of laughter. "Communally," he guffaws; "loosely! *Fnh fnh fnh!*" *"Tee hee fnsk twitter,"* she giggles; "social! kinetic!"

"What on earth," says Porter, folding his newspaper and getting up to inspect, "is all this hilarity over a Scrabble game? Where's the word? That one? C-O-R-E-F-U-C —"

"Hi. Can we come in?"

Jeannie and Mike Katz, and what looks like a formal evening call. That — according to the rules of Southern hospitality — is the end of the Scrabble game. And probably just as well: the boys, bored with TV, have wandered in to inquire what's so funny.

"Well . . ."

The occasion has taken on a hushed and

waiting aspect. The Katzes sip their tea as if it were holy water, gazing deeply into their cups. Obviously they have come to announce another Epiphany (the last time was when they found Jesus. Uncle Tyler remarked that throughout history Jesus was always being mislaid, a record of appalling carelessness; and he for one would be fascinated to know where the Katzes had found Him this time. Uncle Tyler has a philosophical approach to religion and is offended by what he calls uncorseted exhibitions of careless rapture). Everybody waits, politely.

"Well." Uncle Tyler bangs down his teacup as if it were a gavel. Everybody starts. Timmie, who is dozing on the couch with his head in my lap, wakes with a whimper. "Well?" says Uncle Tyler, in whom curiosity and boredom are forever locked in struggle. "Did you have something to announce, or what? You look absolutely pregnant with news."

"Oh wow." Jeannie exchanges a wide-eyed gaze with Mike. "How about that? He picked up the vibes."

"Vibes? Come come come —"

"You're pregnant," Alexandra says flatly.

They nod in unison, solemnly, radiantly.

"Crissake." PJ, reddening, slumps deep into his chair.

"Congratulations." Uncle Tyler hauls himself to his feet. "Well, now that the Annunciation has been made, I trust you'll excuse me."

"Technically" — Mike clears his throat — "technically, she's not exactly pregnant."

"Technically? Exactly?" Uncle Tyler pauses. "You fascinate me. How does one qualify a condition that has always been cited as the one luminous example of the unqualifiable?"

"What's everybody talking about?" Timmie mutters crossly.

'I'm not pregnant yet. It's like, we've *decided* to have a child."

"Gee. Is that what you do, decide?" Stuart inquires.

"Cris*sake*." PJ is now reclining on the back of his neck.

Porter says heartily, "Well. That's quite a decision for a young couple to make." He chuckles. "I suppose this means you'll be leaving us? Joining the work force, now that you're taking on big responsibilities?" He chuckles again, hopefully. "Nothing like a regular paycheck, with a family coming. I wish *we* could provide it, but you know how marginal the operation is here. But if there's any way I can help, put in a word for you in town —"

"Oh, we're not leaving. You don't have to worry about that. We're not into the paycheck syndrome. It's even more important now, with the kid, to hang with liberating alternative commitments." Mike kneads his fists earnestly between his knees. His knuckles have Band-Aids on them. His wrists are bony, raw, young. "With a kid, there's all this beautiful knowingness. This natural poetry, you know what I mean? I mean a kid is where its at, right? Love. Knowingness. You don't corrupt that with, you know, *linearity.*"

"Maybe it's my age," Porter says after a moment, "but I'll never quite understand what's so corrupting about a paycheck."

"Cris*sake,* Dad."

Mike lifts a conciliatory palm. "That's OK, PJ. It doesn't offend me anymore. I mean I understand how you've got this thing, Prof, this materialistic insecurity. After all, your orientations came out of the Depression. Listen, we understand that. It's just not *our* orientation, you know?"

"I could hardly be considered a child of the Depression," Porter observes, "when I wasn't born until 1935. However, I'm not going to argue history with you."

"A useless exercise," puts in Uncle Tyler, "as this generation does not acknowledge that history exists. Except of course to make pronouncements on it. This generation seems to have the impression that it has sprung full-blown, like Minerva, from Zeus's brow. It also claims," he adds severely, "to have invented love. Although I understand it is against bringing children into the world?" He bends a puzzled gaze upon the Katzes. "What with all this doom, pollution, and violence? Not to mention overpopulation?

191

Correct me if this is a misapprehension of your ethical position."

They return his stare with a gaze of such intense radiance that Uncle Tyler is knocked back into his chair. "That's why we haven't had a kid," Jeannie breathes. "Yeah," says Mike, "we've been meditating and hassling it for two years now. I mean what kind of life would a kid have breathing pollutants and eating chemical additives —" "— and radiation, and the bomb, and militaristic —" "— and the energy crisis, with vested interest strangleholds in a faceless monolithic technology," Mike recites dutifully. He takes a breath. "And then all of a sudden there was this Epiphany." "Like Saul," whispers Jeannie, "on the road to Damascus." "Yeah. It was, like, *revealed.*" "Genes!" cries Jeannie triumphantly.

There is a pause.

"It was revealed to you," says Uncle Tyler flatly, "that you had genes."

"Right. It's so simple, you know? So beautiful." Helpless before the simple beauty of it all, Mike shrugs. "We've got

192

these genes, see. The Lord equipped us with these genes — *so we can have a kid.*" "See," breathes Jeannie, "if we didn't, you know, pass on these genes, it'd be like spurning the Lord's gifts." "Like hiding our light under a bushel." "Like negating our human and divine essence . . ."

The two of them, sitting there on the low bench before the fire — he with Band-Aids on his knuckles and she with her boots peeking out pigeon-toed from under the muddy hem of her skirt made from a paisley bedspread — the two of them look so innocent, so dumb, so shrouded in the misty radiance of youth, that my throat swells painfully. *They look as if they owned the whole world; knew everything without being damaged or stained by it . . .*

"For Fundamentalists," Uncle Tyler observes, "that sounds fundamentally Catholic."

"Oh no," says Jeannie cheerily, "I've been on the Pill for years. Now I'm gonna go off it."

"Boys. Time for bed."

"Crissake, Dad. We know about the Pill."

"Yeah," Stuart chimes in uncertainly, "we know about *that.*"

"The thing is, we reject social institutions' control over our bodies. Nobody's going to tell us when and how we make love," Mike declares in ringing tones. "That's our basic civil right."

"It's indisputably your civil right to make babies," Uncle Tyler says, "but what about civil responsibility? In view of your generation's attitude toward crass bourgeois paychecks, who gets the civil responsibility of supporting all these rosy urchins? Or does the Lord provide pablum along with Epiphanies? Purely philosophical inquiry, you understand. Nothing personal."

Some of the Katzes' radiance is dimming. I murmur, "I'm sure Jeannie and Mike feel deeply responsible about providing for a child. I'm sure they —"

"What about that other civil right?" Alexandra, so long silent, cuts suddenly through my little speech. "You haven't mentioned that, Jeannie."

"What other civil right?" Jeannie looks puzzled.

"You know — the right to reject society's institutions."

"Oh, you mean marriage?"

"Yeah. You haven't mentioned you're against that, too."

"Oh, they know that. Everybody knows how we feel about imposing a pre-structured commitment on the love relationship," Jeannie chirps. "It's, like, the freedom to design your own relationship."

Mike says to Alexandra, "I don't quite get your point. What's marriage got to do with it?"

"The point," she says flatly, "is if you have a child and you're not married that makes it a bastard."

"Bastard, that's only a legalistic Establishment concept." Mike moves his shoulders edgily. "I mean if there were no such institution as marriage there'd be no such thing as bastardy, right?"

"That's like saying if there weren't any laws there wouldn't be any criminals," Uncle Tyler snorts.

"What's a bastard? Mother, what's a —"

"Hold it." Porter's tone is quiet, but everybody holds. "Mike, are we to understand that you and Jeannie aren't married?"

"Why do you put the question to Mike?" Alexandra says. "Jeannie's got equal status in this."

Porter reddens. "You understand this isn't a judgment. It's a question. All this time we've assumed you were married."

"Mother? What's a bastard?" Timmie whines.

"Why aren't you boys in bed?" Porter says tightly. "Emily, why aren't they in bed?"

"If you really want to know the truth," Mike says as tightly, "we let you assume it because we knew it'd make you uptight. The way you are now."

"If you really want to know the truth, Timmie," Alexandra says, "*I*'m a bastard."

I close my eyes.

Porter's voice says, "If I'm uptight, Mike, it's not because you're not married, but because you say you intend to have a child. I wonder if you've really considered all the implications. It's one thing to live together without benefit of marriage. It's another thing entirely to bring a child into the world and have it judged, as Alexandra points out, as a bastard. No matter how irrelevant you might consider society's judgments to be, it can be a pretty rough thing for a child to —" He stops. "What was that you said, Alexandra?"

"I said I'm a bastard." Her voice is clear, uninflected.

The ambush: it's sprung.

Who would have thought it would come from her? She harbored our secret so diligently. How could I have ignored what it must have cost her?

"Mother? What's a bastard?"

She has a right to claim me. The child has a right to claim its mother. And the mother a right to claim her child. Eyes closed, I feel myself sinking at last, voluptuously, into relief.

"I'm a bastard," she is saying in steady tones, "and I don't know who my father was, and my mother couldn't take care of me, so she gave me up to be adopted. The people I lived with, I thought they were my real mother and father, they gave me a name I thought was my real name, I thought I knew who I was. And one day, one day, something happened . . ." The voice falters. ". . . and I wasn't. Me. And my father wasn't he, him, not my father. And my mother wasn't my mother. Nobody was anybody, not even my friends. If I'm not me, nobody else is them. I was scared, and they wouldn't tell me. You have to know who your real mother and father are or you don't know who you are. I tried to explain, but they said it didn't have anything to do with *me,* I was an accident between them, my biological parents they called them, that's what you mean by genes. They had me by mistake, they told me. They said it's the people who love me and raised me as their own who are my real parents. But how could they love me if I was just somebody who got born by mistake, some bastard made by two people who didn't love each other —"

"Alexandra." Porter's voice cuts through, sharp with concern. "You don't really believe that your adoptive parents can't love you just because you're a — because of the circumstances of your birth? Honey, they adopted you. Think of how much they must have wanted you, *you,* to adopt you and raise you as their own. You mustn't think —"

"Yeah," Stuart bursts out, "they probably really like you a *lot,* Alexandra."

"How do *you* know?" PJ's voice is raw, suddenly partisan, striving against that for honesty. "Maybe she's trynna say that Uncle Robert and Aunt Whatshername, maybe they weren't very nice to her. He doesn't *sound* very nice, the way everybody talks."

"You've never heard us say anything about your uncle, PJ, much less against him," Porter says.

"Oh haven't I? And how come you and Mother never even mentioned we *had* an uncle until she came —"

"You simply don't know what you're talking about in these matters, PJ.

Alexandra, I think I'm beginning to understand. Frankly, there's a lot that's been puzzling your aunt and me, chiefly because you haven't been able to bring yourself, I think, to trust us —"

"Maybe she was worried about your attitudes on bastardy," mutters Mike. "I mean, it's obvious the poor kid felt uptight enough about it, she'd been brainwashed to think it was shameful —"

"What I'm trying to say, Alexandra, is that it is *not* shameful," Porter continues determinedly, "certainly not for *you,* the perfectly innocent person in all this. But we can understand how difficult it's been for you to talk about it. And I think your telling us indicates that you feel you can trust us, all of us here in the family —"

"And us. Mike and me. I mean we really *feel* for you, Alexandra, all that guilt laid on you by the Establishment. Also we went through this, like, identity crisis ourselves, when we didn't know whether to have this kid —"

"*Laus Deo.* Must everybody seize this occasion to testify?" The harshness of Uncle Tyler's voice is so unlike him I open

200

my eyes. His face is gray. "Must we worry this child's confession around like a sociological statistic? Bastardy" — he seems to strangle on the word, with a mighty effort heaves it out — "is hardly news in this world. Let us not treat it, and her, as if she were the only innocent victim of . . . tragic attitudes." He regains command of himself. "Alexandra, my dear child, you've disencumbered yourself of your secret with great dignity and God knows what cost to yourself. As for the rest of us, I suggest that we not labor that dignity nor increase that cost by tedious dissection. See, we have already made her weep. Child, dear child, ah come now —"

Curled in her chair, she is not looking at him. She is looking across the room at me. Her face streams with silent tears.

A child has a right to claim its own mother.

"Porter." I cannot hear my voice, it is so remote; but it stills the room. "Everybody. Alexandra isn't my niece. She's my daughter."

"Sara." Across the room, the face has

become a dark radiance. "Your daughter Sara."

"Yes. Sara. My own beloved daughter Sara."

PART II

Nine

There was a moment — the first moment after our bedroom door closed and Porter and I turned to face each other — there was this moment when I saw at last my husband's face stripped naked. Then I saw the gleam of bone-naked secrets: like my own, a whole secret life of struggle and desire and pride, of grief and rage and loneliness. *Now,* I thought, *he will hit me.* A blow, now, would be a final act of consummation: a simple animal gesture ripping through the last layer that separated us, connecting us at last in our inmost private parts. I faced him, waiting for the gesture that would bond us, and in the pain of punishment absolve me.

It did not come. He stood there swaying, fighting for balance, the dangerous, fragile balance between the primal and the evolved, between vengeance and mercy, between instinct and decency.

"Who was he?" His voice was thick.

"Nobody you knew. I met him before you. A year before."

"And you loved him."

"Yes. If I hadn't, I couldn't have —"

"You still loved him when you met me."

"I —" No more lies. "Yes. But I loved you too, Porter. I couldn't have married you if I hadn't loved —"

"Security. Respectability. That's what you loved when you married me. That's what you married me for."

"Oh, Porter." A blow would be better. The bone-gleam of naked rage in his face would give me less pain than the shreds of pain he is trying to pull over it, trying to hide it with. "If you could only believe that I loved you. If I needed security and respectability, I needed even more to love you. Everybody I'd loved I lost. There was all this love I had to give and no place to put it —"

"You put it on him." The bone-white

glitter broke through again. "And then when he left you — I take it he *did* leave you, you sure as hell looked alone when I met you — Jesus God. That son of a bitch. If I could get my hands on him —"

"You can't. He's dead. He was one of our first men killed in Vietnam. He was a military observer. One of his fellow officers wrote me. Jim had asked him to, to notify me."

"Jim," he said flatly. "I see."

I didn't see. "He was killed before I met you." Then I did see. "I suppose that's why Jim Randall, when I was sick, the name triggered something," I said dully. "It wasn't anything but that. There's never been anything like that. Not ever, Porter. From the first, when I met you, there was never anything else but you. If only," I said helplessly, "you could bring yourself to believe that."

"God." It came out behind his clenched teeth, a grunt, as if he'd been kicked in the belly. "He was dead when you met me. How can I . . . Jesus God." And as he stood there swaying and fighting for control and understanding and belief,

207

trying desperately to pull the slashed tatters of rectitude back over the nakedness, I saw the last bone-white glitter disappear. Decency had won.

And in the way that pain signals the progress of a disease untreated, I feel the steady throb of unrelieved guilt. His decency does not excise it, does not absolve me. Confession is no cure. Only atonement; but his decency waives it.

He understands — he said, sitting on the edge of our bed with his hands dangling exhaustedly between his knees; the cost to a man of that lifelong struggle for decency was made clear to me that night — he understands that I have suffered. He understands that the cost to me (all those years of love, of guilt, of secrecy, of loneliness) has surely been enough; how can he be jealous of a dead man; without trust and charity nothing good in all of life can survive. "Besides," he said starkly, "I love you. I love my family, I love my children. I guess I'm hopelessly old-fashioned. Maybe a more modern man could overlook something that happened all those years ago. Maybe a modern husband wouldn't care so damn much about what used to be called 'the sanctity of the home.' " He passed his hands over his face. "Hell, maybe I'm an anachronism. I sometimes wonder if I'm stuffy — one of those boring husbands so damn satisfied with himself and his life that he bores hell out of his wife. Maybe I'm a closet sexist, claiming to be in sympathy with women's rights but with these unconscious attitudes — expecting his wife to be satisfied with the things *he's* satisfied with, expecting her to want what *he* wants and spend her whole life providing him these things, on *his* terms, and to hell with what she might want for herself —"

"Porter, please! You're speaking as if I didn't want my life, my family, my home, my husband — these things are just as central to me as they are to you —"

"Central, yeah, but there's got to be something else, doesn't there?" He raised his head; and I saw that the struggle now was with his sense of himself, between self-doubt and hope — hope that he wasn't boring, wasn't a closet sexist; hope that

209

there didn't have to be something else for his wife beyond the central things they shared. "Doesn't there?" he said again, his voice stretched over the opposing pulls. "Have to be something else?"

"I —" *No more lies.*

In my agony of trying not to lie, trying not to discover in myself some sprouted seed of discontent that might (if light were let in on it) spring into a growth that could eventually strangulate me, him, this part of our shared life we call central — in this agony I sank to my knees beside the bed and next to his thigh laid my face in my hands, prayerfully. "Please, Porter, why do we have to talk of this now. I've injured you so desperately and now you chide yourself — Please, all I want is to make it up to you somehow, make some atonement, I love you, Porter, you're my husband, what I want more than anything else is just to do the right thing and be the right kind of woman —"

"Yeah, I want to do the right thing and be the right kind of man." His voice was stark. "It all sounds so goddam dutiful, doesn't it? It strikes me as one of the toughest things people have to do, come to terms between desire and duty." Next to my hand I felt the muscles of his thigh tighten. "I guess I've never had to do that. I always seemed to want what I was supposed to want. And it always seemed to be enough. God, that sounds boring." He gave a short bark of a laugh.

"Porter, please don't keep saying things like that. Do you think I don't value —"

"Security more than excitement. Oh, I know you value me, Em, for my better qualities. I guess I know you love me for them, too." His voice was weary, stripped of the momentary self-pity. "After sixteen years of living together, I guess I know that. It just never occurred to me before tonight — maybe it was seeing you for the first time as a woman who wasn't my wife, the woman before she was my wife, a part of her that was hidden from me all these years — it never occurred to me until now that you've got an existence outside me, and the family, and the boundaries here, marriage I mean." He paused, added sardonically, "Now *there* was a sexist attitude. Classic. I guess I've had more than one revelation tonight.''

On my knees, I pressed my head against his thigh. ''If we could just deal with one revelation at a time. If only we could —''

''Listen. There's one thing I've made up my mind on. You're going to go through with that political campaign.''

I raised my head. ''Porter — no! I don't *want* to anymore, it doesn't *mean* anything to me now, the only thing I want now is to —''

''It means something to me,'' he said grimly. ''If there's anything that by God is going to come out of this, it's not going to be my feeling guilty the rest of my life because I kept my wife chained up like some household drudge. I'm not going to be one of those guys who have to be dragged kicking and screaming into the twentieth century. Whatever else is resolved in this mess, Emily, I'm not going to have that on my conscience.''

''And my conscience? What about *my* conscience, Porter?'' I'd hauled myself to my feet. ''How do you think it'd make me feel, how do you think it makes me feel *now*, when all I want is to do the right thing, make amends — and you turn all noble and sacrificial, and speak of your conscience —"

"My conscience is my concern," he said doggedly, "and yours is yours. If it's right for a woman to have some life of her own outside the family, then I'm hardly being noble and sacrificial in acknowledging it." He too hauled himself up, stood there swaying in a wash of exhaustion. "Enough. Let's forget it now and get some sleep."

There is this to be said about confession and decency: neither, together or alone, grants absolution.

• • • •

An eerie stillness lies over this house. It is like the stillness after an explosion. I keep thinking that my numbed ears will unblock and I will hear the crash of glass, the shatter of devastation, the screams of horror. Nothing. Only this wordless mime, that passes for normalcy.

Sometimes I wonder if anybody *heard* me that night. (Let's forget it now, Porter said, and get some sleep.) He is abstracted, preoccupied with the opening of a new semester; in the evenings he disappears behind his papers. Uncle Tyler continues his studious potterings, in the library stacks, in the kitchen, in the attic where he spends hours going through old trunks, papers, magazines, letters, albums, working on his "family archives." The boys simply continue to do what boys do: living the central part of their lives — school; TV; fights; meals — as if they were citizens of a satellite country (it occurs to me that the young do, indeed, occupy a separate society, with a secret language, a common secret code).

Maybe — it occurs to me, perceiving all this — I've been assuming I was more central to this household than I really am. Maybe women are deluded — and nurtured in the delusion by Guess Who — in believing that we compose the center of the family unit, i.e., the universe, around which all emotional and social security centripetally cling. Have we been propagandized as to the nature of our importance, or, conversely, the importance of our nature? I should be relieved; instead, I am stung.

Porter may as well be lying in this bed alone. He falls heavily into sleep. It is as if, when he finds me beside him in this bed, something strikes him a stunning blow and knocks him out. Lying awake beside him, I feel myself humiliated in a most central part. If this is punishment — and it is; it is — then it fits the crime.

One other fragment of less scrutable evidence: Alexandra has become Sara.

The changeover of names seems to have been made by everybody without effort, request, or reminder. It is as if "Alexandra" has never been quite fixed in their minds — or mine — as entirely real, but rather as a character in a play they had been instructed to attend, and after a perfunctory classroom discussion been allowed to dismiss: she was, after all, only fictional.

All this thrashing around in other people's postulated unconsciousness so confuses, tires, and eventually bores me that I abandon these imaginings, and turn what psychic energy I have left to fighting off a depression whose huge, black density

I can sense approaching. It looks to be so overwhelming that I realize, instinctively, that I'll have to summon all my remaining power merely to continue to *care*. I too seem gradually to be lapsing into that mimelike trance and it scares me. When feeling and even pain no longer matter, all is lost. So I turn to that other source of my pain and caring: my daughter. At least I can now openly express all the love I have so long been forced to hide.

But her face retreats, slowly shuttering closed again. She too seems to be sinking into depression, a kind that I suddenly recognize as anticlimactic, like the postpartum depression that follows the high drama of birth. She has struggled to be reborn into her own reality; *here I am; I am I, Sara*. This announcement has been made, and the world goes on in its same way, unnoticing.

● ● ● ●

I remember in an abstract way that I am expected for lunch at Catherine Tupper's. As abstractedly, as if from a philosophical distance, I am aware of Porter's command: Go through with it.

The whole idea, from this distance, seems laughable. No wonder Porter laughed; how, now, can he insist on such a thing? Does he hope I will lose?

This last notion sends me to the phone. Halfway through dialing Catherine Tupper's number I let the phone fall back onto its cradle. What if I did lose? Would it matter? I sit thinking very hard, trying to feel how much it might matter. I can't seem to feel anything.

It is this, finally, that makes me pick up the phone again, confirm our luncheon date for tomorrow. When things no longer matter — some instinct for survival reminds me — all is lost. I must try very hard. If I do this, I might come to care some, maybe even quite a lot, about Emily H. McPhail, Delegate.

● ● ● ●

"What?" says Porter politely, not looking up from the papers he is correcting.

"I said I'm having lunch tomorrow with Mrs. Tupper and Harry Griffin."

"Oh," he says after a moment, "that's nice."

"Porter —"

". . . Hmmm?"

"— nothing."

• • • •

"Spect me to believe you just got out of a sickbed? You're lookin positively radiant," Catherine Tupper lies in her charmin way. That's what you've got to learn in politics (I note): lie, with charm. Well, I've had some recent practice; now I'll have to learn to do it with charm. She takes my arm in hers. "Don't you worry about contributin to the *technical* discussion just yet," she says, giving my arm a cozy little squeeze, "you just concentrate on projectin your natural self. Harry and Winston just want to get the *feedback,* y'know, of how our woman candidate could be presented." She gives my arm another squeeze and ushers me down her long, charmin hall and into her big, charmin library all padded round with tooled-leather volumes and feather-plump chintz, from which last two gents struggle up, one small and dapper and the other tall and elegant, to be presented with charmin chuckles (Harry Griffin) and murmurs (Winston Langley). I am handed a charmin little stemmed crystal glass of sherry, settled deep into the chintz, and inspected with three pairs of eyes that could spot the twitch of a mouse's whisker from a half mile up.

Half buried in billows of down, I cross my knees — the most visible part of me — and settle back in a charmin but alert pose. As they talk, Winston Langley cases my legs in an abstract, assessing way. I have the impression they, at least, pass. As for the projection of my natural self, I feel rather like Doris Day trying out for a Greta Garbo role. Don't call us, honey, we'll call you . . .

". . . You understand," says Harry Griffin, stabbing a prawn from its nest of rice and letting the Jambalaya sauce drip off it before he ducks his head and snaps it into his mouth — quite like a snapping turtle, with his little curved beak and hard gray wrinkles and ancient little lidded eyes, "you understand, if we back you we'll have to vouch for you with our friends and supporters."

"People we've always been able to *count* on," Mrs. Tupper supplies, "like Winston here, and the interests he represents . . ."

"Uh huh. These people know our word's good as our bond, whoever Harry Griffin supports can be counted on." He dabs at his beak with his damask napkin. "They count on us, we count on them. Some issue comes up later, after the seat's won, we can't turn around and fail to support the people who helped put us there." He looks at me sharply across the table. "That's what politics is all about," and he almost adds "honey," I can hear its expiration hanging in the air between the two silver candelabra.

More or less delicately, I am led through my catechism, probed for assessments of my orthodoxy. "This issue of property taxes," Catherine Tupper murmurs, "is one every *mothah* should be vitally concerned with, don't you think?" She pours a little more chilled Chablis into my chilled stemmed crystal wineglass.

"I understand you've been concerning

yourself with conservation issues, Mrs. McPhail.'' Winston Langley lounges leanly and elegantly back with his lean elegant cigar (''I trust I have the ladies' permission to smoke?'' ''We can hardly boycott the tobacco industry,'' replies Mme. Tupper with a charmin little laugh; ''I was just joshin you, Langley, we ladies just love the scent of those nice little cigars with our coffee, don't we, Emily?''). He has very pale gray eyes in a lean suntanned face. When he turns them directly on me the effect is like having the shutter of a camera clicked suddenly in my face. He does not often do this, but rather moves his gaze carefully over my head, or past my ear, or down into his coffee cup, or along his cigar which he rolls between his long lean thumb and fingertips, gauging its firmness and slenderness the way his eyes gauged my legs. I feel a prickle of animosity. I study the arrangement of forsythia with what I hope is an ungaugeable smile and let Tupper smooth the bump: ''Of co'se conservation's so much in the news now, isn't it? But I can assure you gentlemen, where *progressive* development's at stake, Emily agrees with me that it'd be unwise to make sweepin judgments, or take an unnegotiable position." *Over my dead body, gentlemen, will Seward Creek be rerouted.* "Emily's the kind of thinkin woman who weighs each proposal on its merits." I feel the pressure of her smile, weighting my merits. I recall that among the list of the county's close friends and supporters of Griffin and the party, the name of Jeffrey J. Chauncy leads all the rest. Under the pressure of the Tupper smile I keep my demure silence. But something not demure is hardening inside me.

We go down the line on racism ("Although Emily's from New England originally, she has a really *profound* understandin of the special problems of our state"), on welfare ("I think Emily would agree that it takes considerable study, and she intends to give it a good long hard look"), on corporate tax structures (here I am able to insert that this is something I know little about, and would study, and be pleased to be advised.

I see that this is an important matter and that I have given a good answer; the three exchange glances and there is a noticeable relaxation of the atmosphere. Harry leans back, sticks his thumbs in his vest, and gives the impression that if he were at his office desk instead of Catherine Tupper's table he'd put his feet up on it. Winston Langley turns sidewise in his chair and crosses his long, elegant legs).

"What about Woman's Lib?" Harry gives an expansive chuckle. "D'you think you could carry those gals along with you?" I reply that I think the radical elements would label me Aunt Thomasina. Harry raises his eyebrows questioningly at Winston Langley. "Token candidate," Winston murmurs. Catherine says sharply, "The really *radical* groups are very small, Harry, mostly these little hippie University girls. I explained that to you when we first started talkin about backin a woman. Also you may recall," she adds in a more charmin tone, turning her pressurized smile on me, "that Emily's husband is a well-known scholar and professor at the University, and that ought to be awfully helpful with the intellectual crowd.''

''Uh huh,'' Harry says. ''Well, we don't have too much to worry about as far's these fringe groups go, anyways. They grab a few lines of print here and there, but that don't cut any real political mustard.''

Winston Langley sights down his cigar. ''I don't know, Harry —''

''I do. When it gets right down to it they know who they're gonna have to deal with, who's gonna help 'em get done what they want done, people don't give more'n a sideways glance at these amateur reformists, so-called. Now I know you PR experts and pulse-takers consider yourselves on top of this game, Winston, but you just can't beat forty years of practical, day-by-day, meat-and-potatoes politics, not to mention keepin the party in line, for knowin what counts in an election.'' Harry Griffin snaps his turtle-beak shut with a click.

He takes his feet off the imaginary desk. He finger-hooks a watch out of his vest pocket. The gold chain is fobbed with the small medallion of a fraternal organization. "Well, ladies. I deeply regret havin to tear myself away from such charmin and interestin company," and he flicks his turtle-gaze first to me and then to Mme. Tupper, where it locks for a brief, signaling moment, "but I'm due back in Richmond. Winston — Catherine — anything else we need to ask this little lady here before we wind up the preliminaries? You understand," he says to me with a punctilious chuckle, "all this probin and pryin is just so's we can get to know each other some, put everythin out on the table at the start, so nothin's likely to come up later in the way of a sizable snag, like some basic disagreement, or" — he gives another chuckle — "some deep dark embarrassin secret out of a person's past."

Catherine Tupper goes off into a little riff of laughter as she rises. "That's another thing about havin a lady candidate," she trills, taking my arm and giving it a squeeze. "If you'll forgive my sayin so, gentlemen, there's very little question about embarrassin secrets in a *lady's* past."

Even Winston Langley permits himself a suave smile. "And if Harry will forgive my saying so, Mrs. McPhail has hardly been in politics long enough to have had an embarrassing past."

On this wave of hilarity I am swept out of the dining room and down the hall and into my coat and out the door, where Mme. Tupper gives my arm a final squeeze, this one triumphant. "I b'lieve we've done it," she whispers. "I'll call you the very minute Harry's made up his mind — but between us girls, I know Harry, and I know when he's made up his mind. So you go on home and get yourself a good rest, y'hear? You're goin to need it!"

•　•　•　•

I'm going to need more than a rest. Driving home this late afternoon, I grimly ponder all the qualities I'll have to muster in myself to see this thing through. See it through I will: it's no longer a question of making myself care. As my eyes were opened during these past few hours, so was raised my consciousness — as we women, if not ladies, say. Raised to the flash point.

Some deep dark embarrassin secret out of a person's past — In the past, women were stoned to death for my kind of secret. I tighten my grip around the wheel, around the fury that burns my humiliation to clean hard coals. *No chance of embarrassin secrets in a lady's past.* Lounging like judges behind that elegant table, handing down their righteous judgment. After all these years, Robert's judgment again, its cruel arrogance summoning me once more to the prisoner's dock. Well, the time has come to break out of that dock, where I am forever guilty. With the power invested in me, grant myself amnesty.

Power. I haul the old station wagon, wheels squalling, around the country curves. With the power invested in me as a representative of the people . . . High on a hill, I catch a glimpse of Monticello's white columns. The Jeffersonian dream of reason, of human order. (Sure he kept slaves; he wouldn't now; the order has changed; he helped change it.) My own dream, my own power, are certainly more modest. But surely, they could be of some use. . . ?

I bump off onto the county road. It is winding, narrow, following the bed of Seward Creek, which gushes rain-swollen now in winter, spilling over its willowed bank. Farther upstream where the valley widens, it becomes a broader, gentler serpentine winding through flat patches of farmland, glittering in the blue dusk.

Power and responsibility: little of either would accrue to one token-woman delegate. Porter was right. They see me as a puppet, pulling their own power along my strings. Harry will count the ways, Winston will provide the means, honey, so you just set there nice and ladylike and the gentlemen will all be eatin right out of your hand.

We will see whose hand, gentlemen. Once in that seat . . .

I pull in at Bates General Store and P.O., since 1931, Personal Service Our Motto, C. R. "Boomer" Bates, Prop. Park by the gas pump, step over the two Bates hunting dogs on the stoop. "The girl done already picked up your mail, Miz McPhail," Mrs. Boomer, Postmistress, informs me, leaning her fat elbows over the P.O. counter. "Got herself a Taffy Tuffy Bar, didn't have but three cents so I loaned her the extra twelve," she adds with delicacy. I give her fifteen cents, she waddles around to the check-out counter, punches NO SALE, and gives me three cents change. I abstractedly pluck a couple of cans of soup and a jar of peanut butter off the shelves, and — what else? — a box of cornmeal and some cereal. It's late, late, and I haven't even thought of dinner. "SueEllen," Mrs. Boomer calls sharply, "check out Miz McPhail here!" SueEllen — the Pages' daughter-in-law, eighteen and plump and creamy-skinned and pretty except for one green eye that tends to wander outward (the other eye is dreamy and brown) — comes around from rearranging the chewing gum display and smiles shyly at me. I inquire as usual about her health. She has been married two years and is not yet pregnant, because of what Mrs. Boomer has confided is female trouble. SueEllen says, as usual, that she's feelin sorta tahred, what with her condition and all, she has to stay in bed mostly except afternoons. Mrs. Boomer observes, from her window, that when *she* was SueEllen's age she didn't have time to be tahred, family couldn't afford to take proper care of her even when she was you-know-what, much lessen let her get enough rest. SueEllen blushes and looks grateful. I look pointedly at my watch — Lord, past six! — so SueEllen rings up my groceries, which come to $7.49. Stepping back over the dogs, I reflect on how the people who live around here can afford the personal service of the General Store, the nearest place to buy bread for eight miles around, unless you count the Blue Ridge SuperEtte, Souvenirs and Beer, which doesn't accept food stamps. I am still reflecting as I gun the old car around the bends — and suddenly at the crest of a rise black forms loom in my headlights, I stand on my brakes, the car skids broadside, there is a *thunk,* my right front tire bounces sickeningly, and everything stops.

I come to sitting with my fists knuckled into my ears screaming a long scream that began back there with the *thunk* and carried over past it so the sound of it would be delayed reaching my brain. But it penetrates, *thunk,* right through the scream, which stops now, and I force my arms and legs, violently shaking, to open the door and get me out, it is a matter of will, and around the car where there's a small shape lying in the middle of the road in a widening black pool gleaming in the one skewed headlight with the panicked black cows milling and bawling around so I have to push at their black flanks, their hoofs and tails trampling and lashing, and I am knocked over, and knocked over again, there is this hot smell of animal terror and the road slippery with their steaming stink. I lash at them with my fists and elbows and maybe feet, grunting curses I can't remember knowing, and suddenly they have bolted away. I crawl on my knees over to what is left of the small shape lying in the middle of the road in the widening black pool, surely a child's blood can't be that black? Surely not, not a child's? I see the elongated head in the gleam of liquid black and it is the Cooley dog's.

I try to pick it up but its parts don't hold together, they are all so heavy there is no way I can do this, or carry it. Kneeling in the middle of the road, I feel headlights rake me and I put my arms up around my head and screw my eyes shut. I feel the *thunk* of air as the truck or car barrels past, swerving with its tires so close I hear them hiss through the liquid stuff on the road. It roars around the curve and it is very dark now, and still, and the one headlight beam bores crazily up into the woods. Pretty soon I get up and go around the rear of the old station wagon sticking out halfway into the road and get in and try to start it, but I guess the engine's flooded. So I climb out again and hope somebody will notice the taillights in time not to hit anything. I stumble down the road to the Cooleys' gate and up their dirt lane. The lights are on in the back of the house so I knock on that door. One of the

Cooley brothers, all large heavy men, opens the door and I tell him. Two of the other Cooley brothers come then, crowding behind him and filling the doorway and blocking the light. The first brother says, "She done killed our dog," without turning around. "That was a right valuable dog," one of the other brothers says. "Weren't no other dog round here come up to that'n for a huntin dog," the first brother says. They stand in the doorway with the kitchen light behind them and I can't see their faces. "That was a right valuable dog all right," says one. "And a family pet too," says another. "Be some grievin hearts around *this* house tonight, you better believe that," says another. They all shake their heads and click their tongues, standing in the doorway. I say Please, and how sorry I am and how I'll pay for it, but it was an accident, the dog had got some scared cows running in the middle of the road and when I swerved it darted under my wheel; and I say What we please must do is to get my car out of the road right away, before somebody comes around that curve and there's another accident. I turn and hurry back down the drive, and the three of them get their jackets and slowly lumber after me. I get a flashlight from the glove compartment and tell them I'm going up to the top of the hill and signal oncoming cars, if they'll try to get my station wagon out of the way, I can't seem to start it. "That there's a *heavy* old car," says one of the brothers. "Yeah, get a rupture tryin to lift *that* one," says another. "She just gonna hafta get a tow job on this'n, can't expect us to rupture ourselfs." "Pore old Duke, ain't he a mess?" "Whoo she sure did scramble him up, didn't she?" "*Valuable* dog too." "Yeah, you don't go round replacin a dog like Duke just any old day of the week." I turn back and hand the flashlight to the nearest brother and give him a desperate nudge uphill and climb back into the car and it still won't start. The Cooley brothers troop back to the house allowing as how they'll call a tow truck. I wait a long time in the car but nobody comes. I leave the flashlight on and propped with a couple of rocks on top of the car, cursing myself for not having flares and praying nobody'll come around this curve too fast, and I go and knock on the Cooleys' back door again. They say they'll call a tow truck after I've settled on the dog. I write them a check and go back to the car and pretty soon a kid comes along who says he's the Towing Service and he does something to the car, and it starts. I write him a check and it is late, so late I can't even bring myself to look at my watch. I drive home with only one headlight.

Ten

"It must've been an interesting lunch."

Porter and I exchange stares. His is inscrutable. I don't know what mine is. He moves his eyes slowly over me. Under them my self-sense focuses: standing in the kitchen doorway covered with blood and filth and a ripped coat.

"The political game seems to be turning lively," he says.

I close the door with my foot, move to the table, set down my bag of groceries. He leans against the sink with his arms folded, a drink in one hand, and watches me. I unload the bag. "Have you had supper?" I say.

"I'm heating some soup for the kids. They're starving."

"Uncle Tyler could've fixed you something."

"Uncle Tyler's sick."

"What's the matter with him?"

"I don't know. He felt lousy and went to bed. Catherine Tupper phoned about an hour ago. She wants you to call back."

I fold the paper bag. "Excuse me," I say, waiting for him to move away from the sink. He resumes his lounging position against the cupboard. I wash my hands.

"She said you left her house at four-thirty." There is a tinkle of ice as Porter sips his drink.

"I suppose it was about then." I dry my hands. I get a can opener from the drawer, open the cupboard, take down a tin of tuna. "It was a long business lunch."

"Uh huh. So where the hell have you been?" There is a sharper tinkle of ice.

"It's a long drive from the other side of the town." I open the refrigerator door. "I stopped at the market. On the way back from there I ran into the Cooleys' dog and killed it."

After a moment another tinkle. "That's too bad."

I stare into the refrigerator. "The

Cooley boys said the dog was worth a hundred dollars. I wrote them a check.''

"I'll go to the bank tomorrow." Tinkle tinkle. "You could've telephoned.''

"I couldn't. The Cooley brothers wouldn't let me in the house." I fumble for a bottle of milk, lean down to rummage in the vegetable drawer. "I'm sorry. I wasn't thinking very clearly.''

"That I believe." His voice thickens. "Although it shouldn't have taken too much thought for it to occur to you your family might be worried.''

I straighten and slam the refrigerator door. "I'm sorry," I repeat. "And I'm fixing supper as fast as possible, OK?''

"The implication being that your family's main concern is its supper?''

"It seems to concern you. It was your first announcement when I arrived — that supper was long past due and the kids were starving.''

" 'Announcement'? That's a rather inaccurate description of an answer, which was to your immediate question as to whether we'd had supper. Your concern would've been a bit more touching if it hadn't obviously come out of your feeling of guilt. I mean let's not use the classic ploy of assigning your feelings to the other person, OK?'' Tinkle, tinkle. ''If you want to feel guilty about fixing supper late, don't lay it on me, is all. Hell, I'm not even hungry.''

''So I see.'' I jam the can opener into the tuna lid, give it a wrench. ''You've decided to drink your supper.'' The jagged edge of the can lid snaps up and gashes my palm. I drop the opener, dripping blood, make for the sink. I hold my palm under the running water.

''You've arrived at the conclusion I'm drunk,'' he says in tones heavy with sarcasm, ''and you haven't even been around to count my drinks. Amazing. These wifely instincts can function even in absentia.''

''Like your husbandly instincts.'' The water runs pink off my palm. ''They really rise up strong in the presence of some imagined threat, don't they, like when the little woman spends an entire afternoon away from the house. Imagine, what's the world coming to?''

"I don't know what the *world's* coming to," he says slowly, "but I'm getting an idea of what this family's coming to. And let me tell you I don't —"

"Porter." I close the tap, jerk a paper towel off its roll, wrap it around my trembling hand. "I'm not going to have it out right now. I come home dead tired after a . . . a very difficult afternoon — which, by the way, *you* forced on me —"

"*I* forced on you? I *forced* —"

"— and on top of that a horrible accident, and I'm trying to get supper on the table which nobody's lifted a hand to take care of, and you pick *now* to have it all out. Now that you've fortified yourself with a few drinks." Holding the injured hand with the other to keep them both steady and watching the bloodstain spreading through the paper towel, I hear my voice rise and know I've walked myself into an ambush with my forces scattered and the only way to get myself back together is not to care. "I'm not *going* to have it out now, Porter. So if you can't pitch in and help, go on off somewhere and get drunk if that's what you want to do. Just do it by yourself so the children won't know."

"The children?" His voice is low, hard, engorged with a feeling I refuse to identify. "*You* issuing warnings to *me* about what the children *know*? My God. After the announcement you made to them —"

"And *you* explained to them, I suppose? Took them aside for a fatherly talk about the shameful thing their mother confessed to, laid your own attitude on them —"

"My attitude? You don't even know what my attitude is. After that one night you haven't given any indication that you *care* what it is. You simply made your noble confession and your plea for pardon and then wrapped yourself up in this pious mantle of so-called honesty — floated around the house as if honesty itself invested you with some kind of transcendent virtue, so that nobody could touch you, much less question —"

"*Touch* me? With you going to such elaborate lengths to avoid me — Porter, I can't stand this. I will *not* stand this, not tonight! I haven't even had a chance to

241

get out of my coat and these filthy clothes —"

"Get out of them then. Go on, go upstairs and change." There, in his face: the cold-white glitter of naked rage. This time it is deliberate, knowing, willed, *permitted:* not the hot rage of the wounded animal, but the icy rage of the intellectual man. "While you're at it," he orders, "check on Uncle Tyler. And you might let the kids know you're home. They're up watching TV."

"TV, on a school night?" I try to muster my own anger, but I am too appalled, too clammy with fear, too dazed with fatigue to bring forth more than a mumble. "You must consider this a real occasion, to bend the rules —"

"The occasion," he says with a cold smile, "was an approaching panic on the kids' part when it got later and later and their mother still wasn't home."

"More guilt."

"Call it child chauvinism, why don't you? Then you can feel exploited instead of guilty." He puts his glass down on the counter. "Go on up and change. I'll finish getting supper, if it won't damage my own chauvinist image.''

— but what're we gonna *do?* You just keep talkin and talkin and never even 'splain what we're s'posed to *do,* you guys just keep

Pausing at the door crack of the TV room, I am stopped by Timmie's fretful whine.

— How can I explain if you keep interrupting and blubbering, for crissake? Stuart, stuff some more cereal in his mouth so he'll shut up for two seconds

— Timmie, lissen, pretend we're this gang, see, and PJ's our chief, and he's got this secret plan, and it's really neat, it'll really *work* if we three guys stick together

— well, but what if she's never comin home ever *again*

— Oh, are you ever a stupe! I can't even *believe* it, what a stupe you are. I *told* you, Timmie, she hadda stop and talk to Mrs. Peters, and you already *know* how gabby *she* is, gabbing on all night about her stupid dogs or something

— well, but howdya *know* she stopped

— I give up. I told you she *phoned* me! Crissake, you think I'm a liar or something? A guy's own brother thinks

— He doesn't think that, PJ, heck, Timmie's no stupe, look, he's not even cryin anymore. So go on, PJ, tell us your plan, OK?

— Sheez. My own brother . . . OK. First we write out this paper that we all sign. On this paper it says that we the undersigned are legally adopting this said Sara as our legal sister and *also* a legal member of this said family. So that means this said Sara isn't a bastard anymore, see

— well, but what's a bastard? Nobody ever 'splains

— so that means Mom and Dad don't have to get a divorce. You got that straight? See, when we show them this paper that says she's our *legal* sister, it makes Mom and Dad's *marriage* legal again, and they don't have to

— And we won't have to be orphans? Huh? Will we? We won't have to — Are *we* bastards? PJ, are *we*

— I. Give. Up! If I have to stop every two seconds and explain every other *word*

— Come on, Timmie, you know what a bastard is, it's a . . . Maybe you better explain it to him, PJ, just one more

— If it's somethin awful I don't wanna hear it! I don't *wanna* be a bastard and I don't want Sara to be somethin awful either, cause she's our sister and we *like* her

— Crissake, will you shut him up, she's gonna hear him all the way in her room

— That's what PJ's trynna tell you, Timmie, she automatically won't *be* a bastard anymore if we sign this legal paper that automatically makes her our legal sister. Right, PJ?

— Oh boy. The light bulb finally turned on. My utmost congratulations, Stuart.

— Sure . . . PJ? Maybe you'd better explain to Timmie that *we*'re not, you know, uh, bastards? We don't, I mean *he* hasn't got it straight yet

— Cris*sake!* That does it! That really *does* it! I got *two* stupes on my hands

— Where you going? PJ, where you

— To the latrine. Crissake, a guy can't even take a leak around here without you two stupes asking questions! It's enough to make a guy wanna puke or get drunk or something

— Shh! Shh, there's — Mom? Mom! Hey, it's *Mom*

— Mom! You're home! We were waiting and waiting

— I told you, didn't I? Didn't I *tell* you she'd be home? What'd I tell you guys, next time maybe you'll believe

"It's OK, boys."

When reality breaks down you invent an unreality, i.e., a lie towering enough to act as a shield behind which a spurious order can operate. "I just ran into a dog but I'm not hurt. I'm going to check on Uncle Tyler, and change quickly, and then we'll have supper. You get Sara and go help Daddy in the kitchen, OK? He's a little tired," I add, covering contingencies in advance, "because he's had a hard day at the office . . ." The bigger the lie the better it works. Seeing me borne along on its unreal calm, they simply accept it, bounce relievedly off to obey.

Even Uncle Tyler, mounded under two quilts, seems to accept a blood-covered woman, a murdered dog, and an irate husband as evidence of no more than slipshod planning on the part of the housewife who waltzes off to luncheons that last past her family's suppertime. He rakes me with a baleful, suffering glance and says he hopes *he* is not expected to grieve over a vicious cur that had the whole countryside terrorized.

He looks so miserable I venture to feel his forehead — that he allows me is alarming, as he always resists what he calls "fussing and pawing" — and it is so hot I say I think we should call Jim Randall. Instead of protesting, Uncle Tyler's eyes fill with rheumy tears. He quavers that perhaps I should call the doctor, this is probably the flu and in old people it can turn dangerous. Uncle Tyler has never before referred to himself as old.

I call Jim Randall from the bedside phone and, mustering my remaining strength, get washed and changed and go back downstairs to face what is left of the evening, with what I pray will be a semblance of grace, or at least some form of endurance. If we can only hold together through this evening, Porter and I, and not, please Lord, let the children see. Please, just let it hold one more evening, and tomorrow I promise I will face everything . . .

The boys are sitting at the kitchen table and Porter is struggling to ladle up soup and the report is that Sara is nowhere around. PJ was dispatched to check with the Katzes and has returned with the word that Sara stopped in there a couple of hours ago looking for me — "They said she was awful worried about where you were, she was scared you'd been in an accident, Mom" — and then left again, in the direction of the road, the Katzes thought, but they're not sure.

"She's out there in the dark somewhere?" *Thunk:* my panic punches a hole in the shield. All eyes fix on me.

"Now *Sara*'s gone," Timmie begins to to wail, "and she's *lost* and all alone in the *dark* —"

Over his head I grope, automatically, for Porter's supportive gaze; as automatically, it locks into mine, the long habit of parenthood.

"— and maybe she's had an accident and got killed like the Cooleys' dog —"

Thunk. I flash on it, the terrible sound, the unthinkable —

"Quit that, Timmie." Porter's voice is quiet, almost conversational. "Sara's not lost. I forgot to tell you, Emily, she's over at the Peterses'."

"The Peterses'? Crissake, Dad, why'd you send me over to the Katzes' then?"

"I'm getting tired of reminding you, PJ, not to say 'crissake.' Stuart, will you please pass me Timmie's plate." He dishes soup; his hand is not as steady as his voice. "While you were down at the Katzes' Mrs. Peters called. She said she'd picked up Sara over near the Batesville store and taken her back to her place for supper. I'm going to get her in a few minutes. So eat your soup, and here, Emily" — he splashes some out for me, sets it down on the table without looking at me — "you go ahead, I'd better go over and pick up Sara. Boys, help your mother clean up the dishes and get yourselves to bed without a fuss. Your mother's very tired. Emily, I may stay and talk to Weston awhile, so don't wait up."

"Wait — Porter —"

But he has barreled out the kitchen door, without even stopping to put on his coat. I hear the old station wagon rev up wildly, back with a screech of gears, and rattle away down the drive.

"Crissake," says PJ, blinking, "I betcha he didn't even remember to turn on the lights. That is *weird*."

"Gee. Is he drunk, or something?" Stuart wonders.

"That will do, boys," I say thickly, because my mouth does not wish to move. "Your father is certainly not drunk. He's simply tired. Now eat your soup. I'm going to make a phone call."

"Boy. How come everybody's so *tired* around here all of a sudden?"

Lies. Porter must have been lying. There was such panic in his face. Why would he lie? (I phone Lucy Peters.

"Who? Sara? Who's Sara?" Alexandra, I mean; she wants us to call her by her middle name. "Why, no, we haven't seen her. We haven't seen any of you for ages." Her voice is chilly. "I guess you're over the flu by now? I s'pose you've been just too busy to call.") Lies. One flimsy shield is punched through and now Porter throws up another: why? To shield us? He was trying to hide his panic — *Where is she?* Oh God, he doesn't know either, he went out to look for her and I don't know how many drinks he's really had, and did he forget to turn on the car lights, and oh God, there's only one headlight, the other's smashed, and on that dark road, a person wandering alone, around a curve a small figure suddenly there and the car bearing down and him in it.

Thunk.

Back in the kitchen the boys are bickering wearily over a small bit of ice cream. I divide it and search around and find some — what? — graham cracker and — what else? — an apple. I cut it into thirds and stick some cloves into Timmie's piece to look like a face. Then

PJ and Stuart sort of come through and wash the dishes, while I escort sleep-sodden Timmie up to bed, and check on Uncle Tyler, who has fallen into a fretful doze and groaning (how could it take Jim Randall this long to drive twenty miles), and thank PJ and Stuart as they lurch upstairs to their beds. And all the time I am doing these things I hear, outside the penitentiary this house has become, a muffled *thunk,* which is the sound that the unthinkable makes at its moment of impact.

A solitude ten thousand fathoms deep
Sustains the bed on which we lie, my
    dear*

Wandering the house, I smooth back the coverlet on the bed, arrange Porter's old tweed suit over the valet stand (were his car lights on *Thunk* Oh please), tidy his desk with its papers and lecture notes and office keys and Tums and thumbed paperback, *Introduction to Poetry,* lying open —

Look if you like, but you will have to
    leap,
Our dream of safety has to disappear.*

I push myself on through the thick
stillness of waiting; each time I pause
Time pauses; if I were to stop Time would
stop. I move from room to room of the
weary old house, keeping Time stirred. I
patrol its corridors, I listen at my sons'
doors for their trustful breathing, I check
Uncle Tyler's fretful snores and phlegmy
groans. Back downstairs, I straighten the
library, go out to the terrace for some
logs. Still and black outside (*a solitude
ten thousand fathoms deep*) and
beginning to creak with cold; I can hear
the dried leaves rustle, stiffening
(*sustains the bed on which we lie, my
dear*). I carry in armloads of heavy oak
logs, pile them by the fireplace (*look if
you like, but you will have to leap*);
take the poker and, sitting on the low
bench, prod the drowsing fire awake again
(*our dream of safety has to disappear*).

*W. H. Auden, "Look Before You Leap."

Who would ring the doorbell but the sheriff at this hour? No; please let it be them. The two of them home safe. Please. Nothing more will I ever ask. Nothing else will I ever want. What could I ever have wanted but just that? Just that: the two of them home safe. Please.

I open the door to Jim Randall. He says he's been delayed, an emergency call at the hospital — *an accident on the road Oh which one Surely not both Please* — patching up a couple of brawling rednecks, and what is Uncle Tyler's temperature? He comes into focus going down the hall with his black bag and the dogged tread of a man who has driven twenty miles out into the country as a favor to friends but the patient had damn well better be sick.

Sick Uncle Tyler is. "Why in hell he didn't come in for that flu shot I told him to have when you first got sick," Jim Randall fumes back in the library, where I've brought him a cup of coffee he requested. "He's such a stubborn old bastard — sorry, Emily. I've been on the run the whole damn day. No, Christ, don't apologize, you were right to call me. I don't like the sound of his chest. Somebody his age, and overweight, and probably — well, we won't worry about that now. I called the hospital, they're sending an ambulance out for him. It's a long way and a cold night and he shouldn't go by car, otherwise Porter could drive him — where is Porter, anyway? — and I wouldn't want to even try getting him into my VW. We could wait till morning but I really think it'd be better to get him where we can keep a check on him — Emily? Lord, what's the matter? Look, there's no call to get panicked, it's just that the ambulance is the safest and most comfortable way to — hey, you really are in a state. Come on now. Uncle Tyler's going to be OK, we're just taking precautions, you know that. And you've got your hands full enough, haven't you, running the house with the kids and all, it's just more sensible if you don't have to — Emily, honey, get a grip on —''

"— got to *find* them, let me *go* —''

"Find who? Emily, calm down and tell me —''

"— waiting and waiting and nobody'll let me *go* —"

"Go where? Find who? Tell me calmly, honey, and I'll —"

"— out there all alone, and him in that old car — let me *go,* I have to go —"

"Porter? Is it Porter you're worried about? Come on, get hold of yourself now. Porter's not home, is that it —"

"Porter's home."

Porter's voice. Porter's home! Safe. "Porter, oh Porter . . ." Breaking free, I stumble toward him standing there, right there, in the doorway. "Oh Porter, thank God, you're home safe, and she's — you brought her too, didn't you, Porter? Where —" *Thunk.* "Porter, where is she?"

"Porter's home, yeah." His thick voice: like thunking into a concrete barrier. "Home to his wife. So, Randall, you better get on home to yours. Right now, Randall."

Eleven

Jim says Porter I hope to hell you're drunk. I say Please, please. Porter says he'll give Randall exactly three minutes to get out of his house. He starts counting. One thousand one, one thousand two, one thousand three. Jim says Emily, get out to the kitchen and make some strong coffee and let me handle this. I say But my daughter, she's missing. One thousand nine, one thousand ten, Porter says. Jim says What daughter. I say My daughter, my daughter Sara. Jim says Phone the sheriff, give them her description. I say I can't and he says You have to so don't argue. One thousand twenty-one, Porter says. Jim shoves Porter into the library and closes the door. I phone the sheriff. How old you say the girl is, a man says between yawns. I say she is seventeen but she looks about twelve, she's very small. I say Please don't scare her if you find her, don't shine lights in her face and please don't use dogs, she's very frightened of dogs. He mumbles something and hangs up. Jim opens the library door and barks Pour yourself a drink, Emily, that's an order, and get that coffee on. One thousand two hundred and sixty-nine, Porter's voice is droning. Jim closes the door again. Porter's voice rises and I hear some heavy thuds in there. I put my fists over my ears but I can still hear them, *thunk*. I flee to the kitchen. I put the kettle on for coffee. I try to remember what else I'm supposed to do. I sit down at the kitchen table. Presently I remember and get up and pour myself a drink. I sit down again with it, taking a swallow every few minutes when I remember. I sit staring at the kitchen clock. The two dogs stare at me from their corner.

Pretty soon the ambulance comes and takes Uncle Tyler away. "Don't worry about me," he says tremulously as they carry him out on the stretcher that doesn't seem quite wide enough for him, parts of him are billowing over the sides, "I'm no use to anybody anyway." I kiss him and say that we love him and I will come to the hospital to see him tomorrow. I guess he is too sick to notice how things are. I go back to the kitchen and sit down at the table.

Mother . . .
Cold. It slowly stiffens my joints. When I stir there is a creaking, a whispering, in the stiff joints of this old house. So I stop stirring.
Mother. . . ?
Muttering, the old clock stirs its thick cold porridge of time. Colder. The drink in me has flickered out. My hands and feet are brittle as glass.
Mother . . .
Coldest: a polar wind has risen, howls around my ankles. A door slams with the tinkle of shattered ice.
Mother!
And she. Here. Home.

— Porter, she's home, Sara's home
— He's in there? If *he's* there I'm

not going in

— It's just Dr. Randall, Sara darling, you remember Dr. Randall who came when I was sick.

— Not him, I don't mean him, I'm not going into that room if *he*'s in there

— But darling who? There's just Dr. Randall and Porter

— I won't go in there. He's drunk, he tried to make me get into the car with him, he tried to touch me

— Touch you, Sara, I don't understand what you're

— Join the crowd. She's, she thinks I'm some kind of monster. My God, how could anybody think that of me

— Hold on, everybody. Let's calm down here and

— He can't deny it, ask him, *ask* him if he tried to make me get into his car with him and I could smell he was *drunk,* you think I don't know how they get that way when

— I am not drunk. Can't anybody *see* when a man's had all he can take

— Porter — Sara — please can't we just

— Emily. Let me handle this for now,

OK? Porter, take it easy. Sara? Don't back away, Sara. Nobody's going to touch you. Look at me, Sara, and see if you remember me. Do you remember my name? Never mind now, Sara, he's over at the other end of the room. Look at me and tell me if you remember my name.

— James B. Randall. M.D.

— Hey, excellent. How'd you remember the middle initial?

— It's stamped on your bag. I didn't remember it. And you can stop trying to use child psychology on me. I'm not a child. I'm seventeen. And I'm not hysterical, either.

— Good. If you're not a child and you're not hysterical you can come sit on the sofa with your mother and help straighten all this out.

— *I*'ve got it straight. *He*'s the one who needs straightening. Of course you won't believe that. Everybody's gonna take his word over mine. Everybody always does. Nobody really wants to believe what kids say.

— Sara, sit down. Right there. And right now . . . Good. Good girl. Now everybody's going to stay right where they are and we're going to sit back, and we're going to talk like honest, responsible people.

Honest and responsible people: the two of them each seem to be so sure, in their separate agonies of conviction. It seemes impossible that one has to be lying, or at least shading the central truth.

Maybe — I think, sitting on the sofa with my head turning dazedly from one to the other like somebody observing a tennis match — maybe I myself have been lying for so long that I can no longer distinguish not only truth but reality. Or do we all live in separate realities, and what once passed for truth among us was simply an agreement, smashed now in the general disaster?

Porter says that when Sara turned up missing and wasn't at the Katzes', he realized she must have gone out alone to look for me. She'd been terribly worried, panicking, he says, when six o'clock rolled around and I wasn't home. What he didn't realize until after the Katzes were checked was that Sara must have left shortly after six o'clock, when he'd seen her last. Then he became really alarmed —

"Ask him to tell you what happened *before* I left," Sara breaks in. "Ask him to tell you why I *had* to leave."

"Happened?" Porter raises his head, which he has been holding between his hands with his elbows propped on his knees. He blinks at her with reddened eyes. "What happened?" he repeats thickly.

"He knows what happened. He just won't tell you."

"Anything special happen then, you can recall, Porter?" Jim Randall says conversationally. He looks so casual, so ordinary (it is borne in on me, like the sudden glimpse of a familiar landmark through a shredded hole in a fog), lounging back in his chair, one long leg slung over the arm, exposing a crumpled gray sweat sock and a bony ankle, an ordinary youngish man with thinning light hair and the gray look of too many cups of coffee over too long a day — he looks so solid in his ordinariness that I think, Why, we're just ordinary people, a family with ordinary misunderstandings and troubles, isn't that what everybody's life is about . . . Then the hole closes again, leaving me floating around in that dense whiteness and not one solid thing to set the foot on.

"Happened . . . Jesus, there's been so much, what the hell happened . . ." Porter drops his head back between his hands, rubs his fingers through his hair. "Lessee. I was in the pantry —"

"Pouring himself another big slug of whiskey."

"— yeah, getting a drink. Only it was my first drink, I remember that," he says wearily, "because she came in and saw me and said right off I was drunk. I thought Jesus, I haven't even had a sip yet and she thinks I'm drunk, what would make her think that, she's never even seen me high much less drunk. But she went on and on and I realized she was all upset about Emily not being home, she kept saying if her mother was in an accident it was all my fault for making her scared to come home to a drunken husband. I was beginning to get damn worried myself, because Catherine Tupper said Emily'd left at four-thirty, and what with all that talk about accidents —"

"See? He's not telling you what *happened*. He's trying —"

"Sara, you're interrupting again. Go on, Porter. You were saying she thought you were drunk. But you were just having your first drink, is that right?"

"Just *pouring* my first drink," Porter says doggedly.

"OK. So you were both worried about Emily. Then what did you do?"

"Then I . . . Lessee, I guess I realized she was getting hysterical. So I put down the drink and tried to calm her. I know you're supposed to slap a hysteric to bring them out —"

"Is that it, Sara? He slapped you?"

"No. Oh no, he didn't *slap* me. See, they don't wanna leave a mark on you. Then people can't tell —"

"— but I could never bring myself to slap anybody," Porter says bleakly, "certainly not a woman or a child. So I tried to tell her not to be scared, her mother was probably just delayed somewhere, and she shouldn't let herself imagine things, and she should try to be a big girl —"

"That's what they always say. They say you're imagining things, and you shouldn't be scared, and you should be a *big* girl now." Her eyes are glittering.

"— and she looked so scared and sort of, well, lonely and helpless," Porter plods on, staring down at his hands dangling loosely over his knees, "I guess it occurred to me that Emily — her mother — was the only thing in the world she seemed to have, you know, or care about. It kind of gripped me, maybe because I was so worried about Emily myself, and the idea of something happening to her — anyway, we, the girl and I, we seemed to be in it together. So then I . . . what? . . . Oh yeah, I guess I reached out to pat her shoulder, try to comfort her, and she went all to pieces. Jerking away and screaming about touching her, and something about how filthy drunk men are all alike —"

"My shoulder, oh sure, he'd say he was just petting my *shoulder* —"

"Don't infer anything from this question, Porter, OK? I'm just wondering how come you had to search your memory before you remembered a scene like that. Sure does sound dramatic," Jim says.

"She was hysterical. You don't pay too much attention to what people say when they're hysterical. Maybe I should've."

"Oh, you were paying *attention* all right, touching my so-called shoulder —"

"OK, Sara. Where did he touch you?"

"I didn't touch her. She jumped back before I could get anywhere near her. Jesus, she jerked away as if I were dealing out electric shocks." He puts his face in his hands and rubs them over it. "I know I didn't touch her. I'd know that, wouldn't I?"

"And *I* know he —"

"Hold it. Sara — Porter — I want you both to think very hard here for a moment. Try to visualize, OK? That's the best way to remember accurately, try to *see* it again. Now — was there a movement, a gesture, you may have made, Porter, that you, Sara, could have misinterpreted? Think a moment before you answer. Sometimes two people can interpret a gesture entirely differently, you know. Gestures — the way they're offered, the way they're read — they come out of states of mind. Subconscious expectations as well as intents. For instance, Porter says his *intent* was to comfort you, Sara. But maybe your *expectation* was, well, that he was going to hit you, or act in some hostile manner — maybe because *you* felt hostile toward *him*? So that when he lifted his hand to pat your shoulder, you interpreted it as an intent to hit you?"

"Uh huh. That's really neat, Dr. Randall, except he didn't hit me. I keep telling you he didn't *hit* me, even he says he didn't *hit* me. I mean if you're gonna lay your interpretation on me, instead of wanting mine, which is what I thought you were asking for, you can at least get it straight that he didn't *hit* me."

"I take it we can agree he didn't hit you," Jim says dryly. "OK. We've had

268

Porter's version, let's have yours."

Sara says Porter *touched* her. Jim asks where he'd *touched* her. She says Where did he think, he was a doctor, she shouldn't have to demonstrate things like that. Porter mumbles incredulously that she can't be talking about sex, not like that, he hasn't heard anybody talk that way since his grandmother, and even she wouldn't have considered a pat on the shoulder something unmentionable. Jim says it's Sara's turn, let her tell it her own way.

After she struggled loose from Porter (Sara says) she ran out of the house. "I couldn't stay there with *him,*" she says tautly, "and I had to find Mother. I started out down the road. I figured if I walked far enough I'd get to the place where it goes into the highway to town. I knew that was the way Mother'd be coming back — if she was coming back at all." She stares fiercely down at her fists balled in her lap. The nape of her neck is downy, innocent, frail.

"Oh Sara! Would I ever *not* come —"

"Then," she cuts back, not looking at

me, "I guess I took the wrong turn by the Batesville store, because I walked for a long time and I didn't come to the highway. It was too dark to see but I must've been back in the hills somewhere, there weren't any lights, only a cabin once in a while, and some dogs came out and barked but I threw gravel at them," she says indifferently, "and then pretty soon the road petered out and I was walking on some sort of trail in the woods. So I turned around and walked back to Batesville. I figured maybe somebody at the store would give me a lift, but it was closed and there wasn't anybody around, Batesville's such a dump. So I started walking again in another direction, I was hoping it was the road that went to the highway. Pretty soon this car came along behind me, I saw its lights but it came up so fast it almost hit me —"

"She was right in the middle of the road." Porter winces. "I wasn't doing thirty-five but there was this turn —"

"I wasn't in the *middle* of the road, I was sort of to one side, I couldn't walk in the *ditch* and besides in the dark you can't see even to stay on the road unless you're *on* it," she continues in her steady, toneless way. "So the car screeched to a stop and started backing up. I was pretty tired and I hoped it'd be some woman, maybe, who'd give me a lift. My par — I never hitch rides with guys, a girl I know got — *you* know." Her face is white. "I figured if it was a guy I could run and he couldn't find me in the woods. And it was *him*. So I ran. He got out and looked for me, I could hear him thrashing around calling my name, but I stayed still and he couldn't find me" — she smiles contemptuously — "so pretty soon he got back in the car and drove off. He drove off the way he was going so I figured the other way was home. But it wasn't. So I was too tired to walk anymore so I turned around and came back. I woke up the Katzes and they said Mother was home. So I came home." She stops.

After a moment Jim says gently, "You must be exhausted, Sara. Can I ask one more question? Don't you think anybody, any decent ordinary person, who's driving along a country road at night and sees a

271

young girl walking — wouldn't they just automatically stop and offer her a lift?''

''I know what you're trying to get me to say. You really do think I'm a child, don't you?'' She smiles; her eyes glitter. ''Ordinary people stop for decent reasons. He stopped. Therefore he's ordinary and decent. You think I can't see the fallacy in that syllogism? Didn't you study logic, Dr. Randall?''

''I see you did, Sara. You must go to a pretty advanced high school.''

Her smile glitters coldly. ''You're not going to trap me in that, either.''

''Trap you?'' Jim's face is genuinely puzzled. ''In what?''

''Trying to find out where I go to school. *He* tries that all the time, asking me these casual little leading questions, as if I couldn't see he's trying to find out, and send me —'' She stops.

''Find out what?'' Under his steady gaze the hectic glitter fades, turns ashen. He flicks his gaze to me, then back to her. ''Send you where?''

''Mother . . .'' She turns blindly to me. ''I'm tired,'' she whimpers. ''Mother, I'm so *tired* . . ."

". . . Don't tell him, Mother." I fold back the sheet around her face, which is almost as white and smudged with violet shadows. "Please don't tell Dr. Randall about me. He'll find out everything, I know he will, he'll arrange to make me go back . . ."

I promise her I will not tell Jim Randall anything more. I kiss her, but she is already asleep.

And Porter has already told the whole story.

"Look," Jim says wearily, "you don't have to add to your problems by worrying about what people would think if they found out Sara was Emily's daughter. They'd simply assume, the way I did at first, that Emily was married before and had this child and when they were divorced the child stayed with her father, for some reason."

"What reason?" I close my eyes, rest my head on my hand. "What reason would there be for the mother not to get custody of the daughter?"

"Children always go to the mother in divorce cases." Porter stares at the floor. *So he has thought of that.*

"OK. I'm not going to try to construct an airtight case for your social respectability — which it strikes me you both may be too damned concerned about." Jim is pacing stiffly, trying to get back some circulation in his long legs. His face is grim. "There comes a time when you've got to throw out everything that doesn't matter. The opinion of people you don't care about is pretty far down the list. And the people you do care about — you think they're gonna cut you dead on the street? Give your friends some credit. So Emily made a mistake when she was young. Listen, times have changed —"

"We haven't." *Some deep dark embarrassin secret out of a person's past.* "And a lot of people haven't changed as much as they think they have. Including me."

"And me." Porter says bleakly, "God. Coming in like the husband in a French bedroom farce."

"Let's not hassle that again, Porter,"

Jim says. "I don't think anybody's blaming you." He holds my eyes, like a lawyer pleading his client's case. "That's the kind of mistake a man makes once in a while. There's not a man who hasn't let that kind of idea get hold of him once or twice in his life. Like I said, misinterpreting gestures." He pauses, transfers his gaze to Porter. "So what about that?"

Porter says doggedly, "I can't tell you anything more about that and I can't tell you anything different. I didn't intend to 'touch' her and I didn't touch her. Any way you want it to mean."

There is a pause.

"Emily," Jim says, "this is going to sound rough, but it's the question that's between you two, and somebody's got to ask it so it might as well be me. You know your husband in ways nobody else can. Do you believe him when he says he didn't make a pass at that girl?"

". . . I . . ."

"It's not a question of choosing sides, Emily. It's a question of cold hard honest belief."

"Then I believe that Porter didn't touch her. He just . . . couldn't, that's all."

Wordlessly Porter continues to stare at his hands. Presently in the silence there is the harsh dry strangulated sound of a man weeping.

I follow Jim Randall down the hall. He gets into his coat. He turns to me.

"Look," he says, "I'm no guidance counselor. I'm a family friend besides, you need somebody disinterested to talk with. You people — you and Porter and Sara — are spinning your wheels, and you're all getting sucked down deeper and deeper. You've got to come to some new terms, you and Porter. And you've got to do something about Sara. Honest to God, the number of people I see who go to the most incredible lengths to avoid facing their central problems — Anyway, Emily, if you and Porter can keep on ignoring your own trouble, you've got to do something about your daughter's. There's something in that kid's past, Emily, that may have done her some bad psychic damage. That whole scene with Porter —

I don't know if you noticed, but she kept saying things like 'they get that way when they're drunk' and 'they don't want to leave a mark on you so people can't tell' and 'that's what they always say' —"

"And that nobody ever wants to believe her when she says these things."

"Don't think I — or more importantly, Porter — didn't understand what it cost you to acknowledge that your daughter —"

"Was lying? I don't think she was lying, Jim. I think she really believed what she was saying."

"I agree. I think she was associating so strongly with some previous experience — flashing on it is the expression now — that she was actually reliving it. That's a stress phenomenon we know a lot about," he says grimly, "since the advent of the drug culture." He adds, seeing my face, "there's a lot of bad trips, and flashing back on them, that don't necessarily come from drugs, Emily. The experience of an emotional shock can have the same effect, particularly when there are similar circumstances. She never once referred to Porter except as *he,* you notice that? Just a sort of generalized figure. And she seems to have a horror of a man she thinks is drunk. One way or another, that girl's past has got to be cracked open.''

He hesitates. ''From what I've seen of your daughter,'' he says with care, ''I detect a good deal of what used to be called character. She's highly intelligent, too. She's a girl anybody'd be proud to claim as a daughter. She's a very touching sort of girl,'' he says, ''as Porter pointed out to me tonight.''

''Porter. . . ?''

''When you were putting her to bed. He was telling me about her. She moves him, you know, because she's yours.''

''But not his,'' I say flatly, to flatten my leap of hope.

''No, not his. You're right to understand how that is tough on a man, in his basic gut part. But you're wrong,'' he says as flatly, ''not to give the same guy credit for being more than just a mass of visceral reactions. There really *are* some men who in their very tissues are what you might call evolved — civilized, generous-minded, uxorious, faithful — whatever lofty way you want to describe plain decency. Decency isn't a very dramatic quality, it's not interesting enough for clinical studies, which is, I suppose, why people tend not to take it much into account when they're trying to analyze a guy's reactions."

"I've abused his decency for so long."

"So whose decency is never abused?" He picks up his bag. "Emily," he says wearily, "your husband loves you. Your daughter is devoted to you. I have no doubt everybody else in your family feels the same way. So it could be said that you're a woman who commands a considerable amount of devotion. Instead of feeling so damn guilty, you might start by simply accepting that, and work from there."

"Thank you." I face him stiffly. "And I'm very sorry you were put through this tonight."

"Porter's already taken care of the apologies. Oh — and don't worry about Tyler. I'll check on him on my morning rounds and call you. Good night, Emily."

I slowly climb the stairs, wondering where I can find the strength to carry around this burden of everybody's devotion.

Porter is out on his back on the bed, still dressed. The light from the lamp pours mercilessly down his face, gouging it with shadows. I lean over him. Decency: what, in this grief-scarred terrain, lies under it?

He is your husband. You should know.

In his sleep he moans and gnashes his teeth. He flings out his arm, hits my watching face. At last, the blow.

I could never bring myself to hit anybody.

I get a quilt from the closet and spread it gently over him. I turn out the light. Without undressing I kick off my shoes and climb in next to him. In his sleep he groans and turns to me. I put my arm under his neck and settle his heavy head against my shoulder. I lie on my back staring up through the dark, feeling below us only the bed, and below that an unfathomable solitude.

Twelve

Now why, I think as I awaken, *would I dream I was old. . . .?* I pass my hand over my face. It is wet. Why do the aged weep like children, voluptuously?

I turn my face on the pillow. Outside it is raining; a tepid, soft, voluptuous springlike rain. Like the January thaws of my childhood it has the same dreamlike effect. Ten twenty-five? It does not seem to matter that I've overslept.

Drowsily, voluptuously, I rise, get into my robe, drift down the hall, check on Sara. She too is still asleep, but unstirring. In the kitchen, a note: "Boys off to school. Will phone at noon. Porter." I drift around in my robe, fix some toast and tea, settle at the kitchen table with the newspaper. HIJACKERS SEEK SANCTUARY AT ROME AIRPORT. COST OF

LIVING UP 1.7 PERCENT IN DECEMBER.

I drift into the hall to answer the phone. It is Jim Randall. Uncle Tyler's condition steady, resting comfortably. Flu diagnosis doubtful, doing further tests. Jim's voice is brisk and impersonal; he's got to run. I drift back to my paper. GOOD GRIEF, SNOOPY, IT'S THE RED BARON AGAIN!!!!

Phone again: "Emily? I hope I'm not interruptin you, but Harry just phoned from Richmond and I just had to call —" *They're goin to back us.* "— He's been meetin with his people all mornin, finalizin the reactions, and Harry says most everyone's willin to be persuaded —" *Now is the time for all good women to come to the aid of the party.* I turn to smile at Sara, who is drifting down the stairs in her nightgown. I murmur my thanks to Mrs. Tupper and hang up. I drift into the kitchen after Sara, who sits at the table in her long white nightgown with her long downy neck coming up out of the chaste little ruffle and her sleep-dazed eyes still trusting what they don't yet see, still looking inside at the dream. She is so soft and warm that I smile, and coming behind her chair, I bend to wrap my arms around her shoulders like a shawl, and kiss the sweet nape of her maidenly neck.

She says, "I suppose now they want to send me back."

A pop in my ears and I have surfaced at last from the depths of my own dream. I am not yet old. There are still years to be got through, and here it is not even noon.

". . . see, Mother, if I don't tell you, then they won't be able to find out. And then they can't send me back," she is saying, sitting there in her long white nightie all soft and downy and full of sleep. "If I protect you from knowing, I can protect us both from them, from letting them separate us." In silence I pour her some more tea, and she bends her head and dreamily kisses my wrist. "They'd get it out of you, I know they would. They'd make you feel guilty some way, and then you'd tell."

Guilty. The insight is so shrewd I cannot defend myself. In silence I sit down again.

"Don't worry, Mother." She smiles at me sweetly, trustingly. "I know *you* don't want me to go away. I trust you. That's the one thing I know now, I can trust my own mother. So you trust *me,* and don't worry. If I don't tell you anything, you can't tell them and we're safe. I've got it all figured out."

"Emily?" Porter's voice is reserved, efficient. "I thought I'd let you sleep. How're you feeling?"

"OK. It was nice of you to take care of things. How are *you* feeling?"

"Tired." He pauses. He says formally, "But finally starting to get things cleared. I stopped in at the hospital this morning. Uncle Tyler's holding his own very well. Jim says it's not flu."

"I know. He called."

"Oh. Then you know he's ordered some tests."

"Did he say what for?"

"Just general, he said, X rays and blood tests and so on. You know how vague doctors are. Anyway, Uncle Tyler's pretty depressed. He'd like to see you, and he wants you to bring some things. You got a pencil there, I'll give you the list. By the way, I took the truck in this morning and left the station wagon for you. Maybe you ought to have that headlight fixed while you're in town. The hospital visiting hours don't matter, you can go whenever it's convenient, they let close family in." He dictates the list to me — mostly books — and then he adds, in the same ceremonial and efficient tones, that he has made an appointment for us and Sara for Thursday afternoon with a psychiatrist Jim Randall recommended. And he has also been in touch with a firm of private detectives to try and trace down Sara's adoptive parents.

"They say they'll need a recent snapshot of her, and any more information of any kind she may have given you, beyond what I was able to provide them. They say you should come in right away and talk with them. The man you talk to is a Mr. DiSalvio — Joseph DiSalvio. You don't need an appointment but you should phone before you come to be sure he's in. His office is upstairs behind the Rexall Drug Store off Main Street and the name is the DiSalvio Private Security Agency."

"Uncle Tyler's in the hospital?" Her face pales. "And you didn't tell me?"

"You just got up, and last night — He's much better today," I fib to smother my own alarm at the alarm in her face. "Sara, I didn't realize you'd be so upset —"

"You didn't think I'd care?" She stares at me stricken. "You think I'm the sort of person who goes around not caring about people in her own *family*? You think they don't *matter* to somebody like me, because they're not really my family —" She whirls in her white nightgown and bare feet and, sobbing, pounds upstairs. I follow her, near sobs myself with relief that now I must take her with me to the hospital and so cannot possibly see that detective today.

". . . Is that you, Emily? And who — Sara? Is that Sara, too? Dear child,"

Uncle Tyler quavers, "how very kind of you to come visit an old, sick, useless hulk — *ulk* —" as she darts for his bed and flings herself, weeping, upon him. "Good grief — there, there, child — Emily, what have they been telling her about me — come, there, Sara child, you mustn't take on so *oof* — I must say," his voice comes plaintive and muffled around her shoulder, "one is vastly moved — if you'd just release your clutch the merest bit, dear girl, the lungs, y'know, laboring for air — vastly moved indeed, that youth would take time from its blithe diversions to attend the sickbed of decrepit age. Sara," he says with a touch of his old asperity, "you're getting my nightshift wet. That wretched nurse will pounce on me and rip it off and encase me in a cleaner and even stiffer one. Never mind that one's skin has always been sensitive to starch. Here, blow your nose, there's some tissue on that table, just out of my reach of course, like everything else here, *tout confort* if one can climb out of bed and crawl toward it . . . There, that's better, a wisp of a smile on the sweet young countenance. Ah yes, old Uncle Tyler was always able to make her smile, wasn't he, even now from his narrow hospital cot. Or crib, one should say; they have rails they put up at night to keep one from tumbling out, like an infant. The end of life so appallingly resembles its beginning. The falling curve recapitulates the rising — Oh dear, the child's clouding up again, so sensitive. Come come Sara, one must be valorous, mustn't one? Look at me, for instance; the old can at least set an example, socially if not kinetically, heh heh heh," he chuckles feebly. "That was a good Scrabble game that night, wasn't it? Ah memories. What else is there in the end, save memories and valor? Grace under pressure — *uff,* the pressure of love is a bit heavy, Sara, if you'll just move a little . . . There, that's better. Bring that other chair over here by my bed, next to Emily, then I can see your dear and loving faces. Emily, you brought my books? Good, good. Those other dear and loving faces, books, those old companions come to tend the remaining hours — watchmen, as in

Hamlet, to patrol the battlements, keep the minutes of the night, when the ghost appears — the Old King, in this case one's life, metaphorically speaking. Come stalking back to chide me about its own murder. That's what a wasted life is, a slow murder — no no Emily, let me finish, why must women forever strive to muffle these terminal coughs, these epic clearings of mucus from the soul's passage? — Drat, where was I? Oh yes, wasted in slow murder. . . . No, that wasn't it. I'm tired," he continues querulously, plucking at his sheet with his old plump freckled hands, "and they bring me only gruel and pap to eat. The end of life so resembles its beginnings . . ."

He seems to doze off. "Mother," whispers Sara, rigid in her chair, ". . . is he . . ."

"However." His eyes have popped open. *"She* couldn't have done anything else. Caesar's wife, et cetera. Or was it Cordelia's pearls . . ."

"Mother . . ."

"Emily. Did you bring *Troilus and Criseyde?"* Popping open again, his eyes are clear this time.

"No, Uncle Tyler, it wasn't on the list —"

"Drat! I *must* continue with that translation!" He tries to struggle up on an elbow, falls back with a groan. "Oh *mala fide,* how treacherously the body breaks faith with the spirit. Oh *lèse-majesté* — Sara, dear child," he breaks off to say in crisp tones, "it occurs that the University Library is just across the street from this hospital. Take my library card — it's in my wallet, if they haven't confiscated that too, along with my remaining dignity — in that closet somewhere, and run over and check out *Troilus and Criseyde* for me. The Chaucerian version, mind you, they have a copy, just tell them it's for me . . ."

"Now then," he says after she leaves. "Tell me, Emily, what the devil was going *on* last night?"

"Uncle Tyler, I'm not sure you . . . I don't want to tire you —"

"Tire me? Come come come come come," he chatters irritably, "d'you think I won't shortly be getting plenty of rest?

Why must the old and sick be treated as if life no longer concerns them? Come come come, Emily, d'you think I've got all day?"

". . . Ah, here's Sara. Thank you, my dear. Just put the book over there on top of the papers — you *did* bring me the papers, Emily?"

"The newspapers? I didn't know you wanted them —"

"Newspapers, why on earth would I be interested in the news? People cry News, news, and there is no news. Not when you're my age there isn't. I most specifically instructed Porter to bring me my *papers*. And so of course he sends me these mountains of books. If I needed books I could have them sent over from the Library."

"If you'll describe what papers you want, Uncle Tyler, I'll be glad to bring them to you tomorrow —"

"Tomorrow. Everybody is forever thinking in terms of tomorrow, just as if — The trouble, my dear Emily, is that I need my papers *now*." He fixes me with an eye so desperate, so old, so needful that I find myself saying that I will drive back home and get his papers for him.

"You will find them," he says, sinking back on the pillow and closing his eyes wearily, "in a trunk in the attic." He opens his eyes again. "Leave Sara here," he commands weakly. "You wouldn't mind tending the watch with your uncle Tyler for an hour or so, would you, dear child?"

"No, I wouldn't mind." Her face is pale. "I *want* to stay with you, Uncle Tyler."

"Sweet child, of course you don't want to. Nothing is so terrifying to youth as to be in the presence of infirmity. Now now, no need to protest, my dear, it has nothing to do with affection, which I know you feel. It is simply the instinct of the healthy to avoid intimations of its own mortality, so to speak. But I promise you won't really mind, I shall be as entertaining as possible, and not wander off into morbid philosophizing — What? Emily? Still here? I thought you were off to get my papers."

"If you can tell me where in the attic,

Uncle Tyler, and what trunk —"

"What trunk, *my* trunk of course. With the leather straps and brass clasps and brass plate inscribed with the name *Colonel William T. Talbott,*" he says with massive patience, "which as you may recall was my grandfather's name. Brilliant soldier, my grandfather; cavalry, superb horseman, distinguished himself under Stonewall Jackson and later Jeb Stuart, fell with him in the defense of Richmond. Yes, there was a noble inheritance of valor in the Talbott line. Mustn't forget that, must we, even though I am the last of that name . . ."

Forty miles and an hour and a half later I am back, lugging an old suitcase full of what I pray are the proper papers. I settle Stuart and Timmie in the hospital lobby — they have insisted on coming back with me although I've cautioned them they probably won't let kids into the patients' rooms; but their faces were so anxious and I didn't want to leave them that way and it was already almost five o'clock — and coming out of the elevator, I see Jim

Randall down the hall, dressed in surgical green. He is in a hurry, but he stops.

"Suitcase?" he says. "Tyler's not going anywhere, no matter how much he tries to bully you."

I say I'm only bringing him some things he wants. "How is he really, Jim?"

"He's really pretty sick," he says shortly, as if I were accusing him of withholding the truth. "However, his condition seems steady. We're running some tests, and I'll be checking in on him before I go home." He nods and turns.

"I was just wondering," I say apologetically, "why he seems to sort of slip now and then, and drift away when he's talking —"

"Slip?" He stops. "You mean he seems confused?"

"Once or twice —"

He turns again with a squeak of his rubber heel, strides back down the corridor. I toil after him with the suitcase. "You can leave him his stuff," he says back over his shoulder, "and then go on home. I don't want him tired out with visitors, and I want to check on a few things. I'll phone you later."

"What did you and Uncle Tyler talk about?" Driving home with Sara and the two boys, I try to hide my worry, to be casual. "Or did he just ramble, in his usual way?"

Sara's silence has a tranced quality to it. "No," she murmurs, "he wasn't rambling."

"Boy, he must really be sick if he wasn't talking," muses Stuart.

"Yeah, he's awful sick, 'cause he's in the hospital." Timmie kicks the back of my seat. "I *hate* hospitals."

"You're not supposed to hate hospitals, because they make you well. Right, Mother?"

"That's what Uncle Tyler's there for, to make him well. Sara, did he sound —"

"What if it doesn't make him well? What if he has to stay in the hospital forever —"

"Stupid Timmie, she just *told* you —"

"— and they'll never ever let us see him ever again —"

"Don't be silly, Timmie. When Uncle

Tyler's a little better they'll let you see him."

"— and Sara gets to see him and we don't and *we*'re his *real* family and not bastards either —"

"*That will do.*" But my command is too late. She has turned her head toward the window, looking out into the dark; in the glow of the dashboard lights tears glitter along the profile of her cheek. She stares out the window like the Little Match Girl staring in, forehead pressed against the glass.

"Sara?" Stuart's troubled voice comes presently from the back seat. "Sara? Timmie didn't mean that."

She goes up in silence to her room. In silence, Stuart and Timmie and I stand at the bottom of the stairs.

"Emily? That you?" Porter's voice calls from the kitchen. "Emily? Are Stuart and Timmie with you?"

I strip off my coat, tell the boys to get washed, head for the kitchen. Porter and PJ are making a stab at getting supper. The contents of every cupboard and shelf are scattered over every surface. I roll up my sleeves and tackle it, grateful there's something I must do besides worry.

Porter surrenders the job as gratefully. "Mrs. Tupper called. She wants you to call back."

"OK. PJ, you can set the table. Lord, I forgot to take the meat out of the freezer —"

"Never mind, why don't we just have scrambled eggs or something?" Porter is trying to catch my eye, but I avoid it. I do not wish to discuss problems. I wish only to be a housewife bustling and hustling supper.

"Scrambled eggs it is," I say, bustling to the refrigerator. "PJ, go call the boys, and tell Sara supper's almost ready."

PJ comes back to report that Sara doesn't want any supper. "She sounds kinda like she's crying." He attempts to look disgusted. His face is screwed up with concern.

Porter looks at me. "Maybe I can go up and persuade her to join us," he says. He looks like a man wheeling around at last to face what has been stalking him.

"I'll go," I say automatically. "You and the boys start eating, Porter. Your eggs'll get cold."

"Crissake," PJ mutters, "why don't we *all* go? Who cares about scrambled eggs, anyway?"

She is lying on her stomach across her bed. Her cheek is resting on her folded arms. She does not look up as I crack the door. "I'm just not hungry, Mother," she says thickly. "Please, don't make a fuss about it."

"We didn't come to make a fuss, Sara." Porter stays politely behind me in the doorway. "We came to ask if you'd join us for supper."

She does not move.

"It's only scrambled eggs," Porter says, "but you wouldn't have to eat them if you don't want to."

She is silent.

"We'd all like you to come," I say.

"Yeah, Sara," Stuart chimes, "we're *all* here. See?"

"Crissake, how can she see with Dad standing in the way . . . Stuart, go get it," PJ hisses.

"Go get what?"

"*You* know."

"We won't come into your room if you don't want us to, Sara," Porter says, "but we would all like your company at supper."

"Oh yeah," Stuart is whispering, "where is it?"

"Where is it, crissake, it's in my closet, in that box with the stuff —"

"Go away," she says into her arms, not moving. "Please. Mother, tell them just to go away now."

"They want to tell you how they feel, Sara."

"I know how they feel."

"I don't think you do." Porter is still standing in the doorway, his arms hanging heavy at his sides. *Decent: such a decent man.* "I wish" — he clears his throat and slogs on — "I wish we could all try to understand each other, Sara."

"*I* understand a lot of things." She does not move.

"I'm sure you do. We've tried to be open with you, open to you," Porter continues, fumbling to be right, to be understood and believed, ''so maybe you're more able to understand us than we are you. Sara,'' he bursts out, ''we just want you to come down and sit at the family table with us. Won't you do that one small thing?''

''Family.'' She turns her face down and buries it in her arms.

''Is she crying?'' Timmie blinks anxiously around Porter, his eye patch brushed askew over his brow. ''Oh, now we've made her cry, and she won't wanna be *with* us —''

''Hold it, everyone! Timmie, move over, crissake, will you move it — We got something here for you guys —'' PJ, scowling furiously, looms behind Porter. ''Dad, would you *mind,* we've got something here, it's really important —''

Porter moves aside and PJ clumps through, followed by Stuart. ''C'mere, Timmie. You're in on this too,'' PJ barks. The three of them line up stiffly, with some jerking of arms by PJ, in the middle of Sara's hooked rug. She does not raise her head.

"OK." PJ's face is scarlet. Stuart's and Timmie's are pale, awed. "OK. Now we got this, this legal document here" — he opens his fist to display a tightly folded piece of lined binder paper. He pries open its creases with his raw bony kid's fingers. They are shaking — "which is a *legal* document, signed by the undersigned, which I'll show you in a minute if I can get the stupid thing un*fold*ed, crissake, Stuart, you didn't have to squash it up so a person can barely see it — Anyway, this document, it's legal, Dad, because it's signed with our genuine signatures, right? Stuart's and Timmie's and mine? It says . . . I'll read it. It says."

Scowling fiercely, he holds it up to his face with his trembling fingers and reads rapidly in a loud, hoarse voice. "It says. WE THE UNDERSIGNED, (NAMES) PORTER TALBOTT McPHAIL JUNIOR, STUART HUGHES McPHAIL, AND TIMOTHY McPHAIL —"

"How come *I* don't have three names? Mom? How come *I* —"

"Shut *up,* Timmie! Criss*ake!* —

301

TIMOTHY McPHAIL (END OF SIGNED NAMES) DO HEREWHICH SAY THAT (NAME) SARA ALEXANDRA HUGHES (EXTRA NAME) McPHAIL (END OF GIRL'S NAME) IS THE LEGAL SISTER OF THE UNDERSIGNED. SO SHE IS ALSO AND TO WIT THE LEGAL DAUGHTER OF (PARENT'S NAMES) MRS. EMILY McPHAIL AND MR. PORTER TALBOTT McPHAIL. SO THERE IS NOW (4) LEGAL CHILDREN IN THE McPHAIL FAMILY. SO TO WIT MR. AND MRS. McPHAIL DO NOT HAVE ANY BASTARD AND SO THEY DO NOT HAVE TO GET A DIVORCE SO THEY CAN STAY LEGALLY MARRIED. Then we all signed it here at the bottom. See, there's our legal signatures, right, Dad? So now all we have to do is everybody else has to sign it. We left the space here, see, with a line for everybody — Mom, you sign here, and Dad here, and Sara here on this line. Gimme the pen, Stuart.''

''Pen?''

''Didn't you bring one? Crissake. Why do *I* have to do all the thinking around here? How're they gonna sign it without a *pen* —" PJ's voice cracks anguishedly.

"I have a pen, PJ." Porter's voice steadies. "Show us where it is you want us to sign."

"Maybe," Stuart says timidly, "we oughtta let Sara sign first? Because she's a, you know, girl?"

"Crissake, don't you think we *know* that, Stuart? I was just getting Dad's *pen*. So here it is, Sara," PJ says, holding it out to her, thrusting the paper at her elbow, "so you can sign it first, if you wanna sit up."

We wait. PJ stands, holding the pen out. We wait.

Presently she raises her head, stares at the paper; lifts herself on one elbow, still staring at the paper. Slowly she sits up. Head bent, gropes with her hand for the pen. PJ puts it into her hand and she signs.

Thirteen

"I give up," Porter says, "why does the chicken cross the road?"

"To get to the other side!" screams Timmie, and the table explodes with another round of hilarity.

There is a phenomenon that crops up in the course of long wars: men huddled in the trenches suddenly throw down their weapons, climb out, and stagger across no-man's-land to meet and embrace their opposite numbers of the enemy, who have done the same thing. No treaty has been signed; the crazy moment is short-lived; after they have embraced and exchanged a few garbled messages they go back to their separate entrenchments and have at each other again.

Aware of this, I'm trying not to delude myself. That was no treaty we signed, the six of us; it was simply — like the battlefield phenomenon — an acknowledgment of our shared human condition.

"Hey, Dad, I betcha don't know this one," PJ says hoarsely. "Why does the ocean roar?"

"Hmm. Because the Atlantic's not pacific?"

"Wrong! Mom — why does the ocean roar?"

"To get to the other side?" Another gust, which blows out two of the candles we have poshly set out to eat scrambled eggs by.

"Oh my stomach," Sara gasps. "Oh my poor stomach!"

"You give up? Everybody? Why does the ocean —"

"I know! The ocean roars because it's chicken!" In the ensuing hurricane Timmie falls out of his chair, Porter clutches his side as if he were having a heart attack, Sara throws her napkin over her head, PJ claws the air helplessly, Stuart writhes, and I choke on my coffee.

"Hey — has anybody heard the song

called 'Tony's Push Cart'?''

"Why no, Sara. How does it go?''

"It doesn't go. You have to push it!''

"Push it, oh that's neat, you have to *push* it —''

"What time does your watch say? Dad, what time does —''

"It doesn't say anything, it can't talk!''

"Oh my poor *stomach* . . .''

"Eek, there's a ringing in my ears!''

"That's not a ring, that's the —''

Telephone. I totter into the hall to answer it.

"Emily? I hope I'm not interruptin your supper? My goodness, it sounds as if you're havin a party — celebratin our good news? Well, I feel like celebratin myself! I must say I'm relieved to get hold of you. You sounded a bit distracted this mornin, and then we were cut off — we'll have to get you a private line, what with all the business we're goin to be discussin — and then I did get a teentsy bit concerned when I couldn't get through to you all afternoon. But I understand your uncle Tyler's been taken ill? Porter said you were at the hospital. Well, I trust it's not serious, from the sound of things there. I won't keep you, I just wanted to say Harry thinks we should come into Richmond on Monday or Tuesday. There's a number of people we should be meetin with right soon, get started on the plannin and so forth. Willard'll drive us in, if you don't mind comin over here first? Which would be better for you, Monday or Tuesday?" The line hums. "Emily? Are you there?"

"Yes. Let me close the hall door . . . Mrs. Tupper, you said something this morning about a slogan."

"Oh that." She laughs lightly. "Now Is the Time for All Good Women to Come to the Aid of the Party. Maybe I should've said *A* Good Woman. I'm wonderin if it's a bit too long for a slogan —"

"The problem is, Mrs. Tupper, I'm not a Good Woman. Or at least that'll probably be the opinion of Harry's people when they find out I've had an illegitimate child."

The line hums. Into it I continue, marveling in an abstract way how easy it seems to be, simply a matter of forming words, "I'm not quite sure how it is that the way I loved eighteen years ago has so much to do with my present ability to vote on tax bills and serve on committees and so forth. But I suppose it's because I'm new to politics, as everybody pointed out yesterday. I guess the answer lies in Winston Langley's province of public relations, which is projecting the image of private relations so that the public won't be offended. Anyway. I should have told you this before. There are many things I should have faced before this — long before — and I have no excuse to give you. I can't excuse it to myself either, all I can do is" — the hall door opens; *Hey Mom,* they are calling me; loud calls and laughter — "smile and say thank you, for your efforts on my behalf, and all the people who —" The line sings emptily.

Rock me Baby with a good-time beat
Rock me Baby cause it feel so sweet

In the library, the bouncy thumps of a Golden Oldie, titillatingly tarnished; Porter and I bounce out a demonstration of how it used to be when we jived and rocked jazzily. The kids hoot; Timmie and Stuart waggle their little-boy tails in irreverent mockery; even PJ — crissake! — essays a shambling shuffle vis-à-vis Sara, who is snapping her fingers and writhing everything except her torso, a problem in management her generation seems to have solved (I think with a twinge of envy as one knee cracks loudly).

Rock me Baby like it's Saturday night
Rock me Baby cause it feel so right

"Lord," pants Porter as his jowls jounce, "how'd we ever — *pant* — manage to do this all night?"

"We didn't. We mostly — *crack* — watched, remember?"

"Yeah." He leers as he jerks me to him in a sort of tango swoop. "We got in plenty of action, sitting in the dark — *huff* — watching." He bends me back over his arm, grinning evilly. "What was that?" "My knee." "Jeez, I thought it was a sniper." He flings me out in an abandoned — *crack* — twirl.

Rock me Baby with a fancy roll
Rock me Baby til you rock my soul

"Wow, I didn't know you could dance, PJ, you're really good —"

"Dance, crissake, I'm just sorta standing here —"

"Well, you *stand* really well, I mean it makes it really easy to dance with you —" Sara's arms and knees inscribe blurred circles around her immobile thorax.

Baby O Baby come and rock me please
Rock my soul and knock my knees

"DAD! TELEPHONE!"

"Rock me Baby with a . . ." Porter spins me toward the couch, staggers off toward the hall. I sprawl fanning myself with a magazine.

"Hey, Mom, lookit, this is PJ!" Stuart clanks around like a robot.

"Crissake, you aren't *supposed* to leap all over like a chimpanzee, are you, Sara —"

Porter reappears in the hall doorway.

Face streaming sweat, ashen. His lips move, but I cannot hear. Sara darts to the record player, lifts the arm. The music cuts.

Porter says, "That was Jim. Uncle Tyler's had a stroke."

It is a massive one. He is paralyzed and cannot speak, but he is conscious.

Porter sits at the kitchen table staring at his fists and trying to make sense from what he can recall of Jim's terse explanations. We stand around trying to make sense from the senseless. Uncle Tyler? Struck dumb?

The next few hours, Porter is saying, the next few hours are important. Something about if it's a clot or a ruptured vessel. They aren't sure yet, it's important to know in order to determine the kind of treatment, sometimes a clot can be operated on and sometimes the blood will be, what is it, reabsorbed and sometimes the paralysis gradually loosens a bit here and there; but sometimes, most times

We have to understand, Porter is

repeating, that the chances aren't too

We stand around staring at him, trying to understand.

"Here." Something is shoved into my hand. I stare down at a cup full of liquid and then at Sara's face, which is set in a blank calm. "It's tea, Mother. Drink it." She pours another cup and sets it down on the table before Porter. "Drink it," she repeats steadily. "You'll need it."

She puts one arm around Timmie's shoulders, the other around Stuart's. "C'mon." She nods at PJ. Together they lead the two dazed little boys upstairs to bed.

"Go on, willya," PJ commands hoarsely. "Sara and I, we can take care of things here. Listen, we're not even tired, are we, Sara?" Never have two youngsters ever looked so tired.

They stand together under the porch light as we drive off. Stand watching us until we've rattled around the curve.

Shlick-plunt, shlick-plunt. The rhythm of the windshield wipers beats mesmerically. The night is soft, and black, and damp, with pockets of mist shredded by our one headlight as we wind along beside the creek. Out on the highway it begins to rain, a gentle steady kind of rain that looks to go on forever.

— I wonder why we didn't dance much, back when we were courting.

— There didn't seem to be time. I was working on my degree. I guess it wasn't a very spirited time, back then. It must have been boring for you, my so-called courtship . . .

— You were so handsome. I remember once — Do you remember, Porter, one evening you took me into Boston for dinner, it was early winter and it was the first snow, it was snowing hard and we went into King's Chapel, you wanted to show me the pews all upholstered in scarlet, and the busts of our early American heroes, with their lovely inscriptions — and when we came outside it was so cold. And you put your arms around me, right out there on the street corner, in the snow, and told me how warm Virginia is, I wouldn't be cold there . . .

— I remember.

— Porter? Do you think that was boring. . . ?

Shlick-plunt, shlick-plunt. The dark rain falls gently, like the quality of mercy, not strained.

— I guess it was rough on you, Emily.

— What was?

— The first year or so here. Mother could be hard to please. I should've realized how rough it was, living here with your in-laws in the same house. The whole structure must've been so new and strange to you. I should've noticed more. Lord, I was a selfish bastard. Ever time I think

— I had you, Porter. And I felt so sheltered, there inside your family, what you call the structure

— After all you'd been through. I wish I'd known

— I wish you had, Porter. I'd give anything if you had. But you didn't, because you had no way of knowing . . . Your mother — it wasn't all that bad. I knew that even if she criticized me inside the family, outside there was no question of standing behind me. I remember once at some tea party, one of those women's things your mother used to tow me around to, I couldn't believe my ears, she seemed to be intimating that I was some sort of prize you'd snatched from under the aristocratic noses of the Boston Cabots

— Oh, Mother was a brick wall when it came to keeping up a solid family front. I suppose there's something to be said for solidarity. We all need someplace where we're safe from the outside. Even if it can get rough inside.

— I always felt safe with you, Porter.

— I'm glad. Except that safety's so goddam dull sometimes, isn't it?

— Porter? Last night, when I was up alone, waiting . . . The wait was — so terrible, and I found this poem on your desk, it said *A solitude ten thousand fathoms deep*

— *sustains the bed on which we lie, my dear. Look if you like, but you will have to leap*

— *Our dream of safety has to disappear* . . . Porter?

— Yeah. OK. No more about dull.

He smiles. He takes his hand off the wheel for a moment. Puts it over my knee. It feels warm, steadying. The wipers hiss rhythmically, shlick-plunt, shlick-plunt, as we drive through the soft night rain.

Shlick-plunt. Machinery somewhere, hissing softly, deepens the room's hush. Behind the film the eyes gaze very far ahead. "He's conscious," the nurse says, "but he can't respond." Trapped behind the walls of flesh, the convict's eyes gaze out through gouged holes. "There's nothing much you can do by staying," the warden warns. Trapped in solitary, the eyes gaze out from a solitude ten thousand fathoms deep. "Well then," the warden says, "I suppose you can stay in here if you want, but don't touch anything. Absolutely no smoking. Oxygen's highly inflammable." Shlick-plunt, it hisses.

— and then he said something about how she couldn't have done anything else, and then he mentioned Caesar's wife, and

Cordelia's pearls.

— Cordelia . . . Maybe it was a reference to the Roman matron, who referred to her children as her treasure, her pearls. Caesar's wife, of course, was supposed to be

— above suspicion. That I remember. I wish I'd studied history more. Without the sense of it we seem to be so trapped in the present, so out of context

— He was fond of the Roman period, but he admired the Greeks more. He taught Latin one time

— He did? I didn't know. Everybody's always said he'd never worked

— Only for a half term. At a boy's prep school over in Staunton, just after he finished at the University. As I understand it, he had some disagreement with the headmaster and quit. That was about the extent of his working career.

— But he's spent a lifetime studying.

— God knows his mind's been working. All those projects over the years — I remember once when I was a little kid, about Stuart's age, he had me collecting snails for him. I couldn't figure what they were for, until I finally realized he'd been cooking them — I'd been eating snails in I don't know how many varieties of ways, even deviled in a sandwich I'd become particularly fond of. I remember how indignant I was that he'd fooled me that way. Uncle Tyler said it was stupid of me to be afraid of new experiences, did I want to grow up to be a doltish provincial? If I did, it wasn't Uncle Tyler's fault. Thinking back, I can see how much richness, in his eccentric way, he provided us all. I don't know whatever happened to all the good old-fashioned eccentrics. There doesn't seem to be much latitude in our society anymore for individual quirkishness . . . I remember how he used to take Mother down a few pegs when he felt she was getting too Grande Dame. He'd stare at her feet.

— Her feet?

— Don't you remember, she had bunions, big swollen toe joints, from wearing shoes several sizes too small. "Bunions," Uncle Tyler used to say, "are the Lord's way of demonstrating the comic results of vanity." It seems to me that most of the laughter in our family when I was a kid had its source in Uncle Tyler.

— It still has. Maybe it's because he's not scared to laugh at himself. I suspect he deliberately plays the clown sometimes — Porter, why do you suppose he let himself get so fat? In those old photos he was so slim and handsome.

— I never thought of it. Maybe his main sensual pleasure was food.

— And he never married. Strange, I never wondered about these things before.

— I didn't either. Uncle Tyler's always been just Uncle Tyler. Sort of the way the front porch has always sagged, and the pillars have always kept holding it up.

— I wonder why we need to know these things now.

Porter doesn't answer. I guess that the need to know is by nature a laggard thing, tending to wait until the very moment the pillars threaten to give way and the porch collapse. Shlick-plunt.

— You told Catherine Tupper *that*? My God, Emily, you realize what that means

— Yes. I can't say I don't *care,* but I just suddenly couldn't lie anymore, Porter. Even if the truth never came out about my having had a — about Sara, I would've had to live in fear that someday it might. That, I don't want any more of.

— But you did want, want something else. Didn't you?

— . . . Isn't it strange, Porter, how easy it is to talk now, get things straight out . . . Yes, I did want something else. I still do. I want to be a Delegate, I want to count somehow, I want to be useful, I want to save Seward Creek and keep them from paving over the countryside and building plazas nobody needs, and help girls like SueEllen Page to know more about their own bodies and — Porter? If you had what you call Something Else, tell me what you'd like it to be?

— Well . . . Yeah, I want to count some way, too. Do something useful, something I really care about, that interests me. Like . . .

— Like what? Porter, like what? Listen — listen, Porter, maybe you could. *Do* it, I mean. Maybe we both could, do something *else* too, maybe together? Wouldn't it be marvelous, Porter, working together on something useful and exciting, like the Peace Corps maybe, take the kids with us even, no, I guess that wouldn't work, there's school — but Porter, listen, when they're older, when they're old enough, off to college — why are you laughing? Is it that outlandish? I guess it is.

— I'm laughing because I was going to say that teaching's what I've got, already, that qualifies as Something Else. Emily, Emily, you're something else, yourself.

— Well. It was just an idea.

— What I mean, it's a fine idea. Jesus, it's a lovely idea. Working together on something useful and exciting

— when the kids go off, of course. Oh Porter

— The Peace Corps. You know, I could teach

— *Yes,* and I could, I could — what could *I* do? I haven't had any sort of training

— Training, hell, you could train for anything you wanted, whatever you tackled you could learn

— Porter, do you think we're crazy? I mean here we are talking about joining the Peace Corps and

— No, Em, we're not crazy. There's nothing crazy about new ideas. There's nothing crazy about planning for change. That's what we're all in for anyway, isn't it? Change.

— Porter? Why couldn't we talk this way before?

— I don't know. I don't know how we came to that or how we got to this. But here we are.

— Yes. Here we are.

We smile at each other wearily and get up and go over to the bed again, where the convict's eyes gaze steady out from the holes gouged in the cell wall. We gaze back with our silent message: We are here; you are there alone, but not left alone. The warden comes in and says things need to be done for the charts, so we go out into the corridors and walk around some more; and presently we see the warden coming toward us with her big feet in her white shoes squeaking on the tiles, and she notifies us in her official warden's voice that we can go home now, the prisoner has died.

Fourteen

"He was so amazin. All that energy at his age." Margaret Chauncy blinks her eyes soulfully at Porter.

"Up to the very end." Jeffrey J. Chauncy swirls the ice in his glass of bourbon. "An example for us all."

Weston Peters, pallbearer's carnation in his lapel, clamps Porter's shoulder wordlessly.

Over in a corner of the library Jeannie and Mike Katz sit cross-legged on the floor, softly singing "Rock My Soul in the Bosom of Abraham" to the quiet strum of Jeannie's guitar.

I edge past the clot of graduate students clustered around the buffet, scarfing cold cuts and tuna casserole and discussing in hushed tones the possibility of Porter's canceling next week's seminars. They fall silent, part respectfully for my passage toward the kitchen.

"She's got to have a bigger coffeepot than this," Lucy is directing. "Nancy, look underneath there and see if you can find a hot tray, I know there's one somewhere. Will somebody go find Weston and tell him we need a couple more sacks of ice, he can get 'em in Batesville. What's this heatin in the oven? Take that out, will you, Linda, so's I can get this cheese thing under the broiler — Lord, another tuna casserole. Why didn't anybody think to bring a salad? Margaret, is this s'posed to be warmed? Take that out to the buffet, find a server somewhere, try the silver drawer in the dinin room — Emily, what're you doin in here? You just skedaddle out and let us take care of things. Get yourself a drink and go sit down and rest, y'hear me?"

"There you are." Waylaid in the hall by — Catherine Tupper? She is wearing a mink toque and a determined, signaling stare. She pins me with it, approaching. "Such a shock. Beloved by all. A true Southern gentleman. One of the last of the old school. Such a loss," she says, still pinning me and snapping her fingers at Willis, staggering behind her under the weight of an enormous silver chafing dish around which he flashes a dignified smile. "The dinin room, Willis. I've brought some of my shrimp Jambalaya. Such a gatherin. A real tribute to his memory. Half the county must be here. Where can I put my things and freshen up?" With me mesmerically in tow, she leads me into the downstairs guest room, its bed piled with coats, the only use it's been put to for years. Slipping out of her mink coat, she turns and, pinning me again, says in a low intense voice, "I won't intrude on your grief by discussin things now. I just want to know one thing: Have you told anybody else about this — this secret?"

"I . . ." I mumble that only my family, and the family doctor . . .

"How long have they — I want you to know I *understand,* Emily," she says, breaking into charmin tones and an understandin expression, and I realize that two of the Department of English wives have just come in, women I don't know well except from faculty parties. "When the Colonel passed away," Catherine Tupper continues, "I just wondered what was left of my life. The one thing that saved me, after the Colonel's passin, was *work*." She bends her gaze meaningfully on me. "I just plunged in, all my committee work and the League and the Guild — oh, I just worked myself like a slave. But it's the only thing that helps you forget. That's always my counsel to the bereaved, and that is my counsel to you, Emily, to just roll up your sleeves and plunge right back into some good hard meanin'ful *work* . . . Now you consider what I'm sayin, y'hear? And *do* call me in a few days, will you, about that little mattuh we were discussin. . . ?" And she floats out, leaving me to accept the condolences of the faculty mesdames, whose names I cannot for the life of me remember, and who mention that they have brought tuna casseroles.

". . . Mother?"

"Sara." I've almost stumbled over her,

sitting halfway up the dark little back stairway to the west wing. "What're you doing here, darling, all alone?"

The door at the top of the stairs is tight-closed. It leads to his rooms, his cluttered little study and his bedroom, whose walls are covered with family portraits, framed documents, memorabilia. Perhaps she, like me, has come for her own private ceremony. She doesn't say. She moves over and I sit down next to her on the step. "Why doesn't everybody just go home?" she mutters.

"They will, eventually."

"People all over the place. Acting as if it's a party. Eating and drinking and babbling."

"I know. I can't even get into my own kitchen." I smile wryly. "The one time I could use something to do."

"It's an insult to his memory." She winds her arms around her knees, hugging them to her chest. She begins to rock herself, sitting there on the stair.

"It really isn't an insult, Sara dear. It's a ceremony, assembling after the . . . other ceremony." I hate the word *funeral.* It is so funereal.

"At least the service was quiet. And short. At least they didn't expect us to act sociable there." She rocks. "Here some old guy came up and offered me a drink, and a couple of those college kids wanted me to go with them afterward to some pizza parlor in town."

"Darling, they didn't realize." I put my arm around her shoulders. We sit together on the stair, rocking gently. "Think how we'd feel if nobody'd come."

"At school," she says, rocking, "one of the girls was killed in a car accident. I went over to her parents' house that afternoon and the father opened the door and started to cry and he said for me please not to come in, he couldn't stand seeing any of her friends."

"Everybody reacts to grief in his own way. Tell me, Sara, can you remember why you went to the parents' house? Was the girl a close friend of yours?"

"No, I hardly knew her. She was just a little kid, three grades below me."

"But you went anyway. A sense of ceremony, wouldn't you think?"

"She was in my same school, Mother. I had to do *some*thing, didn't I? I couldn't just not pay any attention, when something like that . . ." She stops rocking. "I guess I see what you mean." She ponders. "Mother? You weren't going to go through his things right now, were you?"

"Not right now. Later. Did you want something of his, darling? I'm sure anything you want —"

"I've got what I want of his. He gave it to me in the hospital."

"He gave you something? That's lovely, Sara." I do not ask what it is. Some ceremonies are private.

"He gave it to me for all of us." In the dim light of the stairway bulb I see that her face is wet. "It's a sort of story. A true one. He wrote it a long time ago. He told me about it, and then we talked, and then he showed me where it was — It was in those papers you brought him. You did bring them all back from the hospital, didn't you?" She turns to me, panicked. "Mother, you brought all his things back with you, didn't you? They don't, they don't take them away or keep them or anything, do they?''

"No, we brought everything, Sara. The suitcase with his papers is'' — where? Where did we put those things, when we came home that gray dawn? — "in the back hall closet. I think that's where Porter put it.''

"I better go get it right now.'' She stands. "Mother? After everybody goes, can I give it to you then? The family, I mean. He said it was for all of us. He said I was to share it with you, after all the — what was it he said — after all the tumult and the shouting died and the captains and the kings depart. I guess he must've meant *this,* this party —''

"Crissake." PJ squints up at us from the bottom of the stairs. "They're all over the place! A guy can't even —'' He lopes off. Some ceremonies are private.

"Emily, you and Porter go to bed. All of you. You're absolutely out on your feet.'' Lucy unties her apron. "It's all tidied up now. I put the leftovers in dishes in the refrigerator — my Lord, there's enough stuff for the rest of the week, at least you won't have to do any cooking for a while. Weston, did you get *all* the plates and glasses from all the rooms? Good. I don't know who a lot of these pans and casseroles belong to — that's the fanciest silver chafing dish I ever did see — but I s'pect they'll be claimed eventually. Wes*ton* — c'mon along now, I swear you're asleep on your feet too. Well. It *was* a nice wake, wasn't it? That's what these occasions do — show you how many friends you got." She kisses us briskly. Her kind face is tired and shining with accomplishment.

". . . Well."

The captains and the kings have departed. The tumult and the shouting have died. The old house stands in an exhausted, but somehow still waiting, silence. (Do houses wait for their occupants' return? It is not presences but absences which populate old buildings. Up in the west wing there must surely be hollows carved out of the rooms' volumes, the way there is a hollow left from the years of his body's weight in the old bed.)

"Well . . ." We occupy the library as restless presences, Porter and Sara and PJ and I (the two younger boys have long since abandoned ceremony, stumbled off to bed). We seem, like the old house, to be exhausted but waiting.

"Mother?" She comes to stand next to me by the window. It has been raining for three days now, a steady gentle springlike rain that has muffled the countryside in amorphous mists; wraps the old house tonight in a soft damp silence, as if it were a passenger liner alone in the middle of the ocean. "Mother? Isn't it time now?" She is holding a large envelope between her folded arms and chest.

"I guess so. Porter, Sara has something Uncle Tyler wanted us to read."

"Now?" Porter, hands in pockets, is gazing down at the embers of the fire.

"He said when everything was over."

"Well, everything's over." PJ is sprawled in a chair with his tie askew and his wrists and ankles sticking out bonily from his good suit, which has since Christmas Eve become an inch too short.

Why — I think with a stab that ruptures some anesthetic coma I wasn't aware of — why, Uncle Tyler will never see this boy become a man. It is like coming out of a surgery begun days ago when a mask must have been clapped over my mouth and nose. I remember when my mother died I did not feel anything until after the funeral when late that night I was crawling into bed and the anesthetic mask was suddenly ripped off and I was gasping in the icy air of consciousness. "Everything's over now," PJ mumbles. "So let's get on with whatever we're s'posed to do."

"Here." Sara thrusts the envelope abruptly at Porter. "You read it to them."

"He entrusted it to you, Sara. You're the one to read it."

"PJ? Would you like to —"

"Crissake." His voice cracks. "Quit messin around and *read* it, Sara."

"April 12, 1922:
"*Non omnis moriar:* These are the words my father is reported to have

uttered at my birth, when he was informed that he had sired a son. *I shall not wholly die:* for it is true that a man lives only so long as his name and his lineage continue, and these are embodied in a son.

"The Talbott lineage is, in the relatively brief history of this land, an unbroken and honorable one. It contains scholars, soldiers, legislators, and a distinguished gentleman of the cloth. (I am recording, elsewhere and in detail, a History of my paternal ancestors. That of my mother's family, the Tylers, must come later. The two lines cross in the person of my grandfather, Col. William Tyler Talbott, whose parents were cousins.)

"My grandfather fell in the defense of Richmond at the age of twenty-seven — only a few years beyond my present age — and my father was born posthumously, in the same year, 1865. I was born at the turn of the century. My father and I were only sons; so that of the direct line I am the sole remaining filament — I hope the pun will be excused — which, if I sired no son, would be snapped and the lineage terminated. And then it would not be I alone who should be wholly dead, but the long ancestral line of my sires.

"The gods have arranged an elaborate jest: with my decease, the Talbott name shall be wholly dead — but the lineage will not. It will continue in my newborn son, who bears, all unknowing and unknown, another name."

— Hey, wait a minute. Uncle Tyler had a *son*?

— It seems so, PJ.

— How come you never told us? Dad? How come you

— I didn't know.

— Crissake. There sure is a lot goin on in this family people didn't *know*

"My son was christened today with the name of another man. It was a pretty ceremony, in the school Chapel, with the moving little touch, so common to christenings, of the babe's indignant screams as he was shocked awake by the dash of cold water on his pate. I silenced the schoolboy titters around me, with my Latin Master's frown. My son roared lustily in the arms of the Headmaster, who looked as smug as any man who holds his firstborn son, and believes he sees upon that blunt visage the intimations of his own Immortality. And standing beside him, the mother of my son demurely bent her long, lovely neck.

" 'I christen thee Randolph Terence Ackeroyd,' the Reverend Doctor intoned; and in the name of all that is Holy, my son became another man's. And the joy with which he was conceived died in me.

"If I am not to be permitted to die of it, Joy I must eschew, for Joy and Life and Mollie are one in me, and I cannot eschew one and not the others. So farewell, Joy: I bequeath thee to my son, who was born of it. And farewell, Life: I bequeath what remains of thee to the endless sea of Time, for Time alone is Life's measure now. And farewell, O my beloved, my beautiful

Mollie: I bequeath what of thee that was so briefly mine to thy Virtue; for that above all — above Joy, above Life — commands thy duties.

"My duty is to depart. But I take my Mollie with me, hidden in my breast — my heart's Wife, I her constant Husband. While I live, she cannot wholly die.

"*Ackeroyd:* how the gods must titter, that the last of the Talbotts must bear such a name!

"*Omnis moriar.*"

"Well." A deep, shaky breath from somewhere. Porter stands staring into the ashes of the fire.

"What's he saying? All those fancy words," PJ says hoarsely, "like *achew,* it sounds like a sneeze —"

"It means to shun." Porter's words are professorial, his tones not. "The language is old-fashioned, PJ, but the feelings aren't." He adds as if to himself, "Words change, but human passions don't, do they?"

"Particularly youthful ones," I murmur.

338

"Yes," Porter says to the fire, "particularly those. He was twenty-two. Renouncing love at twenty-two."

"But he knew how to love, didn't he? All those years, just one woman . . ."

The room falls silent again. The dying fire sighs.

"What'd he want us to *know* for?" PJ's voice is raw under the burden of his knowledge.

"So he would not wholly die." Sara's neck is bent, as if she too bore a burden. She smooths the paper over her knees. "He told me you don't really die when you live on in people's memories."

"What'd he — want us to find his son, or something?" PJ blinks fiercely. "Did he want us to find him and tell him the truth? Crissake, that'd be a *shock* to a guy —"

"No. I asked him that and he said no. He just said he wanted us to remember him, and to remember . . ." She hesitates, staring at the paper. ". . . to remember we have to trust each other with our own truths, or we'll have to live alone with our secrets all our lives."

"*I* haven't got any secrets. I mean, no

339

important ones, I'm too young to have any *important* secrets, aren't I, Dad?'' PJ's face is white, scared.

''I'm the one Uncle Tyler meant, PJ.'' Sara stands suddenly. *How small she is,* I think with a clutch of apprehension. She walks over to Porter. ''He said to burn this. But first,'' she says steadily, looking up at him, ''I have to — I *want* to, he didn't tell me to — say I'm sorry I felt that way about you. It wasn't really you, it was somebody else. Uncle Tyler explained it to me. So I don't feel like that about you anymore.''

''I'm . . .'' Porter turns back to the fire, moves his shoulders once in a mighty heave. ''I'm very glad, Sara,'' he says thickly to the fireplace. He stares at the papers in her hand. ''You're sure he wants us to burn this?''

''He said to.''

Formally, we come to stand with them by the fire. Formally, Porter stoops and lays the papers on the glowing ashes. The edges curl a moment, then burst into a small bright flame. We stand gazing at the flame until it's devoured, whitened into powdery ash.

PJ mutters, "If *I* had a name like Ackeroyd, I'd throw up."

Staring at the ashes, I think: *Mollie Ackeroyd*. He mentioned her only once . . . The day she died she wanted her papers brought to her from the attic. Had they found them? And among them would there have been very old letters, flowery and passionate, written by a very young man? And were there still, in some family's attic, in some dusty corner of an old house —

"I have a name," Sara's voice is saying, "that I have to tell you now. It's my other parents'. They're Mr. and Mrs. Stephen Alexander. They live at 1233 Oak Road in Winchester, Massachusetts."

Fifteen

· I stare into the refrigerator. If there are eggs in here, a bottle of milk, I'll have to unload everything to find them. Food: this kitchen is a delicatessen. And I can't think, can't think of anything except last night

— The telephone number? It's 617-729-1970. But please, please don't call them

"Mother? Can Timmie and I have this for breakfast?" Stuart is holding out a plate on which repose the remains of a cocoanut fudge cake.

"You know you can't have cake for breakfast. You'll have eggs, as soon as I can find them —"

— They'll come and take me back with

them, Oh please don't call them please

— I promise you, Sara, your mother and I will do everything we can. But we have to let these people know you're all right. Think how they must be worried

— They know I'm all right, they already *know* that

— But Sara, how could they know? Unless you've written or called them — and if you have, I can't understand why you don't want us to call

— Or why *they* haven't contacted us

"But we didn't get *any* last night, or even any of this pie," Timmie is whining, "we hadda go to bed and PJ got to stay up and now he even gets to sleep in and miss school —"

"That has nothing to do with it, Timmie. Stuart, hold this a moment, I think I see the milk —"

"We could have some milk with the cake. That's got vitamins and stuff in it, hasn't it? Mother? Hasn't —"

— I said they know I'm all right, I didn't say they know where I am. I called

343

them a few times — I couldn't stand thinking of them worrying, she gets these awful migraines, and he

— You called them, Sara? But if

— Not *direct,* Mother, there's this Emergency Line for, for runaways, you can call them and tell them who you are and your parents, you don't have to say *where* you are, you just tell them you're OK and they call your parents and tell them, and there's no way they can find out where you are. That's the *point,* kids wouldn't use this Emergency Line to let their parents know they're OK, if they knew they could be traced and made to go back

"Oh Stuart, please don't argue. I've got so much to do today — go see if Daddy's through shaving, and ask Sara to get up. Ask her nicely, Stuart, she's very tired, she was up late —"

"How come *we* didn't get to stay up? And *we* don't get to stay home from school — Mother? How come PJ gets to and *we* —"

"Oh Timmie, please . . ."

— Surely it wasn't that bad, Sara, that you're afraid to go back? Sara? Was there anything you haven't told us about these people?

— Crissake, maybe they beat her up or something! Listen, Dad, why'd you have to phone them? Why can't she just stay here with us

"He was our uncle Tyler too." Timmie's whine rises to a wail. "We shouldn't have to go to school after our own uncle's just dead and everything! We feel just as bad as PJ —"

"Oh Timmie dear, I know you do." I close the refrigerator door. I bend to put my arms around him. "But we all have to be brave. We have to get back to normal as soon as we can. PJ was up very late and he's tired. But you're not tired, really. I know Uncle Tyler would want you to go to school, to show how brave and grown-up you are. Besides, some people are coming today, and we have to go to the airport to pick them up. We're all going to be terribly busy, and you and

345

Stuart wouldn't have anything to do. And you know you really like school. So hush now, darling, and let me get breakfast . . ."

— Sara? Are they — the Alexanders — somehow frightening to you? Is there some reason

— No. But . . . Oh, I don't want to talk about it

— If there is something, we should know about it. We have to contact these people. But I want you to understand, Sara, you don't have anything to be afraid of. I guarantee, I'll see to that. You'll never have to be with people who aren't good to you

— Oh Porter, maybe we shouldn't call right now. Maybe we should wait, and try to check

— Maybe they'll *make* her go back, Dad! I mean if they adopted her, isn't it like they legally sort of *own* her

— Nobody owns a child, PJ. They just have legal custody. And that custody can be remanded, if it's proved the child's been abused

— Oh *please*. They're not — They . . . Oh *please,* I just couldn't stand it if I had to leave my own mother after all I went through to *find* her, you don't know what I

— That's another thing, Emily. Why haven't these people been able to find Sara? A runaway kid shouldn't be all that hard to track down. The only thing I can figure is, maybe they don't care

— Oh they care. They care, do they ever *care*

— Of course they must, darling. But Porter's just wondering why they haven't been able to find you

—I told you, the Emergency Line doesn't even know, you call this central number, it's in another state. I told them to tell Daddy *not* to try and find me, if he did I'd just . . . run away for good. That's one of the reasons I had them call, so Daddy wouldn't notify the authorities. He wouldn't want to anyway, he'd only do it if he was so worried he was desperate. Daddy wouldn't want anybody to know

— That you'd run away?

— That I'm adopted. He'd have to tell the authorities that, because I think he knows I was trying to find my real parents

— He doesn't want anybody to know his child's *adopted*? What the hell kind of people would be ashamed of having an adopted child?

— It's not that they're ashamed, it's they . . . don't like thinking about it, they don't even want to know it, they never wanted me to know it, they just can't face the idea that they . . . Oh please, why do we have to talk about this, I don't even understand what I'm talking about, not really, I just want to stay here

— Sara. How can we *not* call these people? In the name of human decency, honey, we've got to resolve this. We can't let it go on this way, with them not knowing where you are or if you're ever coming back, and us not knowing what kind of people they are — and you hiding out here like some kind of escaped criminal. Honey, it's possible we might even be liable to charges, harboring a runaway child and not notifying her legal custodians.

— Oh Porter

— We can hide her out, Dad. They'll never be able to find her, if we hide her out and never tell

— Hide me out. That's what you'd really be doing, isn't it? Now that you know.

— Yes. But that's not the important thing, Sara. The important thing is that for the sake of everybody involved — and you most of all — there can't be any kind of real life, if you're hiding out from what's real. Wasn't that what Uncle Tyler was trying to tell us? And wasn't that why you finally told us? Listen, Sara, it was a very brave and trusting thing, telling us tonight. And now you're scared — we *all* are, because we care for you, you've come to be a member of our family

— Oh Porter

— But I'm asking you to trust me when I say this: you don't have to be scared. I won't let anything bad happen to you. If these aren't good people and if for some reason we can't work things out right, I

promise you, even if I have to take it to court
— Call them. Call.
— Oh Sara. Porter. Are we *sure*
— Call. Call them. There's no such thing as sure, anyway. Call and tell them I'm OK. Tell them, tell them I'm with my mother and my own family.

"Mother?" Stuart is saying. "Mother?"
I put down the egg I've been staring at. "What, Stuart?"
"Mother?" His face is scared. He is holding out a piece of paper. "Sara wasn't in her room. This was on her bed. I guess it's supposed to be for you."

I can't face them. I can't go back with them. I can't stay here and get you into any more trouble. Tell them I'm sorry. I'm sorry about so many things. I'm sorriest of all if I hurt you Mother by doing this. I love you so much, you are just the way I hoped you would be all the time I was looking for you. There's so much more I want to say but it's beginning to get light and I have to go before everybody wakes up or I never could. I'm sorry to turn out to be such a coward but I can't stand facing them or getting you into trouble because I ran away. I guess I am just a cowardly person always running away but I want you to know I will always love you. I love them too, please tell them that. They probably won't understand but I hope you will. *Do not worry,* I promise I'll be OK.

Your devoted daughter
SARA

PS. They call me Janie. But Sara is who I'll always be.

PPS. Please give my love to the boys and to Porter. I am really sorry about being scared of him, I didn't mean to lie that night, I was all mixed up but I know now he is a really good person, and maybe even likes me altho I can't see how he could.

"I'll go look for her. She can't have gone too far in an hour or so." Porter hastily buttons his shirt. He has traces of shaving cream under his chin. His face is gouged with dark hollows. "I'll take the truck, leave the wagon for you."

"I can't — Porter, I can't go to the airport alone." Meeting them alone, facing their faces, having to explain. "And she's not going to be where we can find her —" *I can't face them.* "And she promised she'd be OK, we just have to trust —"

"OK." He gives my shoulder a quick squeeze. "Get dressed. The plane gets in at ten, we should leave in a half hour. I'll get the kids off to school. And I guess I'd better wake PJ, and tell him, in case . . ."

She changes her mind? *Please Sara,* I pray, change your mind and come back. Come back, be brave, face it with us, help us all face it bravely together.

Raining. Rain drips from the old eaves, gurgles in the gutters, streams steadily down the windows; wraps the great magnolia tree, darkening the whole wing, in a gray-green undersea mist. As I dress I keep praying, as if she can hear my whisper, Please, did you take your raincoat, and your sweater, and your warm wool pants and your boots, not your sneakers, they'd get soaked and muddy, please, darling, be sensible —

Half dressed, I think to check her room: her boots are beside the door, her pants and sweater on a hook in her closet. Rummaging through it wildly, it strikes me how pitifully few clothes she has, as if nobody really expected her to stay, as if she'd been a transient come knocking at our door, and we'd hastily assembled a few garments, just enough to cover her nakedness decently and tide her through.

I begin to weep, realizing how it must have been for her all these weeks, gathering so little of permanence to herself, occupying a room in a house that must have seemed to her neither refuge nor habitation, but a way station on a journey she must desperately have hoped had ended here.

Shlick-plunt. The windshield wipers beat out their computer rhythm. Porter and I sit staring out at the wet highway, trying to compute a workable prediction from the fragments of data, last night's telephone call.

— If this is some kind of hoax, there's no way you can pull it. No way. If it's blackmail, you can forget it. If you've kidnapped my daughter — let me tell you, fella, if you've harmed her you're gonna end up sorry. Every last one of you

— We're hardly a gang, Mr. Alexander. We haven't kidnapped your daughter. She came here on her own, and she's been staying with us

— With your connivance. Which means you've been secretly harboring a runaway. There's laws against that, fella. Just who are you people, anyway?

— Our name is McPhail. I'm a professor of English at the University of Virginia in Charlottesville. My wife is

— Her mother. I'm her mother. She came to

— Her mother. That's interesting. Her mother happens to be standing here next to me. Let's cut the clowning. Put my daughter on the line.

(No

(Sara, you have to, they have to hear your voice so they can believe us, and they'll know you're all right)

— Janie? Is that you, Janie? Are you all right?

— Hello, Daddy. Is Mother there too?

— She's right here, baby. Oh God, Janie, Janie-girl, are you OK? Tell me you're OK

— I'm OK, Daddy. How's Mother?

— She's right here. Oh God. Oh God, baby, you don't know what we've been through. How could you put us through this is what I don't understand. What've we done to make you put us through this hell, if you'd only tell us Janie-girl.

— I'm sorry, Daddy. I really am. I

(Can't. Talk any more. Please I can't)

— Here's your mother. Speak to her, Janie. Tell her, tell her why you, she's suffered so, you know how she

— Janie. Janie? Speak to me, Janie.

— Mrs. Alexander? This is Porter

McPhail. I'm sorry, but she — Janie — can't seem to speak to you right now. She's pretty upset. Maybe if we give her a moment or two . . . My wife's on the extension, if you'd like to speak with

— I understand. We're rather upset ourselves. Steve, Janie won't speak to me. Will you get hold of yourself, please? You'll have to talk to these people.

— OK, McPhail. So what the shit am I supposed to say now, you got Janie down there and she won't talk to us, won't talk to her mother, so it seems you got her pretty well brainwashed

— I guess the first thing you can do is calm down, Alexander. Sara — Janie — hasn't been brainwashed. At least, not by us she hasn't

— Porter, please, Mr. Alexander . . . we mustn't talk like this, as if we were enemies, surely we can

— Who's this? Oh yeah, you're the one claims to be Janie's mother. Well, like I said, that's pretty interesting, because her mother happens to be right here

— Mr. Alexander, I'm her natural

mother. Your . . . daughter is adopted. Surely you can't have forgotten that. Surely you can't be denying that?

— Lady, *I*'m not on the witness stand here, *you*'re the one making all these claims. So maybe you can give me some facts

— Boston. Mass. General Hospital. November third, 1957. 3:37 Sunday morning. Baby girl, weight six pounds five ounces. Born to Emily Elizabeth Hughes, age eighteen, unmarried. I'm Emily Hughes McPhail.

— Those records are supposed to be sealed! You could've got to them somehow, you could've bribed some clerk, you figured you could blackmail us

— Blackmail you, Alexander? What kind of people are you, thinking you're exposed to blackmail if you've got an adopted child? What in God's name kind of *shame* do you think you have to hide? How in hell can you

— Porter, please, can't we just

— because if that's the way you feel, Alexander, if having an adopted child's a big shameful secret you have to hide from the world, then let me put you out of your panic. We'll take that girl off your hands, Alexander. We'll adopt her ourselves. And let me tell you something else, *fella,* we'll be proud to announce to the world

— *God* . . . I . . . God, man, you don't understand

— Porter, maybe we have misunderstood. Please, can't we all give each other a chance

— Yeah, yeah, McPhail, let's . . . give us all a chance here for a minute. God, you got to realize it's a . . . shock, you know? All these weeks we been going through hell, you don't know, nobody could possibly know — and then tonight. Hearing her voice again. Knowing she's all right . . .

— Mr. Alexander? Maybe if I could talk to your wife a moment

— I. Naw, I'm OK now. She isn't . . . up to it, she's not too well, Mrs. McPhail. And this has just about killed her, this thing with — Listen. The only thing I can do right now is take your word. You say you're Janie's natural mother, you give me the facts and figures such as they are, which are supposed to be sealed, maybe they are, so I don't know how else you'd . . . And you know who we are, our name and phone number anyway, she hadda give 'em to you, so . . . All I ask before we go ahead with this is one thing. Let Janie tell me herself who you are.

(Oh please, why can't he just take your word, I don't want him to talk to me, he'll ask me why again.

(Sara, he won't believe me unless you tell him, don't you want him to believe)

— She's my real mother. She's Emily Hughes. I traced her here myself, she knows all about when I was born, she had a baby on my birthday and it was me, Daddy. She's my real mother and I'm her daughter. Please Daddy, don't say anything, just listen. I had to know who I am, you wouldn't tell me, and now I know. Tell Mother I'm sorry, I love her too but it's not the same. Please Daddy that's all I can say now so goodbye.

— All right, Steve. Tell them we're flying down to wherever it is, Virginia, tomorrow morning.

— For God's sake, Helen

— Mr. McPhail? This is Helen Alexander again. Would you be so kind as to make reservations for us for tomorrow in a good hotel there? We'll want a double with connecting bath. Would you please check with your airline there first, we'll be coming in on the earliest connection from Boston. We'd very much appreciate your having Janie there at the hotel when we arrive. With her things packed, of course? It'll save everybody considerable awkwardness if she's said her good-byes to you, and won't have to go back to your house. I'm sure you've been awfully kind to her, and as she's inclined to be rather demonstrative, as young girls are apt to be, it'll be much easier on everybody simply to

— For God's sake, Helen, will you let me handle

— But Stephen dear, it's all handled.

There, you see? how much simpler it is when you let me take care of things?

Shlick-plunt. Waiting at the red light to make the turn onto Airport Road, I feel my mouth go dry, my heart begin to thump heavily. "Porter?"

"Ymn." He is staring through the wet windshield, his knuckles white around the wheel.

"What do you think they'll do when they find out Sara's not with us?"

"We'll know that," he says grimly, "in about twenty minutes."

"Maybe they'll think we've hidden her."

"I'd rather we had." He guns the car violently as the light turns.

I know what he means: What kind of parents would a child run away from, rather than face?

"We'll know," he says again, as if he had heard me, "soon enough."

Sixteen

"Decent of you to meet us."

He grasps Porter's hand. His gaze has grasped Porter's face in the same swift powerful way, released it to sweep the airport waiting room. He has not looked at me. He has acknowledged me only with a crisp nod directed over my head. He is a big man: big reddish face, big reddish nose, huge red hands, raw and powerful as a laborer's, incongruous with the clipped gray moustache and hair, with the smooth suavity of the dove-gray suit and gray fur-lined overcoat he carries over his arm.

But it is not he, commanding as he is, who commands my wary glance. She: this woman who has for seventeen years commanded the name Mother of my daughter.

Helen Alexander stands silently next to

her husband, and it seems to me she exudes a certain light, trapped as it is luminous, wrapping her in a kind of isolation. She is a very tall woman, very thin, in a very severe and chic black coat. She must once have been beautiful, before — what? Not age; she's only a few years older than I — something wore it away, so that there is now sheer architecture, a terse and elegant refinement of structure. But the light is the same self-isolating kind I have seen some beautiful women wrapped in, for fear that a touch might shatter that image.

"Where is she? Where's Janie?" The man's gaze is still sweeping the room, powerfully, as if anything in its way could be flicked aside. "I suppose she's waiting for us at the hotel. OK, let's have the bags picked up. Is there a porter in this place? Hell, I'll get 'em myself, only a couple of overnighters. You driving us into town? Sorry you had to trouble yourselves." He talks as if there's a machine inside him he's dictating to. All the time his eyes stab around the room. I catch a flash of them as they flick swiftly over my head.

They are blue, deep-sea blue, the color of a drowning man's eyes.

"What do you mean, she's not here? You didn't bring her to the hotel?" In the front seat he swivels his massive shoulders, his prow of a nose, toward Porter. "Look. You knew this was gonna be rough on everybody. Why'd you want to drag it out for?"

"We're going to have to have it out," Porter says evenly, "even if it drags out." From the back I cannot see his face, but I can see his knuckles whiten again around the wheel. "When I say she's not here, I mean we don't know where she is. She left sometime early this morning —"

"Left. What do you mean, left?"

"I mean departed. Split. Any way you want to put it."

"You mean run away."

"If that's the way you want to put it."

"Or is that the way *you* want to put it, McPhail?"

Their voices are hard, controlled. They're saying kids' things, tough blustering boys' threats, but their voices are men's. It is scary, when boys' threats are made by men's voices.

"The way I didn't particularly want to put it," Porter is saying, "is that she's run away to avoid facing you."

Shlick-plunt. Helen Alexander sits beside me with her hands folded, wrapped in her shimmering aura, looking out the window: composed, isolated. Surely this must scare her, too?

"And you had nothing to do with it, I suppose," Stephen Alexander says harshly. "You're utterly in the dark as to where she might be. Right, McPhail?"

"Right, Alexander."

"And you expect me to believe that." The tones are flat, hard. "You expect me to believe that she's been with you all these weeks, this morning she disappears and you haven't a clue as to where she'd be. I'm supposed to believe that."

"I guess I don't expect you to believe anything. You seem to have a lot invested in thinking this is some kind of hoax. Then you don't have to deal with any alternatives, do you, Alexander? Because if it's not a hoax, it's got to be something else, doesn't it?"

Shlick-plunt. Shlick-plunt.

"OK." The big shoulders heave once, as if trying in one mighty, final spasm to shake off something that rides them. He slumps back against his seat. "Skip the hotel for now, will you? We might as well go straight to your place. Maybe she's back by now. Maybe she'll be coming back," he says wearily, and the rock-hard voice has broken up, and has a sound like the sea rasping on a graveled beach. "Maybe she'll be coming back any time now. We have to be there when she comes back."

"Nice place you got here."

We have driven the twenty miles in besieged silence, ticked off by the drum of the wipers, the hiss of tires on the wet highway. The car winds around the drive, stops under the sagging porte-cochère.

"Big. Real old Southern mansion." Stephen Alexander sits for a moment, staring at the peeling white pillars, the red brick crumbling under the tentacles of English ivy, stripped now of leaf. There is a steady drip drip of water on the car roof from the leaky porch ceiling. "Quite a spread you got here. You buy the place?"

Porter opens the car door. "My family's lived here since the Civil War." He goes around back to open the tailgate, get the two bags.

"Civil War. How about that." The big man sits a moment. He sounds as if he's trying not to be impressed. Now why, I think as I gather my purse, slide over, begin to climb out, should he be impressed? Everything's so ramshackle.

"Stephen." Helen Alexander's silence — so long unbroken that I had become unaware of it — is, in its breaking, like a shatter of glass. "Stephen," she murmurs, "I'm getting the aura."

The effect on her husband is electrifying. He wrenches open his door, heaves himself out, goes swiftly around to her door, opens it, leans in over her. His heavy face is engorged with — what? "I've got your pills," he says, "right here in my pocket. We'll get you right inside, Lovely, we'll get you to a real nice room, and a big bed, and we'll draw the curtains

— You got a big quiet bedroom she can lie down in," he says to me, "she's gotta lie down where it's dark and absolutely quiet, she gets these migraines —" He turns back to her, puts his huge arm around her shoulders. "Come on, Lovely, easy now, let Stevie help you, we're gonna get you right into your nice big dark room . . ." and he slides the other arm under her silken knees; and tenderly, without disturbing a hair of her dark smooth head or a fold of her chic black coat, he lifts her out of the car and up the porch steps. She does not recline against him, but is borne sitting upright, as if she were in a sedan chair, smiling faintly, graciously, blindingly.

"Lunch . . . ?"
"Sure. Fine. Anything's fine." Without turning from the library window, he lifts his hand in a vague gesture. "Don't knock yourself out, or anything."
It's the first acknowledgment that he's a guest in this house. For the last hour he has been commanding, preempting: the "guest" bedroom won't do ("These're

twin beds. She needs a double bed, she gets claustrophobic without a lotta space") and the old nursery is too far from a bathroom ("It's a mile down that hall, walking that far makes the pain intolerable, she sometimes won't let me carry her"). After hesitating, I showed him the only other room that was presentable on such short notice — the other unused bedrooms have long since been turned over to that principle of nature that fills available space — and I did not tell him it is Sara's. I bundled up Sara's few things in case they might notice, shutting my mind against the fresh stab of pain at how very few they were, and the superstitious sense of their removal, as if the appropriation of her room by these people stripped her of her Sarahood, and she became Janie. *Symbolism is not reality,* I told myself fiercely, but something had happened, something was ruptured when they entered this house. I got out some fresh sheets and brought them in, but Stephen Alexander took them from me, saying that there was a way she needed the bed made that only he could manage. I felt a stab of a lower sort, that a woman need only to have a headache in order to turn a husband, and an entire household of strangers, into body servants. Then I felt ashamed and went downstairs, where Porter was carrying in logs for the library fire. We said nothing to each other, but busied ourselves with small chores, our way of collecting ourselves for our next duties, whatever they were, as hosts or innkeepers or maybe even hospital staff. PJ had left a note saying he was down at the Katzes', and I silently hoped he would stay there. When Stephen Alexander came downstairs he handed me the bundle of sheets he'd taken off the bed and they smelled of Sara, her young-girl's skin, a faint smell like unripe fruit, peaches or apples. He didn't seem to notice this. It was strange because the delicate odor was so mnemonic, it flooded my brain with her essence. "Lunch . . . ?" I asked then.

So here I am in the kitchen again, staring into the refrigerator — where did this weird profusion of food come from?

— and remembering with a third stab why it is here; and the back door opens. I whirl; but it is PJ, dripping in his yellow slicker and boots coated with red mud. He pauses in the doorway with a strange, cagey glance, then mutters, "Hi. Dja pick up those people?"

"Take off your boots on the paper. The Alexanders are here. They — you haven't seen any sign of Sara, have you?"

"Crissake, you brought them *here?*" His face is taut. "How come you hadda bring 'em *here?*"

"They thought maybe Sara'd come back. PJ, you were supposed to stay in the house in case she called."

"I did stay, and she didn't call. Crissake, Mother, she's not gonna *call* —" he has leaned over to take off his boots but now he hesitates. "If those people're here, I guess I don't wanna see them. I guess I'll just go help Mr. Garrett or Will or something."

"No, you won't. As long as you're here, you might as well have some lunch," I say distractedly, "and make yourself useful. Go ask Daddy to find out from Mr.

Alexander what she'd like for lunch.''

''Who's she? You mean Mrs. Alexander? Crissake, can't she talk?''

''She's not feeling well. She's lying down upstairs. So please be very quiet. I guess she'll need a tray — PJ, be nice to them, be *polite,* and don't ask a lot of questions. And when the boys come home from school, keep them sort of out of the way, will you, find something for them to do, but not anything noisy —''

''What is she, sick or something? Crissake, why'd she hafta come *here* to be sick?''

''PJ, please! She didn't plan it. Now go ask Daddy about lunch, and I guess you can set up a card table in the library, the dining room's so cold, I think the furnace must be on the blink —''

''Everything's on the blink around here, if you ask me,'' he snarls, and slopes out reluctantly to be nice, to be polite.

''Great stuff,'' Stephen Alexander says. ''What is it?''

''Shrimp Jambalaya.''

''How about that. Cooking up something

372

like this for lunch." He is forking it away rapidly, as if it were a stoking operation to be got through in the least possible time, clearing the decks for more important action. Yet he eats on and on, the way people eat who love food and can't stop. He does not look at me but inclines his head slightly toward Porter. "You eat like this all the time, or only on cook's day off?" I can't tell if this is meant to be humorous. His voice is neutral.

"Maybe you'd like a glass of wine with it," Porter says.

"No thanks. Never touch it. I don't drink. You got some Coke or something, I could use that. With a twist of lemon peel, if you got a lemon. What'd you say is the name of this shrimp thing?"

"Jambalaya." I get up. "But I didn't make it."

"Stouffer's then, I bet. Frozen. They got a great line of frozen food. I do a lot of cooking myself, use Stouffer's all the time. You ever try their spinach soufflé? You whomp that up in the oven, barbecue a big thick rare steak, toss a salad together with those packaged cheese croutons and a few anchovies, and you've got yourself a gourmet special."

I go out to the kitchen, find a Coke — there is a six-pack, thank heaven, among the delicatessen leftovers — search for a lemon, give up, notice that PJ has left half his lunch on the kitchen table and departed again, and return to the library, where Stephen Alexander is telling Porter the recipe for his special barbecue sauce.

He talks about food, obsessively but with a strange indifference, for the rest of the meal. Then he switches to appliances ("They got this new gadget out now, French thing just coming on the market, you can peel an onion and then either slice it or chop it up, any size pieces you want, in a minute flat") and then — pacing restlessly around the library, while Porter and I sit captive, tranced, waiting behind polite host-masks for something, anything, to happen to break this knot we're all tied together in, and start unraveling whatever it is that must be disentangled before any of our lives will be straightened and we can be quits of each other — then he goes on to talk about sports, about ice hockey, the Boston Celtics, and basketball, and players with names like Orr and Havlicek; and all the time he is talking it is as if into a dictaphone — he even interrupts himself once in a while to say, "You got that?" — and he keeps flicking back his cuff to check his wristwatch; and still talking, he pauses a moment to stare at the rain out of one of the tall windows. The only time his voice stops is when he leaves to go upstairs and check on his wife; Porter and I sit comatose staring into the fire; he comes back to report tersely that she is "as well as we can expect, given that she's in excruciating pain"; and then he begins pacing and talking again. Nothing of what he says reveals the slightest fact about himself, or his wife, or their adopted, runaway daughter. Nothing in his words or tone acknowledges that he is in the presence of the woman who bore that child and then surrendered it to him — or even, indeed, that she exists.

The day drags on. There is a numbing timelessness to it, the suspended quality of idleness of rain-trapped Sundays, of extended weekends wherein houseguests — who have arrived expecting to play tennis, or take nature walks, or swim, or drink up a party — are reduced to wandering about with their hands in their pockets, staring out streaming windows; and hosts flee when possible to the kitchen, desperately serving up meal after elaborate meal earlier and earlier, in order to use up time which expands — according to theories of management and house space — in direct ratio to its own rate of consumption.

Once when Stephen Alexander is upstairs Porter goes into the hall and I can hear him on the telephone. He makes several brief calls. When he returns I ask him, listlessly, who he was phoning, and he hesitates, and then he says he was checking the bus station and the airport and the railway station. Nobody, he says, has seen anybody of Sara's description buying a ticket. "Oh Porter —" "No," he says, answering my alarm, "I didn't call the sheriff. She's not going to be wandering around the countryside in this rain. Besides," he adds, coming to lay his hand on my shoulder for a moment, "she's smart, Emily. She's not going to be where she can get picked up, as you said. And as you also said, she promised she'd be OK, and we have to trust that." He waits; and I nod wordlessly, stuffing down my panic with the need to trust. "That's the only thing we can do," he says bleakly, "trust, and wait."

Sometime during the afternoon I find myself in the little hall back in the west wing. I pause at the foot of the stairs. There is a quiet murmur of voices coming from the half-closed door up there: Porter's, PJ's. *Why,* I think, *Uncle Tyler's dead.* I sit down on the bottom step for a while, wanting to go up and sit there quietly with them; but I sense that the father and son are speaking of things they may never have spoken of before to each other, and that years may pass before they can speak of them, together, again.

Then there is the far tootle of the school bus down the hill and Stuart and Timmie burst through the kitchen door, streaming in their boots and slickers. I am helping them off with their things when Stephen Alexander rushes in. His face is afire with expectancy. The fire goes out.

Prying off Timmie's boots, I introduce the boys. He comes over to shake each of their hands in a formal way. "Stuart, is it?" he rumbles. "Say, you're a big fella. Hefty. I bet you're gonna play football when you get to high school, right?"

"I dunno." Then, obliging as always, Stuart adds, "Maybe I will."

"I betcha won't, Stuart," Timmie says jealously. "You don't even *like* football."

Stuart's red cheeks turn redder. *"You* don't know what I like, Timmie."

Stephen Alexander laughs easily. "That's right. Don't let anybody lay anything on you fellas. They used to ask me if I was gonna play football, I used to tell 'em how the heck did I know. I figured if I knew what my game was gonna be, I didn't have to let anybody in on it. You wanna make up your own mind, right?"

"Right," Stuart and Timmie chorus obediently. Then Timmie blurts, "Mother? Who's he?"

"Why . . . Mr. Alexander, dear." Still kneeling, I pry at his boot. "Timmie, hold your foot stiff. Stuart, will you hang up your coat on the porch —"

"Me, I'm Janie's father." His voice cuts through mine. "My name's Stephen, but you can call me Steve." He is standing with his hands in his trouser pockets, looking peculiarly like a kid hanging around the outskirts of a sandlot game. "Forget that Mr. Alexander stuff."

"We're not supposed to call old people by their first name," Timmie says.

"It's OK if they *ask,* though," Stuart says. "Mother says it's OK if they ask, don't you, Mother?"

"I . . ." I find myself appalled at the idea of intimacy.

"Forget it. I don't wanna come in here and blow anybody's routine." He jams his hands back into his pockets, turns and walks out of the kitchen.

"Gee. Now we hurt his feelings." Stuart's face is dismayed. "He was just trynna be nice, Mother."

"But who *is* he?" Timmie persists. "How come he's here? Are we having another party or something?"

"Shh, no, Timmie." I jerk and the boot comes off.

"Whattawe have to whisper for? Is everybody asleep? Is somebody sick? How come" — Timmie's voice rises as he gropes for some question to give form to what he senses isn't at all right here — "how come PJ didn't have to go to school? Mother, how come he — And where's Sara? I bet she and PJ got to *go* somewhere, and you didn't take us! And how come that guy's here" — his voice rises to a wail, cracks into sobs of grief — "and Uncle Tyler's not! He died and he's not ever coming back and I WANT MY UNCLE TYLER —" he roars as some anesthetic wears off and he finds himself struck with the icy air of reality.

"I'm sorry to hear about your uncle," Stephen Alexander mutters. "I didn't know you'd just had a, uh, tragedy in the family. That's too bad. Yeah," he says, shaking his head, "that's the way she goes sometimes, isn't it?" He unconsciously flicks a glance at his wristwatch.

Seven P.M. Another meal: company meal (leftover casserole of indeterminate composition except for tuna and black olives) formally at the dining room table. The boys are silent, cagey. I assume that Porter or PJ has explained who the Alexanders are and why they are here. There have been no more questions, not even about the unseen lady who lies suffering behind the bedroom — Sara's bedroom — door. There have been no more questions about Sara's absence, or speculation on where she might be. While I am grateful for this, I am uneasy. It is unnatural; their silence seems not to ease the tensions but to increase them. There is not even a complaint about the presence of olives — vile contamination! — in their actual food.

"... maybe you'd allow me," Stephen Alexander is mumbling, "... make a little contribution to his favorite charity. Or yours, if you got a favorite charity. Gesture of, ah, sympathy. Too late for flowers, stuff like that."

"Very kind of you," Porter says stiffly. "But it's not necessary."

" 's OK. Don't wanna come in here and blow everybody's routine," he mutters again, with a lift of his massive shoulders that may be intended for a shrug but looks more like a wince.

We bend in stricken silence to our plates.

"Emily? I'm sure I'm not interruptin your supper this time, seein as how it's so late." There is a pause. I can think of nothing to say. What can I possibly say, now, to Catherine Tupper? But it seems she has something to say to me.

"I've been thinkin over that matter, that matter of what you told me the other day. And I've come to the conclusion that it doesn't have to be a factor."

"Mrs. Tupper —"

"Nothin's a factor if it doesn't *have* to be a factor," she says with portentous stress. "You understand what I'm sayin? I mean, I know of a great number of, ah, *factors* in the business we're speakin of, other people's little *factors,* so to speak, not necessarily of the same kind of co'se" — she gives a dry little laugh "— but which have simply been absorbed, I guess you might say, into the practicalities."

"What you're saying, Mrs. Tupper, is that in politics there's a lot of hidden scand —"

"Oh gracious me, here I am babblin away about nothin, tyin up your party line like this, what I called for was to ask if you could come to lunch tomorrow? A very quick one, won't take long, just the two of us? I *know* this is a tryin time for you, so sad, but as I was sayin yesterday, there's nothin like work, is there, to begin the healin process. Nothin like rollin up the sleeves, gettin interested in somethin useful, to take the mind off —"

"Mrs. Tupper. There are too many important things right now, in my life, they have to be settled —"

"— sorrow and bereavement, is there? I remember after the Colonel passed away I thought —"

"I can't go on ignoring them. They have to take precedence —"

"— I would perish of boredom, you can't imagine how it is, after so many borin years, I mean to say fulfillin years of co'se, how you can come up all of a sudden starin boredom right in the eyeballs, as the Colonel used to say. Referrin to other matters of co'se. While he was just sittin there —''

''These things take precedence with me, Mrs. Tupper, because they're part of a prior commitment. At the time I was married I made a commitment to my husband, and a way of life, and a family —''

''— drinkin himself to death and slowly killin me along with him. I started out so brave and bright and wantin to be useful. Oh, I was such an energetic girl —''

''— and to myself. Nobody twisted my arm when I married. I wanted to be committed. I still do, even if there are other things —''

''— he used to say, 'Calm down, Catherine, you'll have enough to keep you busy soon's the babies start arrivin.' But they didn't. I began to wish they would, just so's to have somethin to set my hand to —''

''Everybody has to make some kind of commitment. My husband made a

384

commitment when he married me, and nobody twisted his arm, either —"

"— boredom, nobody knows the hell a woman can go through, day after day and year after year with nothin to set her hand or mind to. 'Why, honey, you don't need to lift more'n one of your pretty little fingers,' he used to say, 'that's all *my* wife needs to do to get anythin she wants,' he used to say —"

"And it's not just a question of duty. There's a part of everybody, man or woman, that needs the central things in love, and marriage, and children. Mrs. Tupper? Excuse me, but all of a sudden I think I know what it is you're trying to say to me."

She says in flat, rational tones, "I'm tryin to say we need a woman candidate."

"You're trying to say *you* want a woman candidate. You want somebody to stand in for you, Mrs. Tupper. Somebody you can direct, and guide, and turn into your . . . surrogate, I guess is the word. Mrs. Tupper? Why don't you run for that office yourself?"

"Why," she says, after a little pause, a

little tinkling laugh, "why, that's a sweet thought. But don't you know? I'm too old."

"Surely that doesn't —"

"All these years sittin on my hands because I'm a woman, now I'm free to do somethin, I'm an *old* woman." She laughs again, a little wildly. "So you see it's quite out of the question now. Quite ridiculous. There's nothin quite so ridiculous as the idea of an old woman settin her hand to somethin new. Particularly if it's useful or important things, things like men do. And particularly if she's got some real feelins about it, and a mind of her own. It's all very well for a young woman, while she's still attractive, you see, and useful in *other* ways if you know what I mean, to try to be useful to the world in general. They may even indulge her some, particularly if she's charmin and modest and tactful, and doesn't start actin like any real threat. But for an *old* woman, whose main usefulness is plainly long past, if you know what I mean, it's just flat-out ridiculous. I take it you're withdrawin from the race, then."

"I have to. This race, anyway. Maybe when I've got more time, and things are more settled, and the children are a little older —"

"Nothin is ever settled, honey, for a woman." The voice has gone stale, weary, indifferent. "Least of all not the kind of woman you are. I always did suspect you didn't have your whole heart in this. The other — your little revelation — you would've kept to yourself, you wouldn't have told me, if you'd *really* wanted . . . Well, never mind. I'll just have to look around" — her voice trails off vaguely — "try to find somebody younger maybe, a young woman without other commitments . . ." And the line goes dead.

A rustle on the stairs: the dark figure of Helen Alexander, descending. I am still sitting at the little hall table, staring at the telephone.

She descends into the light in a long wrapper of soft, ruby-red wool. She wafts past me, trailing her pain-dazzled, abstracted smile.

"You're feeling better?"

"Where's Stephen?" She wafts on. I clump down the hall after her.

"In the library. Straight ahead."

Stephen Alexander and Porter have taken up their aimless pacing again. The boys, whom nobody has thought to send off to bed, are slumped in varying postures on the couch, following them with their stares, faces secret and watchful.

"Stephen," she says as she enters, "I called you but you didn't come."

"Helen! You're up! Are you all right, Lovely? God, I didn't hear you, I should've checked — Here, let me help you back upstairs —"

"Stop that, please." Her smile is impersonal. "I'm not going back up. I've been waiting. I'm quite tired of waiting, Stephen, and nothing's getting done. I can see that. Somebody" — she rakes the room with her impersonal smile — "has to get things done, don't they? So I guess it has to be me."

"But, Lovely, you're not in any

condition —"

"It usually is me," she murmers, bringing the smile to rest on Porter, "who has to see that things get done. Stephen's so impractical." She eludes her husband's big, pleading hands and wafts over to the chair by the fireplace, where she seats herself, upright but graceful. She transfers the smile from Porter back to Stephen Alexander. "Sweet, but impractical. Aren't you, darling? Would you give me another of my pills, they're in your pocket. I couldn't very well get one myself, could I, while they were down here in your pocket. You see what I mean," she says to the boys, suddenly transfixing all three of them with the smile, "he's impractical. And who are you?"

They gape at her wordlessly.

"These are our sons," Porter says. "Porter Junior, Stuart, Tim. Boys, this is Mrs. Alexander."

They stare.

"Stand up, boys," Porter says sharply, "and say How do you do to Mrs. Alexander. And then I think you'd better be off to bed. It's a school night.''

"Stephen, it would be much easier to swallow this pill with a glass of water, don't you think? Please don't send the boys to bed just yet. I like children. Stephen and I both adore children. We'd have loved to have had a son.'' The smile is rueful, fond, dazzling. "How lucky your parents are, having such nice boys. And three of them, that's even luckier, isn't it? Three hostages to fortune, that's what children are, aren't they'' — she releases the boys, and turns the smile on us — "instead of just the one Stephen and I have. Janie's an only child, you know. So I'm sure you'll understand the suffering it's caused us, taking Janie away from us like that. I'm sure you must realize now that whatever your reason was, it was a cruel mistake. You don't look like cruel people,'' she says, brushing all of our faces in a final encompassing sweep, "and I'm sure you regret your mistake. That's why I'm willing to negotiate with you like this, myself, instead of taking it to the authorities. If you'll give Janie back to us now, tonight, we won't bring kidnapping charges against you.''

She turns her dazzling smile toward her husband, who has returned with her glass of water and is standing in the doorway. ''There, Stephen. See how much simpler it is when you let me take care of things?''

Seventeen

"Talk to me." She lies on the bed in her ruby-red robe, its folds etched in the dim light from the hall, her long frame outlined in draped hollows. She lies with her legs straight and her arms at her sides, with a dampened cloth over her forehead and eyes, like a bandage. He instructed me how to arrange it, before he went out with Porter to look for the boys. "Please talk to me," she murmurs. "Tell me about your sons. Such nice boys. I didn't mean to frighten them."

But she has. What can I say to her? Their terrified faces: they thought she was really going to call the police, have us all thrown in jail. And now they've bolted, and they're somewhere out there in the cold and rain and dark, like fugitives from justice. And Sara may be out there too, a fugitive from this same woman. What can I say to her?

"I love children," she is saying tonelessly. "I would never cause them pain. Maybe I caused her pain, without meaning to. How could I mean to when I love her so much? Please talk to me?"

"Perhaps it'd be better for you to have quiet."

"No. It doesn't make any difference."

"It must be terrible, the pain of a migraine."

"Yes." There is no trace of self-pity in the flattened voice. "Terrible, like the pain of having a baby, I suppose."

"I don't know. I've never had a migraine."

"I don't know either. I've never had a baby. I just have migraines instead."

There is a silence. Presently she says, "It's my fault, you know."

"That you have migraines? Surely you can't —"

"That we didn't have a baby. It's my fault. Nobody knows why, but it is. They can't find any real reason why I can't have a baby. They said it must be hidden in my mind somewhere, that I didn't really want a baby." There is another silence. She murmurs, "So it's my fault, really."

I say, "Do they say it's your fault you have migraines, too? If they can't find a cause they figure it's all in your mind?"

Beneath the bandage her mouth twists into a wry smile. "I suspect they do. I can't imagine why anybody'd want to have migraines, or not want to have a child," she says conversationally, "but that's the way it keeps on being. So maybe they're right."

"Do you *feel* they're right?" Despite myself, I sense a stir of pity for this woman.

"No."

"Then you don't really believe them when they tell you it's all in your mind?"

"What else is there to believe? You asked how I felt," she says wearily. "What I feel and what I have to believe are two different things now. I guess that's where the trouble is. All my life I always felt certain things, like wanting a child, I felt so strongly and deeply about it

394

it was more than just a belief, it was part of me. It was part of the way I knew I was. And could trust what I knew." Still there is no trace of self-pity in the matter-of-fact voice. "What kind of woman wouldn't want a child, when she feels this love for them? But all those years I couldn't have a child, and all those tests I took, how many tests, over and over, they all said I should be able to. So what else is there to believe, except that I'm not the woman I always felt I was. I can't even trust that anymore. It's my fault," she says steadily, "and I have to face up to it."

Guilty: they have handed down their judgment. She must accept it, because there is no other. They have taken her physical measure, found it innocent; so they have pronounced her spirit guilty. A jet of anger spurts in me.

"There are some things," I say as evenly as I can, "we can't let them lay on us. If we can't trust what we *know* we are, then we aren't anything but what they decide we are."

"I know." There is another wry smile, a

twist of pain. "But sometimes it's easier just to let them decide."

"And feel guilty all your life?"

"My husband is a good man. A good, kind, loving man. He wanted children so badly. Whether it was my body or my mind that prevented it, I'd feel guilty enough that I couldn't give them to him."

"But maybe it's him — maybe he's the one who —"

"No. Not him. He was tested too . . ." Her voice fades, turns fretful. "I don't want to talk about this anymore. Could you wring this out with some more cold water . . ."

I bring the bandage back, lay it gently over her forehead and eyes again, sit in the chair beside her. She lies in silence, utterly still, in a sort of coma that may be sleep. But presently she murmurs, "Talk to me. Tell me about what it was like, when she was born."

"Sar . . . Janie, you mean?"

"Yes." The mouth smiles. It is not wry, but gentle. "She was so small and new and marvelous when I first held her, she was three weeks old by then. Tell me how she was when you first held her and she was just born."

I tell her. She listens intently as she lies on the bed, wrapped in pain the way she has been so long wrapped in guilt.

• • • •

"I'm sorry, Alexander. How else could I explain it to them? Those kids were scared out of their wits. They really thought she was going to have us all thrown in jail."

"I know. Jesus, I know they did. I hope you don't think she — we like to go around throwing little kids into a panic. But Jesus, for you to tell them she's crazy —" Stephen Alexander sits at the kitchen table with his head in his hands, his elbows propped, water dripping off the elegant gray sleeves. He and Porter are both sitting, drenched through, too weary to care. It is almost eleven o'clock. I'm boiling water to get some coffee into them. Upstairs, Helen Alexander has drifted off into a wordless trance that may or not be sleep. The boys, after a quick hot bath to warm them, have been bundled, exhausted, off to bed. They were found down by the Katzes' cabin, brought back soaked and inarticulate. PJ worries me most: feverish, distraught, teeth chattering. "Dad said not to worry," he chattered. "Dad said she's not really gonna *do* anything, he says she's crazy, you don't hafta pay any attention to what crazy people say —"

"She's not crazy," Stephen Alexander is saying. "It was just the pain, and not knowing where Janie is, she didn't realize what she was saying. Helen'd never scare little kids on purpose, she's the last woman in the world to do a thing like that."

"Well, she did, and it was a damn crazy thing to say," Porter snaps. "Frankly, I'm beginning to understand why Sara — Janie — wouldn't want to face that kind of thing."

"God," Stephen Alexander groans, "you don't understand."

"I don't think we really do, Porter." I pour out two cups of coffee, set them on the table. "I don't think Helen intended —"

"Intended or not, the effect's pretty

obvious. It's time we had some explanations from you, Alexander."

"You been talking to Helen?" The big man has raised his head, is looking at me with his drowning, deep-sea gaze. "She feeling any better? You know she didn't mean to scare the kids, don't you?"

"I know. She — she feels terribly guilty about it." I hesitate. "She feels guilty about a lot of things," I say, "that she really shouldn't.'"

"Like Sara's running away?" Porter has his two hands clenched around his coffee cup. "I think I'd feel guilty, if I had a kid who ran away twice."

"Listen," Stephen Alexander pleads, "there can be two different reasons, can't there, for a kid running away —"

"Seems to me that two reasons for running away are about two reasons too many," Porter says. "No matter what the reasons are, and none has been forthcoming. None *I*'ve heard, anyway." He stares down into his cup. "I'll grant you, she wanted to find her real mother. But why'd she have to run away to do that? Listen, Alexander. I'm not trying to be cruel. But we care for that girl. We feel responsible for her. I meant it when I said on the phone last night that we intend to protect her. Your wife cited the laws against kidnapping. Well, there are laws that protect kids against unfit parents, too. If we found that's the case here, we wouldn't hesitate to take it to court. I'm sorry."

"Jesus. Oh sweet Christ Jesus," he whispers.

"I'm sorry," Porter repeats. "You know we're not kidnappers. We've got to know you're not unfit. We've got to know you're not somehow mistreating that girl."

"Mistreating her. My God," he says brokenly, "we love her. She's our daughter. You don't know what we went through to get her. She's the only thing we have. She holds our life together." His face is gouged, like naked granite which has, for countless seasons of sun and snow, simply endured. "We love her," he repeats.

There is a silence. "Porter," I say finally, "I have to believe him."

Porter says nothing. I can see that he, too, has no other choice: he has to believe this man.

"You got to understand," he says again and again.

But belief is not understanding. There are still things — I think as we sit around the kitchen table, the three of us, bargaining so painfully for insight — that elude belief, when its components remain obscure.

"The thing is," Stephen Alexander says, groping back for roots, "Helen and I, we got this feeling about families. We were gonna have our own kind — the one thing we weren't gonna have was the kind of families *we* had. That's what we're beginning to see might've been the basic problem here." He hesitates. "We been seeing this psychiatrist, since — the last few weeks. I mean, Christ, Helen's migraines for one thing, they got so bad she's been spending half the time flat on her back. She's had 'em on and off for years, we tried everything, those jackass doctors couldn't do a thing for her. So now they got so much worse I finally decided whatthehell, we might as well let the shrinks take a shot at it." He says defensively, "I never had much use for those witch doctors myself, but nowadays everybody goes to the shrink, you get a broken fingernail and you run for the shrink, it doesn't mean you're nuts, y'know. Anyway, this guy we're going to, he seems to have a lot of common sense, frankly I was surprised. None of that mumbo-jumbo stuff they hand you, about how you were potty-trained wrong so you're scared to make decisions, that sort of blather."

Now that Stephen Alexander has begun to talk again, he flows steady and unstoppable as before. "What we're beginning to see, Helen and I, is how this family thing's been working on us. Helen was raised so damn strict, to begin with. You get a woman like Helen, sensitive and beautiful and intelligent — Helen's got an IQ of one fifty-two," he says, opening and closing his fists around his coffee cup, "which the shrink says makes it even tougher for a woman, although I frankly don't see why the hell it should. I'm not stupid either and it sure hasn't been any handicap to me. The thing is you get a fantastic woman like Helen, and you raise her to believe all kinds of nutty things she instinctively *knows* are nutty — I mean Helen's mother was beyond belief, one of those dames who thought, y'know, men're only after one thing.'' He laughs, a short harsh bark.

"She was scared to death of men when I met her. No wonder, I practically had to beat 'em off even to get within shouting distance of her. Well, you've seen her. You know how beautiful she is.''

Porter and I exchange a cautious glance. *The eyes of love are blind,* it's said. Maybe Stephen Alexander's first look had blinded him; and love had fixed her image, unchangeable, on his retinas.

"The first time I met her,'' he is saying, "it was at this big party, some Boston charity bash her mother made her go to — she was always trynna wedge Helen into the upper crust of the society pie, her old man had plenty of dough but it wasn't the right kind for Boston, he was a new Irish who made it big in the construction business horning in on the old Irish — anyway, there was Helen backed into a corner by this pack of party wolves. I could see by her face she didn't want any of *that.* I guess I know how to break up a wolf pack." He grins, without humor. "I know how to protect her. That's one of the great things we got, Helen and I. She knows I can protect her from any guy who's stupid enough to try and hustle her."

Marriage as a Protectorate: this view of it might be touchingly gallant but it could also serve to isolate a woman in her sense of herself. *Sometimes it's easier just to let them decide,* she said. How much we have to learn — men and women, all of us — about living together. Out of a sudden sense of pity for us all, I blurt, "All these problems you seem to have with your marriage —"

He doesn't let me finish. "Problems?" Instantly hostile, defensive, his face turns granite. "We got problems, sure. But we're dealing with 'em. How about you?"

"I didn't mean —"

"We've dealt with ours." Porter's face is like a blade. "And it's not ours that's under consideration here. I think we've got a basically healthy —"

"Healthy. Yeah, what you got, it'd have to be pretty healthy. It isn't every guy who wouldn't put up some kind of squawk about his wife having a kid that's not his. I suppose you'd say that's a healthy attitude. What they call modern and enlightened. Me, I wouldn't guarantee I'd be all that healthy about it, myself. Maybe I'm too damn basic, or something."

I have lurched up, grabbed the coffeepot, am making dumb stabs at offering it. *Why,* I think confusedly, *this is the way wars start.* Somebody mumbles something that's misunderstood, a jab in a sensitive spot — "Coffee?" I babble, "More coffee?"

"It's OK, Emily." Porter hasn't moved. He looks steadily across the table at Stephen Alexander. "Nobody's going to start fighting over your virtue. That's the oldest kind of holy war there is, and we've been through it. We've come to our own terms. And you," he says to the other man, "you've come to terms with your own wife. You love her, I love mine. So let's quit the manhood question and get on with the question that's on this table" — he raps it sharply with his knuckles — "which is why that girl won't face you."

There is a silence. Then — my trembling legs give out — Stephen Alexander's granite visage crumbles. He lays it in his palms. "I don't know. Christ, if only I knew."

Presently, out of the silence, there come the broken grunts of a man trying not to weep. "I keep asking myself over and over, and I don't know." Across the table, Porter and I once more consult wordlessly: once more, we have to believe him.

"She always had such a . . . trust in her, a lovingness," he says wonderingly. He has begun to speak as if to himself. "Even when she was a tiny baby, God, she was the littlest thing, she had this way to stare at you, as if she knew who you were, and trusted you. And then she'd try to smile, this was before she even learned how, it'd break you up seeing her try to smile — and comical, she'd wiggle so hard trying, and thrash her little arms and legs, and then the smile'd break out sudden. I remember once Helen was holding her over her shoulder, burping her, and I was standing behind trying out a funny face on her — and she burped, loud. And I laughed, and then she started laughing too, and it struck us all so goddam funny we were all laughing, me and Helen and the baby. We laughed so hard Helen almost dropped her, and then the baby got the hiccups, and that cracked us up. God, it still cracks me up to think of it.'' His face has cracked into a huge grin.

"Tell us more," I plead, "about when she was little."

But the grin is gone. "I dunno," he says wearily, "I keep thinking about her now" — he glances at his watch, back in his mechanistic gesture; it is late, late; how could we have forgotten how late it is getting? — "maybe holed up somewhere, all alone, loaded down with whatever it is . . . Jesus, she's so young. She's too young to be loaded down with troubles. It's tough enough when you're old and beat-up and been through so damn many things, like I have." He passes a hand over his face.

"Like everybody has." Porter picks up his empty coffee cup, stares into it, sets it down again. "Trouble seems to be the human condition."

"She used to come to me when she had troubles. Helen — well, Helen tended to get kinda tense with her, she tried too hard sometimes, always worrying about doing the right thing for her. Trying to be a perfect mother, as if just being herself wasn't good enough for the kid. You'd think a woman like Helen would know how great she is, you'd think she'd trust her own instincts about herself. Well, I blame it on Helen's mother. What kinda example of motherhood did *she* set, is what I think. I told Helen that, I don't know how many times. She could've handled a dozen kids, and had a great time doing it. Hell, when we were married, we wanted a dozen kids. And then . . ." He stops. There is a haunted look in a big face.

"You could have adopted more," Porter says.

"Yeah, well, she — Anyway, you can't believe the hassle trying to find a baby to adopt. It took us years just to find Janie. We wanted a girl, and we wanted her with dark eyes like Helen's, and intelligent, from intelligent-type people, maybe a college girl with a good background —" He stops. "I'm sorry," he mutters. "This must be kinda tough on you. You, uh — We didn't specify a redhead, but it was like an extra bonus," he says with painful gallantry, not looking at me, "besides her being so pretty . . . Well, like I was saying, she used to come to me with her troubles, and I used to explain —"

Once again he stops. He hauls in a great, shaky breath. Lets it out: "Christ, if only I couldda explained that one thing to her! If she just wouldda listened! I tried to tell her — my God, how she couldda imagined something like that, it was as if she couldn't even recognize me anymore, as if a couple words on a piece of paper made me somebody else, a stranger, a guy off the street, who'd —"

"Wait a minute." Porter has been slumped in his chair. Now he straightens. "Hold it. When was this you're talking about? You said something about a couple of words on a piece of paper —"

"That goddam birth certificate. I don't know how the hell she ever found it. I didn't even know Helen had it. I thought we'd burned everything, everything —"

"She found her own birth certificate? Is that what you're talking about — what happened when she found it?"

He drains his cold coffee in one gulp, bangs down the mug, shoves it away. "Xerox copy of her birth certificate, hospital certificate. Name of attending doctor, name of mother, father's name unknown. All that stuff that's supposed to be sealed forever. I don't know why Helen'd want to keep it. I don't want to know, why she'd want to keep the evidence for something we spent seventeen years trying to forget." He falls silent.

"So," Porter prompts, "she found it. And she hadn't known she was adopted. She told us that. Evidently it gave her one hell of a shock."

"Shock. Yeah, it was a shock."

"So what did she do?"

"Do?" he repeats dully.

"When she found out. Is that when she ran away?"

"No. No, she didn't leave then. Not until, Jesus, I don't know, a couple of weeks after. But it was as if she didn't live there anymore. In her own house."

"So." Porter's tones are dogged. "What did she do right after she learned she was adopted? She came to you?"

"Yeah. She brought the paper to me. She asked me what it meant. I didn't wanna — She kept on, she was all upset. She'd already figured what it meant. She figures things fast. Sometimes too fast, she jumps in feetfirst and then she finds she's all wet, and then somebody hasta pull her out, and it was always me. She always came to me to set her straight," he drones, "only this time she, I, I couldn't make myself say it, that she was right, she was adopted. She said she'd ask Helen if I wouldn't tell her. So then I had to say yes, that's what it was. And she fell apart. Right there in front of me she went to pieces. Screaming about how could we have lied to her all these years, how could we not have told her who she was, how could she ever trust anybody anymore, how she was — nothing but a bastard, what we must of thought of her all this time, knowing she was a bastard and her real mother a whore . . ."

"She was hysterical." Porter glances at me. "People don't mean what they say when they're hysterical. So go on. What did you do?"

"I tried to explain," Stephen Alexander drones on, "I tried to explain, but she wouldn't listen. I tried to tell her we never thought of her any way except as our own daughter we loved more than anything, it would never even of occurred to us to think of her like — She was just an innocent little baby, how she was born didn't matter to us —"

(Didn't it? Didn't it have to be intelligent, from intelligent-type people, maybe a girl with a good background? Dear God, how little we know of our unconscious attitudes)

" — but she wouldn't listen. Wouldn't listen, she, she kept backing away from me and when I tried to touch her, comfort her you know, hold her and make her stop feeling so terrible and all, when I tried to touch her she — acted as if I was gonna hit her or something, she — shrank away with this terrified look, it tore me up, and she said I was . . ." The machine falters. Once again there is the deep blue of the drowning man's eyes.

"Tell us one thing." Porter leans forward. "Had you been drinking?"

"Drinking . . ."

"You said you didn't drink. Were you drinking when this happened? Could she have got the impression you were drunk?"

"Drunk." He stares down at his fists. "Drunk? No, I couldn't of been drunk. I've thought and thought about that, it's strange you'd ask, because that's one of the things I been beating my brains out trying to figure. But I can't see any way I could've been drunk that night. I quit anyway. Haven't had a drop since. But Jesus, all I'd had was two one-ounce drinks. And I've *always* had just two drinks before dinner, and a brandy after. That's hardly gonna make a man my size drunk. Christ, she never saw me drunk in her life. I never got drunk at home, a couple times out maybe, but what kind of guy gets drunk in front of his wife and kids? Except guys like my old man," he says, putting his head in his hands and rocking it slowly from side to side, "and I had enough of that when I was a kid, I know what it can do to a family. The one thing when I was a kid, the one *thing,* I wasn't gonna be that kinda man if I ever had a family of my own . . . Drunk. No, I couldn't of been drunk that night. Could I?" He raises his head, blinks painfully at Porter. "Could a guy get drunk on two light whiskeys and one brandy which he's had every night for years? All of a sudden, and not know it? Like maybe something went haywire with his insides, it suddenly has this effect?"

"Not unless he had more than he thought. No way."

"Jesus." He drops his head in his hands again. "I don't see how. I'm always so damn careful. I always know what I'm doin. Listen, you're raised with an old man like that, you don't wanna be like that. You're careful. You always got it in the back of your head, it may be in the genes, or something. There's no way I could've had an extra drink and not know it. I'd just finished that one glass of brandy when she — But I quit. I quit cold that night and I haven't touched a drop since. I mean she looked at me as if, as if I was like my old man, or something. That filthy bastard,'' he says without inflection, ''that dirty louse, the way he treated my mother. We kids were tough, but my mother, she was sensitive, she was a classy woman, she — Forget that. I gotta ask myself, what else can I do, if Janie thought I was drunk I gotta ask myself if I was. I never kidded myself on anything. Only dimwits kid themselves. I couldn't kid myself on this, my God, my own daughter —''

''Maybe she just caught the brandy on your breath,'' Porter says, ''and in her emotional state she latched onto the idea you were drunk. Listen, she —''

But he is not listening. "Maybe she *wanted* to think I was drunk. Maybe she was scared of something else and didn't want to think it. How do I know? I been over it and over it a million times and the only thing I can figure is what I absolutely can't believe," he says exhaustedly, "which is maybe she saw me for a filthy bastard like my old man. Except even my old man wasn't that filthy."

"What you mean is she accused you of 'touching' her," Porter says.

"Yeah." He shudders, an involuntary spasm. "I can't even imagine it. Me. A thing like that. I can't even imagine it."

"I can. She accused me of the same thing."

"You? The same —"

"She was hysterical. The circumstances were pretty similar, now that I think of it. She was worried sick about Emily, and I was just pouring myself a drink, and — I guess she must've flashed on it, as the kids say, relived it, because of the strong associations — I reached out just to touch her, comfort her, the way you did. And I swear to God when she accused me

416

afterward, there was a moment —"

"When you wondered yourself?"

"Right. I wondered, what *did* I do? What *was* in my mind —"

"Yeah. And you begin to wonder if you're crazy. If maybe there's this animal streak in you." Stephen Alexander laughs, unsteadily. "My mother used to say there's an animal streak in all men, even good ones. Sometimes it seems like I've spent my life like some kinda lion tamer, whip in one hand and a chair in the other, trynna make some poor dumb beast inside me roll over and lay down. You get what I mean?"

Porter grins, bleakly. "I get what you mean. They call it 'decency.' "

"In women they call it 'virtue,' " I blurt. "And in everybody, it's how people tell us we are, no matter how we *feel* we are."

"Uh?" My face heats under the glance of these two men, exclusive in their newfound brotherhood.

"Yeah," Porter says politely, "I guess you could put it that way."

"Then I will." I suppose my anger is

directed more at the way things are — and probably always will be — than at these two good men, so bewildered that their feelings should be misunderstood. "I'll put it that the same thing that makes men question their own decency is what makes women question their own virtue. And that comes from the unconscious assumption that it's not *natural* in people to be the way they should. I don't know if you realize it, Stephen, but Helen's somehow come to believe that she lacks the maternal instinct." He starts to interrupt, but I bumble on past him, determined to make myself — if not anybody else — put some sense together. "I'm not saying it's you, it was probably some well-meaning doctor who figured he knew all about maternity because he delivered babies. The way my brother Robert felt he knew all about virtue because his two children were legitimate. My baby wasn't, so I was a slut."

I pull in a good big breath. "And Sara. If you try to think what a girl, a young girl that age, might feel, when she finds out all of a sudden that her father's not really her father, she's not really his daughter. All her life she'd *felt* he was her father and she his daughter. If there was one thing she could trust it was that. Then all of a sudden this central thing she trusted about herself and him was shattered. And somewhere in her mind she's got these half-formed, scary ideas . . . All these unconscious attitudes about sex — about virtue and decency and what you two were saying just now about feeling like lion tamers — these attitudes are powerful. They seep through to kids, who're just getting conscious of themselves . . . Girls, you know, getting conscious of themselves as women — Listen, I don't think kids are as sophisticated nowadays as everybody thinks, about sex and freedom and all that. Kids are natural conservatives, and all these unconscious attitudes they absorb are certainly not liberal, they're *traditional*. Like you, Stephen, all your life worried that you might have your father's traits in your genes. So she — Sara — could've picked that up, and when she found out she was illegitimate, all these mixed-up notions about being a bastard —" My voice has begun to wobble, my anger liquefied into a general sorrow. I press on, wearily.

"And then this man who's suddenly not her father makes a fatherly gesture. And because she's in a state of shock, and self-revulsion, she misinterprets. If she can't trust who she is anymore, she can't trust who anybody is. She said that herself. Remember, Porter?"

"Yes. Yes, I remember."

"Anyway." I'm too exhausted to raise my head from my hands. "I don't think her reaction was all that abnormal. And I think she realized that herself, before we did."

"My God. What've we done?" The big man's voice is stricken. "We shouldda told her. When she was little. We shouldda told her. We just wanted so much to protect her. And —"

"Daddy."

" — ourselves, from any feeling that she wasn't ours. And she *was* ours. Just as much ours as if —"

"Daddy." She is standing in the pantry

doorway. She is wearing a yellow slicker three times too big for her, under it a long calico skirt with a muddy hem. And beside her stands PJ in his slicker, pajama bottoms rolled up over muddy untied sneakers.

"She didn't really run away," PJ blurts wildly, "she was at the Katzes' all the time, they promised not to tell but I hadda go tell her they were gonna have us arrested, Stuart and Timmie didn't know, it was only me and the Katzes, Sara said it was OK, she was gonna come back anyway, she said nobody was gonna be arrested but if there is I'll go, I'm the one who helped hide her."

Sara says, "It's OK, PJ. You're the one who's brave. I'm the one who's the coward. I was a coward, Daddy, for not wanting to face you and Mother. It was just that I felt so bad about hurting you. I just couldn't stand seeing on your faces what I'd done to you. But I have to. I love you. Where's Mother?"

Eighteen

Sat. June 7. My dearest daughter: A burst of real summer today, sun leaping up like a bridegroom (as some poet put it), and I leaping up with it to weed the veg-garden before the weeds leap up their daily 2 in. in this steamy clime. Now I *think* I've cleared what remains of the afternoon to answer your long, lovely letter with what might be a disjointed ramble — unless everybody really *is* out helping Porter mend the fence. At 5 we're going to "drop in" on the Peterses, continuing Porter's Social Expansion & De-Insulation Program — think I wrote you he decided we'd become too housebound and familified over the winter, he says families can be *too* self-sufficient & ingrown. Although I'm not sure walking our own fields isn't

422

to be preferred over inspecting a new dog run. Oh well, the Peterses *are* good friends.

I know this coming week's a tough one for you cramming for those comprehensive exams, which sound formidable. I used to know a girl at Radcliffe who'd likewise gone to St. Mary's Country Day, and she said after surviving those Sr. year comps, no mere college exam could ever

"Mo-therr!" The strangled tones come floating up from the region of the back porch. "They won't let me *garble* with the *squawkle* . . ."

hold any terror for her again. But you are so *smart,* darling — which undoubtedly is why they're letting you take the comps despite all those weeks you lost — so have confidence in yourself, keep hanging in as you put it, and

"Whyncha *answer* me?" Timmie, ruffled and outraged and eye patch askew, glares at me from the doorway.

"Because you weren't going to interrupt me when I'm up here. Remember?" I lean back in the chair, stretch, beckon him. "OK. What won't they let you do?" I drape one arm around his skinny shoulders. His T-shirt is inside out and backward again. For years I have pondered the scientific mystery of how, against odds which I figure are four to one, little boys manage to get into their T-shirts thusly, reversing the odds.

"They won't let me help hold the wire and Stuart gets to hammer and I don't and PJ's bossin me around and —"

"Daddy's supposed to be bossing that job, darling. So I'm sure if you take your grievance to him, he'll —"

"He's not payin any 'tention, he's just leanin around talkin to Mike, and Stuart and PJ won't let me do *anything* —"

Thus is ever the way that men mend fences. I arrange for Timmie to deliver to them two beers, the portage and ceremonies of which should take at least a half hour.

in just a little more than 2 weeks (2 weeks! I can't believe it's this close at last!) back you will be with us, and the whole summer to relax in! It's so lovely here in the summer, so different from those long winter weeks of rain. Looking back on them is like looking back on a prison term, all of us locked in here together in this house. But we can look *ahead* now, with so much behind us (as you say in your letter), and summer coming. And after that, off you go to college. Hard for me to imagine, having a daughter in college; I can't help wishing it were going to be the U. of Va. right here — and I certainly sympathize with Steve's and Helen's similar wish that you were going to be someplace close to them such as Radcliffe — but we all bow to your special wisdom in deciding to "go out to a wider world," as you put it. I've been thinking a lot about this recently, which is perhaps why I keep remembering that night you came back. I remember you said it was not a question of splitting yourself in two like the child in Solomon's judgment, but of being part of both. And then you said — how simple and practical it sounded; a flash of your grandmother's New England common sense — that if a person couldn't be split in two, Time could. Time back with Helen and Steve and finishing St. Mary's; Time back with us this summer; Time to start your own life in college . . . Here we'd all thought *we* were the ones who had to negotiate for you, had to make choices for you. And you stepped in and simply made your own. It was like waking up out of a long confused dream

"Mother! Guess what?" Stuart, red-cheeked, panting, T-shirt ripped (never was a fence mended without a shirt needing it), bursts in, bursting with news. Stuart loves news. "Mother, guess!"

I put down my pen. "The cows got out."

"Only three. But Mr. Garrett found 'em down the road and they're back now. But guess *really* what."

"Mr. Garrett wasn't mad?" That would be *really* news.

"Noooo! You want me to give you a hint?"

"I want you to give me the whole thing."

"He's gonna get married!"

"Mr. Garrett? But who —"

"Mike! He and Jeannie're gonna get married!"

"Oh. Why, isn't that" — with her almost five months pregnant, my reaction is not so much boggled as elusive; does one celebrate the triumph of Society or mourn the surrender of Dissent? — "nice." I am surprised at how nice it strikes me. I must be more Victorian than I suspected.

"Dad said it was about time. I heard him and Mike talkin. Mike said he's been thinkin a lot," Stuart reports with precocious journalistic accuracy, "about the baby, and, uh, lessee, what's he call it —"

"Legitimacy," I supply, firmly.

"Something like that, I guess. Anyway, Mike told Dad they decided to get married so the baby wouldn't be a —"

"Burden. That is *nice*," I say,

sweeping him in with my arm and giving him a hug, "and you can go tell Jeannie I'll come talk to her tomorrow, she may want me to help with the plans —'"

"Well, but *lissen*" — and he squirms away — "they're gonna get married *today*. Just as soon as everybody can get ready — that's what Dad told me to tell you, we're all gonna go up to the church this evening and help them get married, because Mike says we're their family, and we hafta get into our good clothes, and Dad says we'll come back here afterward and have a wedding supper —"

Sun. Afternoon. Interruption. It's taken me all morning to tidy up after guess what: a Wedding Supper. Consisting of scrambled eggs, some anonymous but posh "side dishes" I found at the bottom of the freezer (one still in a fancy stoneware casserole — I wonder which of the Good Ladies of Mercy thinks I've decided to keep it after these 5 months, hope it's Lucy's but suspect not, she'd have come right out long ago and asked for it back), and some champagne

Porter had stashed away back in Nov. for our anniversary & somehow forgotten . . . . But it was a good party, just family (Mr. Garrett and Will of course) — *Jeannie and Mike,* I forgot to note, were bride & groom. They both looked appropriately shy, radiant, and uplifted. The Ceremony was very moving and expressive. They held it outside the church, in that meadow next to it, the old apple orchard. I'm happy to report that (1) the preacher was most dignified, modulated his Amens which he kept at a minimum, and (2) the herd of cows they keep in there were over at the other side of the field and didn't notice us until the ceremony was almost over — when they ambled up I got between Porter and PJ & was brave, even as 2 of them stood quite close, staring at me the way they do. Jeannie wore a flowered skirt and a shawl and isn't showing *too* much yet, but enough so that Mr. Garrett had a hard time not looking appalled — it struck me strange that he'd been accepting, in a farmer kind of way, of Jeannie's condition until she stood up to get married ("in front of God and everybody," I heard him mutter). Well, attitudes *are* strange and inconsistent, aren't they? Automatic, reflexive, forceful as a heartbeat. It is so irrational how we keep confusing attitudes with ideas —

Which makes me think of something else you said that night. You were telling us how you found me, traced me here — the search you had to make through all those Bureaus and Offices and Records. You said you kept coming up against stone walls, hostility, refusals, after you admitted you were adopted and were trying to find out who your natural parents were. It was incredible to us all — even to Helen and Steve, who had so much to face that night — how attitudes toward adoption are still so confused and (reflected in some of the laws) inhumane. It's still hard for me to imagine how you were forced to lies and deception simply to find out who you *are*. As if the information were so shameful and dangerous that nobody could be trusted with that knowledge — least of all you yourself, 17 and within a year of your legal adulthood! If it hadn't been for that sympathetic clerk who let you see your Order of Adoption — and only through the accident that she happened to have been adopted herself, and understood what it meant to you to *know* — and, above all, your own courage and determination . . . I can't bear to think how it might have been for us all. So many old and painful secrets growing like boils; now they've been lanced, and begun to heal

"Emily? I hope I didn't get you in from the garden."

"No. I was upstairs and I wasn't sure it was the phone." There is a pause. "How are you, Mrs. Tupper?"

"Fine, thank you. I'm callin to ask a little favor. Knowin your interest in community affairs, and of course understandin how busy you young matrons are," and she gives an understanding little laugh, "I'm wonderin if you and your nice husband might be willin to lend

your names as members of my Sponsorin
Committee. It wouldn't demand anything
in the way of time or work, just —"

"Sponsoring Committee? Sponsoring
what, Mrs. Tupper?"

"Why . . ." She hesitates. She says
dryly, "Our candidate, of co'se, who's
been persuaded to take your place. I
thought you knew. You're the one who's
responsible, y'know."

"Candidate . . . ?"

"Me," she says in the same dry tones.
"Oh, I know what I said when you first
suggested it. And I was right, of co'se.
Absolutely right." She gives a dry little
laugh. "But I got to thinkin. All this
stirrin around of Woman's Lib, y'know? It
bein the comin political revolution?
Well, I said to myself, Catherine Tupper,
if women have to fight for a place of their
own in the world — and I know what that
fight's goin to be, my dear, because I was
fightin it before you were born, even
though I didn't know it at the time — why
then, why shouldn't an older woman fight
for the older women's place in the world?
Which will doubtless," she says wearily,

"prove to be the longest and losinest fight in history. Long past my time, and probably yours, and maybe even your daughter's. However. At my age, I haven't anything much to lose but my dignity, and I'm not sure it ain't worth the sacrifice, as the Colonel used to observe about another related matter." Another dry laugh. "Anyway, it'd be a help to me here in the county if you and your husband wouldn't mind lendin your name to a worthwhile if losin cause. If you'd like to talk it over with him first —"

"I don't have to talk it over with him. We'd be honored to be on your Sponsoring Committee. And may I say" — I clear my throat — "right *on,* Mrs. Tupper?"

"You may," she says crisply.

even though each of us has had to revise some of our conditioned reflexes. And it's wonderful to know that things are so much more relaxed there now, the three of you getting the feel, as you say, of a new balance. We are too — mostly me, as I'm the one who's felt so off-balance all these years, toting around all that guilt and secrecy. Like carrying a hidden bomb and expecting it to go off any moment. Well, it *did* go off, and painful as it was for all of us it shattered that uneasy balance, and made a new footing possible. The mere fact of not being afraid anymore

"Hey, Mom!" My pen inscribes a loop. A cry, startlingly close — where? — "Mom!" From the second-story window? "Hey, Mom! Over here!"

I rush to the window: PJ's face, framed by green leaves. "PJ, get down out of that tree! Those branches are old and brittle and you'll —"

"You *said* not to come in the room while you were working, didn't you? Lissen, can we go swimming in the pond?"

"The water's still too cold. PJ get *down* from there —"

"I'm not gonna fall, for crissake. The water's not cold, we felt it. C'mon, Mom, it's so *hot* —" A sinister crackling of twigs.

"PJ, *please* get down from that tree

434

this very —"

"But can we? Huh, Mom? Can we go swimming in the" — a sharp crack; loud thrashing; face disappears — "pond?"

I open my eyes, unclutch my shirtfront. "Oh, all right, go swimming — get down from that tree *carefully* — but remember you and Stuart have to keep an eye on Timmie, and no jumping in, and —" The rest of my cautions are lost in a volley of crackles, thrashing, and screeches of victory, *Yay!*

is like starting life again as a new person. It must seem like that to Helen, with those migraines starting to release their grip, and realizing that if they were partly in her mind, it was from the tensions of worrying about herself as a mother

"I guess I'm interrupting you." Porter stands at the doorway, hands in pockets, looking as if what he wants most is to interrupt me. "If you're writing to Sara, give her my love."

"I will." I smile at him. "It's such a

beautiful afternoon, isn't it, we really should be outside," I hint. "I'll be out as soon as I finish this letter."

"The thing I was thinking," he says, leaning against the doorway and looking around the room, "was maybe this'd be a good time to clear the decks here, so you'll have more space."

"I don't need more space, Porter. Just the desk." And a little uninterrupted time; but who does not?

"I was thinking it'd be nice," he says vaguely, "if you'd like to turn these couple of rooms of Uncle Tyler's into a study, or something. For yourself, I mean. I've got my own study, why shouldn't —"

"Porter dear, what would I do with a study?"

He shrugs. "Hell, I don't know. Maybe just sit and think." He jiggles the coins in his pockets, gazing around the room, stacked with Uncle Tyler's things, books, papers, old albums, clipping, folders . . . a pair of cuff links in a tarnished silver tray on the highboy, the edge of his old blue bathrobe caught in the closet door —

as I follow his gaze I return all at once into an awareness of what, all those months ago, was so painful to be aware of: the presence of Absence.

"The thing I was thinking," Porter mutters, "was that maybe this'd be a good time to —"

"Tidy up." It has taken me a time to grasp it: there arrives the moment, after due and appropriate time, for a final ceremony. What's past must finally be passed. It does not wish to linger, querulously plucking at the Present's gaze with its poor remnants left behind — these unimportant, rumpled parts — until even the loving gaze is blunted, and what is vital to remember, lost. "You're right, Porter. It's time to get things tidied away. He was such a tidy man."

"I'll bring the trunk down out of the attic." He turns, hesitates, turns back. "Listen. If you don't want a study, how about turning these rooms over to Sara when she comes? For a place of her own, I mean." He adds sternly, in case I should mistake simple practicality for something softer, "Kids should always have a room of their own to come home to, no matter how old they get."

I rise, come to him, kiss him.

He frowns. He rolls up his sleeves in a businesslike way. "I'll get the trunk," he mutters.

Later: almost time to get supper together, the boys have been swimming and they're ravenous — you'll love swimming in the pond this summer — and Porter and I have been tidying up Uncle Tyler's rooms. We now have 3 old trunksful of mementos up in the attic, all neatly labeled for some future Historian (possibly Stuart, he was helping us and he was fascinated with the old photos and journals). Anyway, guess what. We agreed that you are to inherit Uncle T's rooms — if you'd like them, of course. There they'll be for you, dearest S., as long as we're a family & here in this old house

"Mother! When're we gonna have supper?"

Must hurry & finish. Did want to say what I keep forgetting in all this rambling — by all means invite your friend down for a visit this summer. He sounds like a splendid boy (or should I say young man, for that's surely what a Harvard Freshman must be!) and we could certainly use some help around the farm this summer, what with Mike going to work in town — forgot to tell you he's got a job in one of the campus clothing shops (!) & hopes to save enough money before the baby's born to go back to Graduate studies *if* Jeannie can find a job and somebody to take care of the baby part-time. Anyway, warn your young friend he might have to mend a few fences, but from your description of him — athlete *and* conservationist! — that should hardly tax his energies or conscience

"Mo-*ther!* It's almost six, when're we gonna eat —"

speaking of which I also forgot to say there's a drive on here to save

Seward Creek which I'm spearheading as they say, as Chairman of the Conservation Committee they've formed which will mean battling it out eyeball to eyeball with JJ Chauncy and H. Plante and the rest, I can just see all the county hostesses trying to figure the seating at dinner parties, everybody's splitting into factions

"Mo-*therrrrr!*"

but it's certainly worth the try. Porter says go ahead and take 'em on, he's all for me. Anyway, you'll be here this summer to help, and the boys are

". . . hunnnnngry, Mother, when're we gonna *eat* —"

● ● ● ●

"Eat," Porter commands, "and stop complaining."

"But this stuff's too hot. Why can't we just have scrambled eggs or soup or something?"

"Soup's hot, for crissake."

"PJ, stop saying crissake every other word. I'm getting tired of having to tell you."

"But this stuff tastes funny, and it's burnin my mouth —"

"Take a drink of milk, then. And it's not all that hot, Timmie. When I was your age my mother used to fix curry every Sunday for supper, and that was —"

"Porter —"

"— considerably hotter, and I didn't complain. When your mother goes to the trouble of fixing a special stew —"

"Porter?"

"— you could show your appreciation by not complaining. What is it, Emily?" he says patiently, laying down his fork.

"Curry."

"What about curry?"

"That's what this is, curry. I tried your mother's recipe again. I guess I still haven't quite got it right."

Porter picks up his fork. He clears his throat. "Boys," he says, "when you are grown men, and your wives ask you what your mother used to give you for Sunday supper, I trust you'll have the gentlemanly decency to say that you do not remember.'' He plunges in his fork.

The forgiving laughter swells.

The publishers hope that this Large Print Book has brought you pleasurable reading. Each title is designed to make the text as easy to see as possible. If you wish a complete list of the Large Print Books we have published, ask at your local library or write directly to:

G. K. Hall & Co.
70 Lincoln St.
Boston, Mass. 02111